GORÉE ISLAND

ISLAND OF NO RETURN

Saga of the Signarés

RICHARD HARRISON GORÉE

Gold Leaf Press

Gorée Island: Island of No Return
Saga of the Signarés

Richard Harrison Gorée

Cover design: Mark Sandell
Cover art of Signaré: Walter "Rap" Bailey

Edited by: Elissa Hannam
Copy editing by: Jack Kuiper

Published by:

Gold Leaf Press
33 Crocker Blvd.
Mt. Clemens, MI 48043

10 9 8 7 6 5 4 3 2

Library of Congress Catalog Card Number: 96–079858

288 pps; Perfect bound; $19.95
ISBN: 1-886769-08-7

Dedication

This book is a memorial to the millions of Africans who died during the Atlantic slave trade and is dedicated to the following:

My Lord and Savior, Jesus Christ
My great grandfather, Harrison Gorée
My wife, Paula S. Gorée
To my children: Richard, Tracie, Rachel and Sasha Farrah
My grandmother, Mrs. Mamie Boyer
My father and mother, Harry and Hazel Gorée
My dear sister and brother

Thank you all for your love and support!

Acknowledgements

I would like to acknowledge the following people without whose assistance and support, this book would not be possible: Richard Harrison Gorée II; Tracie J. Gorée; Ruben & Ruben Powell IV; John O. Adams; Joseph M. Gorée; Candace, Joseph II & Jessica Gorée; Rachel Humpries; Kenneth D. Watson & Rita Ross; Kimbely Camp & Dean Ham (Museum of African American History, Detroit, MI); Ray C. Johnson (Paul Robeson Academy, Detroit Public Schools); Eileen Julian (Indiana University); Catherine D. Abraham; Dr. George Brooks Jr. & family (Indiana University); Earl V. DeShazor, Pauline DeShazor & family; Dr. Robert Bland (Lewis College of Business, Detroit, MI); K. Frank DeShazor; Iona Graves; Leslie Graves; Mr. & Mrs. Louis Graves; Dr. Frank Ware (Wayne State University Press); Kenneth S. Gadd; Vicki Gadd; Aunt Ida Bell Wilson; Renee Bell; Rochelle Bell; Regina Wilson, Ramona Wilson & children; Larry Glenn; Warren Hollier & Baiyina Omar (African Heritage Cultural Center, Detroit, MI); Matt & Nellie Adawi; Dennis Paul Jones; James S. Maxell; Sister Mary Melton Brooks; Pastor Victor Melton & family; Gina & Michael Morris; Algene Manson; Cynthia Pearson & Anthony E. Scott II; Robert & June Malburg; Emma & Lisa Sanders; Michael & Linda Williams; Paul Sanders; Tyrone Hinton; Sako Ujama & family; Troy & Wanda Thurman & family; Keith Lindsay; Michael Johnson; John Richardson (Hanna's Book Shop, Mt. Clemens MI); Ali Abdulah; Roy Ayers; Assata & Tupac Shakur; Sylvia Johnson; London Winters; Louis Wood Jr. & family; Kurt S. Eschenburg & family; Hargis Thomas; Prof. David Blight (Amherst University); John Franklin Jr. (Smithsonian Institution); Harold Blake & family; Aunt Thelma & Jame Green & family; Leon F. Heard; Celia Washington; Kamaal A. AmenRa; Mojo-Charles Johnson; Fred Gorée & family; Paul Gorée; Edward Gorée; Niki Gorée; Langston James

Richard Harrison Gorée

Gorée; Mayor Janie Glymph Gorée; Laura Hill; Jarda Alexander; Habiba Owens; Queen Mother Dr. Osum Dara; the late Bishop David L. Ellis; Marion Crawford; Carol Gibson; Rosita Gainey; Dr. Paul Egbo & family; Leon Shearer; Anita Johnson & family; Monica McCoy & family; Sharon Wallace; Steven A. Cleaves; Bob Tillman; Darlene Tillman; my friends and co-workers of Goodwill Industries of Greater Detroit; Joseph N'Diaye (Curator of the Slave House on Gorée Island); Walter Rap Bailey & family (for the cover illustration of the Signaré); Mark Sandell (for the cover design); and my publisher, Rebecca J. Ensign.

Foreword

Twenty-five years ago, inspired by a photograph of my great grandfather, Harrison Gorée, I began delving into the Gorée family tree. What began as curiosity quickly became a full-scale commitment—to my family, my ancestors and ultimately the heroes, victims and legacies of the Atlantic slave trade. The result of my commitment is this historical novel, set in the 17th century.

The theme of my story is "the two-sided coin" of slavery. I emphasize "two-sided" because it often happened that one person's freedom was purchased at the price of another person's slavery. This tale of Gorée Island, during its French occupation, is a strong, unique illustration of this.

The slave trade was a booming business in Africa and was usually carried out for the benefit of traders and tribal chiefs. However, a group of African women of mixed African-French lineage managed to place themselves in a powerful position in the slave business due to a strange twist in French law. In effect, this twist forced anyone wishing to engage in the slave trade on Gorée Island to marry one of these mulatto women.

My story illustrates this nuance of African history by focusing on the (fictional) life of one such woman—from her childhood, through her awareness of her position in her world, to the influence she wielded on other women in her position as they successfully manipulated their circumstances to their advantages. While these women triumphed in their endeavor, the question raised, of course, is simply: Is the price they paid worth what they actually bought?

Richard Harrison Gorée

I leave that to you, the reader, to determine. My objective is to cast another shade of light on the travesty of slavery while also showing that survival and control of one's destiny are universal truths of human nature and have been realized throughout history in the most adverse of circumstances.

Richard Harrison Gorée

Gorée Island: Island of No Return
Saga of the Signarés

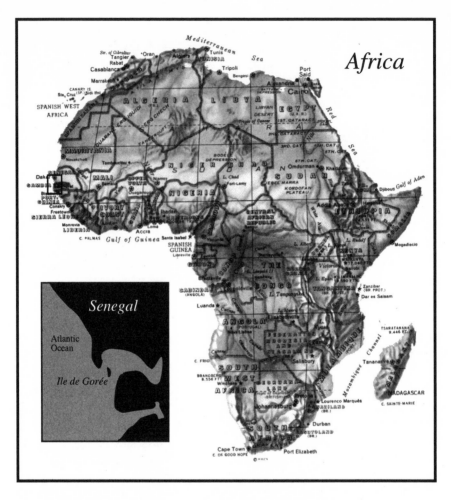

Gorée, Senegal, two miles out west in the Atlantic Ocean, was the main point of embarkation for slaves shipped to the Americas from West Africa. In 1588, Gorée was occupied by the Dutch who named it "Goede Reede" or "Good Harbor."

Because of its strategic position, the island was in constant political turmoil. Portuguese, Dutch, British and French each had control of Gorée at one time or another. Today, the island is considered a memorial to the black Diaspora and provides the backdrop for this story.

Prologue

The African woman had been in the process of giving birth since the moon rose. Now, with the silver disk at its brightest, she thrust the baby from her womb. She didn't hear her own cry. Instead, she was listening intently for the other cry she awaited, the sound of life from the newborn.

"It's a girl!" a quiet voice said beside her.

The African woman looked up through the dulling, aching pain to see the light, odd-featured face of the creche-girl who had been assigned to her. Then she saw her child being wiped and wrapped in a thin cotton blanket.

"I didn't expect you back so soon," the African woman said softly.

"The Captain was very drunk, and what he wanted was quick to do," she replied.

"Which captain was it?"

"The pockmarked one whose breath stinks."

Even in her pain, the African woman found a laugh.

Richard Harrison Gorée

"They all stink that way. They put a foul-smelling root in all their cooking. I've had to make food ready for them, food I couldn't eat myself if I were starving." She paused to breathe. "That's the captain of the ship that will take us away... tomorrow."

The creche-girl handed the African woman the squalling bundle.

"She will not cry long, then she will be hungry."

"I understand and I'm ready."

The girl paused. "The captain is said to be a hard man."

"I'll deal with that tomorrow."

Silently the creche-girl moved away, out of the slave-pen where the women were kept apart. The African woman saw her approach the guard, pass briefly out into the light, and then disappear. And when the girl left, the African woman forgot about her, and bent to her burden. This wasn't easy when one's ankles were chained by iron to a stone wall.

As the creche-girl had predicted, the baby's cries soon faded. But even as that cry died down, the African woman was aware of other sounds in the night. Though they sounded like the cries of beasts, they were not; they were the moans and groans of men, accompanied by the clank of chains in a regular rhythm. She knew well enough what these sounds signified.

The chains were coming off the walls in the stockades below, and they were being linked together so that the carefully guarded men, the valuable cargo, could be moved into the hold of the waiting ship.

She, too, would go. It would be a while before she knew what her destination must be; but as she had said, she would be ready.

The moon set, and the sun rose, and by the time it did the captain of the great trading vessel was well satisfied. He would be under way before the heat of the day. Entrancing as the African

2

night might be, with its pale mild moon, the African sun brought only one thing to a man's senses: unbearable heat, leading to thirst and fatigue.

With a practiced eye, he watched his men finish loading the ship. The last of the Africans came out of the fort's stockade, through the passage that was known as the Door of No Return, and down a steep staircase, shuffling slowly. At the foot of the stairs a man waiting by a hot fire thrust a branding iron onto the passing shoulders, burning each man forever with the initials of the French Company of Senegal. A few cried out; most only stared into space at this violation. Then, up a narrow gangplank they went, not under whips this time, but under the prods of sticks and growls from the deckhands. The Captain remained pleased. Keeping the men tightly chained did slow down the loading somewhat, but with a little prodding they could be made to move with adequate speed. Better that, the captain decided, than to use the sloven method of herding the men over the narrow gangplank unchained. That method had proved ineffective in the past. Some of the slaves had jumped. No doubt they knew they faced certain death in the shark-infested waters west of the island. Nevertheless, some had jumped.

Now the last of the male slaves were loaded, and the women were brought forth separately. It was not thought necessary to chain them, for they rarely caused any trouble.

Calling to one of his officers, the Captain stepped down from the ship's quarterdeck and walked over to the launching point. Carefully he inspected the women as they came aboard. Most of the women looked at their own feet. Only one pair of eyes rose to meet his intent glance.

The Captain studied this African woman with a flicker of interest. There was a look in her eyes that he had seen before, a look he couldn't place at that moment. She was a dark mulatto, with curly, black, silk hair, skin like roasted coffee, clear eyes of dark brown. On her finger was a gold ring. The Captain paused as his eyes caught its shimmer. That ring--it seemed vaguely familiar to him, as did she. His thoughts wandered to a night a few months ago, a night..... Smiling smugly, he glanced down at the bundle she held in her arms.

3

It was a baby, a newborn, hardly more than a few days old. The smile left his face.

With three gruff words he signified to the ship's officer to take the baby from the woman. The mother would fetch a high price. She was young, strong, handsome. But the baby...no, it must remain behind.

When the officer approached the young mother, she seemed about to protest, to resist, but once he had grabbed the baby from her, her arms fell to her sides. The baby began to cry loudly as the officer took it down the gangplank, but the mother paid no heed. Instead, she stared at the Captain, and in that instant he recognized the look in her eyes.

"Stop her!" he called in alarm, but it was too late. The woman was already in the water, a jump ahead of his men, and she was out of reach. She swam in a straight line, away from the harbor, with strong quick strokes.

Silently the Captain cursed himself. How could he have forgotten that look, the look of the enslaved men who chose death in the water in preference to a life in chains? It was rare in a woman, but nevertheless...

As he mulled over these things, the Captain saw the large dorsal fins appear and begin to close in.

The captain turned his attention from the matter and ordered the loading resumed. He was not one to dwell long on his own failings. He had little time for that. By the time he left the harbor, sailing westward, she would be forgotten. Perhaps it was for the best anyway. Sure, he had lost a valuable commodity, but such a spirited woman was a common source of trouble aboard ship. More than one like her had goaded the men into savage revolt, and the voyage was a long one.

As for the child, it lay in the arms of Mama-Lise, the island's Nurse Mother. She rocked the baby girl gently, admiring the coppery glow of her skin. Then, with a snap, she handed the baby to the young girl at her side; the same young girl who had helped the pregnant mother the night before.

"Take her to the creche, Helene-Marie. I will be up shortly."

With that, the old Nurse Mother sauntered away in the direction of one of the captains waiting on the pier. Mama-Lise had business to take care of. As she strolled away, however, she looked over her shoulder, unable to ignore the bellowing cries of the newly-born baby.

Such a fiery child, she thought to herself. Definitely a lion's cub.

Griots, travelling storytellers and musicians, were the traditional oral historians of Africa.

Chapter One

Hadithe Zakale, the teller of tales, sat close to a roaring open fire and gave no thought at all to where his next meal was coming from. He concentrated on the story of the moment, measuring his effect by the eyes of his hearers and making adjustments as he went along. This was a tale he had told many times, that of the blind man and the cripple; yet there were many ways to tell a tale, and in a way it was fresh each time he told it.

It was only when he had finished the tale, reaped the applause and sat back to watch the dancers who came next on the impromptu program of the village's harvest festival that Hadithe Zakale gave any thought to the future. He was reasonably content with the way things were going here. For another week yet he would be honored, entertained and splendidly well-fed here in the village that the natives, in their own odd tongue, called Hard Earth. After that, he would resume his travels, and as the season of harvest moved north and west this time of the year, he would follow it.

He had become, to some extent, a creature of habit, but these were easy habits he had to follow. He had no family at home, because basically he had no home, and yet he was at home wherever he went. He never lacked for food or drink, and if he needed a place to sleep or blanket to make sleep possible, he would get that too. He had few possessions, because he had no reason to carry necessities with him. They were at his command wherever he went.

Hadithe Zakale, the teller of tales, was no longer a journeyman at his craft. Nearing the age of forty, he was a master; and the decorations on his few possessions proved that to anyone who didn't know him by sight. King, or prince, or tribal chief, village elder, or commander of a troop, or trading mission, those who entertained him each gave him some token to add to his collection of what a later age would call testimonials. They decorated his cloak, his long necklace, and, most of all, his drum.

Idly he wondered what sort of token he would carry away from Hard Earth. It would be best to have something small, and strange, and very much inappropriate on the face of it; that would make it easier to associate the token with the village. It had been a long time since the teller of tales had visited a village so resoundingly misnamed. The earth thereabouts was anything but hard, and it was so fertile that there would be another harvest later on, far out of season for the general area.

At least that was what he'd been told by his host, the High Chief Kwame-Uhru, in the course of an explanation of the village's name.

"It is never wise to boast," the old chief had told him after taking much thought with Hadithe Zakale's question. "Some god might hear the boast, and be moved to jealousy. I don't know if your gods would feel that way, teller of tales, but mine have been known to."

The storyteller considered those words, and they made sense to him, for he had heard a great deal in his travels about various kinds of gods. It wasn't easy to distinguish them, in many cases, from the ranks of the demons and other evil spirits; sometimes the gods themselves seemed a bit confused. But such confusion always made for a good story.

"There is wisdom here," he had said at last to his host. "But what happens when a man's woman has given birth to a strong and healthy son? Dare he boast about that?"

"Oh, of course. But not too much. And not too loudly, you understand."

Hadithe Zakale had been a guest in many places, and there was a long list of hosts he was bound to remember in case, as often happened, the same host would one day greet him again. Kwame-Uhru was one he would remember well, for he was a man of uncommon parts. In the past few days the storyteller had seen him demonstrate good judgment, forbearance, generosity and on two occasions, necessary hardness. Even now, sitting in a place of honor to the north of the fire, Kwame-Uhru was demonstrating yet another fine quality of a chief: rapid dispatch of business between the dances.

What made this all unusual to Hadithe Zakale was that in at least two senses, Kwame-Uhru had no business being there at all. His rank was too high, and his status too low, for the post of a village chief.

How that could be might seem strange, and it had seemed strange to the storyteller until he pieced together (as he was bound to do) the parts of the tale. Kwame-Uhru was a high chief of the Ashanti nation, but his rank was a courtier's rank, not inherited at birth or conferred by a village, but stipulated by the Ashanti King. He was one of many such who were assigned, on request or perhaps in spite of it, to govern a community during the minority or incapacity of the rightful village or tribal leader.

But rank was one thing, status another. Kwame-Uhru did not try to hide his lack of the latter. The second part of his name was not a family name, but a descriptive; it was a corruption of the Swahili word *uhuru*, "free," and it described the only status Kwame-Uhru had ever achieved. In fact, the High Chief of the village of Hard Earth and the surrounding territory had been a slave of the Ashanti King.

Perhaps, Hadithe Zakale thought as he watched the dancers and the crowd and the undistracted attentiveness of Kwame-Uhru to business amidst the action, things had a way of balancing out. But he

9

had best be thinking of the next tale of the night; the dance was coming to an end. He let his eyes dig deep into the crowd, trying to judge the mood, trying to guess which of his myriad tales would go over best at the moment.

"Teller of tales, have you truly traveled from one end of this world to the other?"

Hadithe Zakale looked up with a start. This was not the cue he had expected. It was a moment before he realized it wasn't a cue at all, but a polite and straightforward question from a man of no nonsense: The High Chief.

The storyteller inclined his head, a brief bow appropriate to his own status and that of his interrogator.

"I haven't been to the world beyond the ocean," he replied. "But from here I've been north to the desert lands where the sand stretches out like mountains; east to the high lakes where the Great River arises; south to beyond the land of the lion and the elephant, where the trees grow together in one mass like the tangle of an old man's hair; and west to the great ocean, where the waves rise higher than those tangled trees and the fish can be larger than a house, longer than a thrown spear's measure."

The old Chief chuckled. "There you see our problem, teller of tales. We seem to be right in the calm and quiet middle of things. All wonders are far away from us, at the edge of the earth. For although I have heard of a land beyond the ocean, I don't really believe it exists. Well! Will you help us get as close as you can? Tell us of the West, and the great ocean, and the people who live by it."

The teller of tales nodded; he would have done so no matter what the request, for such a man as himself was supposed to know a story of every kind, or be ready to invent one on the spot, if he didn't. In a way, he was glad that Kwame-Uhru hadn't asked in detail about those big fish in the ocean; he'd only heard of those, not actually seen them, and his lies might have had to be extensive.

Still, he must give the High Chief a second shot at asking about them, since protocol demanded such.

"High Chief, the honored Kwame, I've often traveled to the shores of that ocean, and I have seen many things both wonderful and commonplace. What will you hear?"

"Why, both the wonderful and the commonplace would be good, for the one will excite us, and the other, remind us that it happened among people like ourselves."

"And is there more?"

The High Chief appeared to consider for a moment. "Yes, let me ask you one more thing. For I had a dream the other night. I had a dream that there was an island in the west, and that people who came to it never returned; the women stayed and ruled, and the men were taken away in huge ships by men with white skins. Could this be a true dream? Can you tell me?"

Hadithe Zakale's eyes widened slightly, as if in mild surprise, which was appropriate and misleading, for he was much more surprised than he was willing to let on.

"I think it is a true dream, honored Kwame, for I know of such a place. I haven't been there for many years, but I will tell you what I know.

Chapter Two

Down below the fort, the sounds of afternoon preparations for the evening meal dominated the half-dozen mud huts that alone existed to justify the term "village".

Helene-Marie, a young mulatto woman, was behind in her work. Preparing lunch for the garrison commander and the Factor had made her so. She didn't really mind, however, for she found the duties of cook and waitress a great deal less bothersome than creche-work. She had been engaged in creche-work for nearly eight years, and while she liked children and missed the bustle of being a nurse-maid to some extent, she liked the kitchen work better. Besides, she had two children of her own now, and an adopted third, a seven-year-old girl she had named Sasha.

Sasha had been born to a slave woman. Helene-Marie had been there that night. She had helped the slave mother give birth. Helene-Marie remembered that night so clearly. It was the night the storytellers had come... Helene-Marie caught herself before she became too engrossed in her thoughts. How silly of her to think of that now. She had dinner to prepare and the children would be home from the creche soon.

Helene-Marie's own children, Jeanne and Andre were three and four. Those were not their real names, of course, any more than Helene-Marie was the mulatto woman's own real name. Rather, they were labels the whites had insisted on attaching to them, as they did for everyone on the island: native, European or mixed. Somehow, a name was not really a name to these strange northern people unless it was French.

Except, Helene-Marie reflected as she worked over the cooking pot, for Sasha. Three years ago, when Father Philip had prepared a baptismal register and handed out the names, he had put her down in the records as Marianne. Sasha, however, only four years old at the time, insisted that she knew her own name and it was not Marianne. She made such a fuss over the change that, at least in the village, it never stuck. Any adult who called her Marianne got a cold stare: any child, a kick in the shins, if not a blow from a small fist. The name Marianne remained on the fort's records but, at least among her own people, she was called Sasha.

Idly, Helene-Marie glanced up as Sasha came bursting into the kitchen and without a word began cutting up some vegetables. The young mulatto woman had long ago given up questioning Sasha about her comings and goings. The girl knew when she was needed, and was always there. If she wasn't needed, she was nowhere to be found.

Like all the island children, Sasha was given a great deal of room to roam as soon as she was old enough to walk. It was, after all, a small island and very difficult to get lost. Some of the island children took more advantage of this slight freedom than others; Sasha was one who took full advantage of it.

"Isn't that ship in the harbor the one with the captain called Tremblay?" Sasha suddenly asked, not looking up from her vegetables.

Helene-Marie looked up, surprised. Like all household servants, Sasha had a good ear for gossip. Obviously she had made the connection between the ship and the man who was master.

13

"Yes, that's Captain Tremblay's ship," Helene-Marie answered quietly.

"Then I suppose he'll ask for you, as he always does."

Helene-Marie shrugged. It was not a matter of great concern for her, although that particular Captain did indeed ask for her when his ship called at the island. In fact, he was probably responsible for the existence of Jeanne, if not for Andre. But there was no certainty in such matters, and on the island it made little difference.

"If he asks for me, he asks for me. What of it, Sasha?"

"I just wondered. All the other captains go from one woman to another, sometimes in one stay. Sailors are even more that way. Why does he want you all the time?"

Helene-Marie was tempted to say something harsh and dismissing, to stress that it was none of the child's business, but somehow that didn't seem right. It was a question she had wondered about herself, so it was perhaps natural for the child to wonder about it, too. She didn't consider herself any great beauty (Sasha, when she grew up, would have far more of that), and she had little of the thing Frenchman called *allure*. Yet there was an explanation, or so she thought.

"He's an older man than most," she responded after a moment. "An older man wants the same things a young one does, but he's less concerned about it. I don't think he seeks adventure, new things, with the same drive. I suppose Captain Tremblay has grown used to me. I make him comfortable, and he is content with that."

"He always wears those great rings on his fingers. Five or six of them. Wouldn't you like to have one of them?"

Helene-Marie cast Sasha a sharp glance. "He doesn't have to give me anything. Or didn't you pay attention to the things Mama-Lise has to say about that?"

"Nothing is due you," the child replied, mimicking the voice of the old Nurse Mother whose word had always been a kind of law for the islanders. She had, after all, raised most of the people who had been on the island for any length of time...had raised Helene-Marie herself, and Sasha too, from the time her mother had flung herself into the sea.

"But they do give things," Sasha went on. "Sometimes they do. Captain Tremblay has given you things."

Helene-Marie nodded. "Useful things, Sasha. Food, sometimes, and a thing or two for the house. But nothing of that kind."

"But you would like to have one, wouldn't you? To wear, I mean?"

Helene-Marie sighed and laid aside her ladle, wiping her hands.

"Yes, I would like that, but it is unimportant."

"Why not ask for one then?"

The young mulatto woman regarded the child in astonishment. She met a matter-of-fact stare, as if the suggestion was the most ordinary on earth. She was about to reply, not knowing what to say, but being forced to say something, when in the distance a bell tolled. The moment for speech passed abruptly, almost as abruptly as Sasha did; the hour bell was the signal, among other things, for mothers who had children at the creche to come and get them for the evening. Sasha had appropriated this task long ago and went in search of Andre and Jeanne.

Helene-Marie picked up the ladle and resumed work over the cooking pot. A lion's cub, Helene-Marie scoffed. Mama-Lise had been correct in her assumption of Sasha. The child was fierce and unrelenting. Zealously, she tried to put the entire conversation out of her mind. She tried, and tried again, but somehow her thoughts always came back to it, and most of all to Sasha's last words. She found she couldn't get them out of her mind at all.

"Helene! Helene-Marie! Hurry up with that wine, before we die of thirst!"

There was no immediate response, but Lieutenant Etienne Desjardins didn't doubt there would be one. When he raised his voice, it could be heard the length and breadth of Fort St. Francois,

15

and generally understood, even if it had to pass through wooden walls. For a man who was accustomed to drilling his small garrison as if it were a guards regiment, it was a source of pride to be heard clearly.

His companion might have been impressed, but, having spent more than a year and a half on the island, he had grown used to the Lieutenant's ways. They were two men of very different natures. The Lieutenant was tall, a bit overweight, a light-skinned man from the north of France whose face glowed red from overexposure to the sun. Henri Aubrisson, by contrast, was from the south of France, a Provençal by birth. He was small, olive-complected, and unusually quiet for a man with such considerable authority. One would never have guessed him the Chief Factor of the Senegal Trading Company, the *Companie du Cap-Verde et Senegal.*

The two men got along well despite their many contrasts. It was fortunate for both of them that they did. Each knew this and, when necessary, worked consciously at it. Each had independent authority, and there was no one, save the King of France himself, who could have issued an order binding both. More than once in the brief history of French control of this island, the limited space had been too small to hold both an opinionated garrison commander and a stubborn company factor.

The wine arrived in due course, brought by a tall, slender mulatto woman whose mixed blood was reflected both in her features and her skin color. Trailing behind her, as always, was a young girl with the same coppery skin, bearing a basket of bread.

They didn't speak, but merely set down their burdens, bowed politely, and scurried away. Aubrisson watched casually as they departed. They seemed to move almost in unison, and one might have thought they were mother and daughter, but this wasn't so. The woman, Helene-Marie had two children of her own. The child, Sasha, was a former charge of hers, an orphaned child left to the care of the creche when her mother flung herself into the sea. Although Aubrisson was not on the island when all of this occurred, he had heard the stories. The stories of the woman who would live freely or not at all. Aubrisson wondered if the child had the same spirit. There was something in her eyes, something strange. But then again, all of the island people seemed strange to Aubrisson. He left it at that; he wasn't quite interested enough to try to understand these people.

After the two men had drunk the customary toast to Louis Quatorze, the King of France, and the Lieutenant had executed his customary smack of the lips in appreciation of the wine, he cocked his head to one side and favored Aubrisson with an amused glance.

"So, *M'sieu* Aubrisson! We have done everything properly, and spent our dinner in pleasantries concerned with the climate. But now we have the wine. So out with it, my friend!"

Aubrisson's eyebrows went up ever so slightly, but, adopting his companion's bantering tone, he responded playfully.

"Why, whatever do you mean, Lieutenant? Out with what?"

"The news! As you well know. You spend ten days in Saint-Louis de Senegal, where ships from France are forever coming and going, and you pretend you've come back here with nothing to tell me?"

"Um, well, I did receive some orders to process. Some new policies of the company to put into practice. Also a new pair of shoes that might last three or four weeks, given the pleasant climate you mentioned. That sort of thing?"

Lieutenant Desjardins sighed, and then burst into loud laughter.

"All right, all right. I will be so blunt as to ask. What news of the wider world, Henri?"

"Oh, that. Well, I have news of a caravan, and a priest, and a revolution. The caravan and the priest are close by and will affect us, and the revolution is far away and probably won't...so I suppose I should deal with them in order. How say you?"

"I say, by all means proceed as you suggest."

Aubrisson did so, launching into a detailed description of the caravan that was now wending its way westward through territories claimed by France. Word traveled quickly through the African lands, much faster than men or beasts of burden, and when it touched on possible trade goods, men like Aubrisson were quick to size it up and make preparations. The Lieutenant nodded appreciatively at the details of what this caravan contained, with an eye to what part of it he

17

might acquire that would suit his needs. It was of more interest in its entirety, however, to Aubrisson himself. It would be Aubrisson's business to see that the caravan reached the coast off Gorée, and that ships would be available to take its cargo.

"That's very interesting," the Lieutenant said when Aubrisson had finished. "Hides and gum and slaves. Yes, I can see you will be busy as usual. But what of gold and ivory?"

Aubrisson shrugged. "Ivory, some certainly, it's been seen and it's been reported. But you know how it is about gold. They keep that as quiet as they can until they're actually on the point of trading it. Many of these tribal chieftains are little better than robbers." He shifted in the hard wooden chair that was all too typical of garrison furniture, in no way comparable to his own stuffed chair in the Company Factor's offices a few yards away.

"But don't worry. Our warehouse is full of trade goods, and there's a great deal in your own account, as in mine. Whatever they bring, we will each have a full share of it, and the King and company will be happy, too."

The Lieutenant snorted. "*Eh bien*, let's make it so. Well, so much for the caravan. Now what about this priest you mentioned? Surely a priest is not news. They're always sending one up from St. Louis. He gets tired, and he gets frustrated, or his native laziness gets to him and he goes way off somewhere else, at which point we are at peace until they send a new one. Look at Father Philip. He was here for less than five months."

"I know. But this one, the one that's coming on the *Durance*, he is from France."

"From France?" Desjardins echoed in astonishment. "They send him to this place? How could they do such a thing?"

"It seems he requested the assignment."

Aubrisson paused while his companion took that news in. He knew what the Lieutenant must be thinking. Ever since the time of the Portuguese there had been a priest in or near the island to conduct services for the small congregation of garrison soldiers, free Africans, mulattoes and visiting sailors. But most of these priests were of native blood. Some were Europeans of mixed backgrounds, others temporarily assigned to Gorée before returning to Saint-Louis or going on to some other African post. A priest straight out of France would be unique.

"I suppose," the Lieutenant said, "we had best get the women to clean the cobwebs out of the chapel. Although I must admit it hasn't really been that neglected, priest or no; there are always candles burning before Mary's altar, at least."

Aubrisson nodded. He was not at all sure those candles really signified what a European imagined they did, but he let that issue alone.

"If he asked to come here," the Lieutenant continued, "He must have some idea about doing things here. Could that be a problem?"

"I doubt it," Aubrisson replied quietly. "I've met this priest; he's called Father Charles. You wouldn't think him old enough to be anyone's 'father' if he weren't a priest. He wanted to come here immediately on the trading skiff that brought me back, but I begged off. As you noted, we need time to prepare...and perhaps to get ready to let him down gently. Still, he seems to have a head on his shoulders, so I think he'll get a quick grasp of how we run things here." Aubrisson permitted himself a chuckle. "This is the kind of missionary territory, if it is that, that would have driven St. Francis himself to madness."

Talk drifted then into a familiar discussion of the nature of the island and its people. It was a port, a slave depot, a military garrison, a minor naval base, peopled by such a mixed lot of folk as perhaps existed nowhere else south of the Sahara. The two men became so engrossed in this line of conversation that they were on the verge of returning to their separate duties when the Lieutenant captured the one hanging thread.

"Did you not mention a revolution, Henri? What, and where? Were there any battles worth noting?"

"Hardly. I don't think a shot was fired. A few months ago, it seems the English thought their king might be returning to the True Church, so they threw him out."

"Ah! Another Cromwell episode, eh?"

"No. They didn't boot the monarchy, only the monarch. They dethroned James Stuart and then turned 'round and gave the crown to William of Orange."

"The Dutchman? Impossible! The English would stand for a plain usurper like Cromwell before they'd put up with a Dutchman."

"It's true, my friend. It may not last, however, since our own King is a friend of James Stuart. King Louis has welcomed the exile at his court. But the English seem determined."

"*Mon Dieu* ! The English are fools!" The Lieutenant paused to reflect on the matter in military fashion. "If they see no danger, they are fools...or else, as you have said, determined men, and men who think the people are with them. But they may live to regret that decision. I think they have not heard the last of the House of Stuart. It may come back, as it has before. Meanwhile we may have to think about defending this island. Who knows what might chance?"

He got up and strode to the one window of the garrison office, a window that overlooked the island's protected anchorage. There were no ships in the harbor now except for the small trading skiffs that went back and forth ceaselessly between the island and the mainland, bringing the necessities of life. Foremost among these was water. The island itself was barren of streams, except for a small trickle off the south end of the high hill on the opposite side. There was a well, but not a very productive one. What little food was grown on the island depended on the infrequent rains, or minor irrigation projects which were rarely followed through. Because of these conditions, it was easy for the island to change hands. It had in fact changed hands many times already and might do again. Lieutenant Desjardins concentrated on the defense tactics. It would not be easy to storm the island. Gorée was equipped with two forts and several cannons. It would be difficult to attack, but then why would anyone bother to attack, really, when it could be starved and parched with dramatic speed?

After a few moments the Lieutenant turned from the window, and Aubrisson, thanking him for dinner, took his leave. Both had work to do.

20

Some games are as old as the human race, reinvented by new generations of children if they haven't been learned. Hide-and-seek is one such game, and the children of the island played with great skill and perseverance. Not all participated of course, but those in the range between six and eight had a regular session every day as the sun began to set. Dinner over, they were once again free to roam.

One of the favorite spots for this activity was a long ridge on the west side of the island, where the ground was rough and rocky. No one on the island had much use for the territory, so the trees and undergrowth were left to nature. The children loved the unruly playground it afforded.

Two girls and two boys, Arsene, Sasha, Denis and 'Tien, were busily searching for a third boy, Vincent, when he accidentally gave himself away. He didn't do this by showing himself. Rather he let out a cry of anger and pain from the midst of a thick clump of grasses, and followed that with a series of epithets that were part of the privileged inheritance of children who live in a place sailors frequent.

The other four, converging on the grass-clump, found Vincent sitting on the ground, holding his right foot, rubbing his big toe. Something had caught in it, twisting and tripping him.

"Clumsy," Arsene said.

"Oh, yes, of course," the boy replied, wincing still. He pointed at something sticking out of the ground. "Who put that trap there?"

'Tien, a very light-skinned boy about eight years old, reached for the object. It was an iron ring of some kind, and to his surprise, he could not pull it out of the ground.

"It's stuck on something," he said. "Let's all pull."

"We can't all pull," Sasha said. "There's not enough room for all of us to get a grip on it, stupid."

"Who's stupid?"

"You are. But I'll help you, 'Tien. Somebody always has to."

Ignoring the boy's response, Sasha reached over and with two youngsters pulling, there was suddenly movement. It wasn't what they had expected. The ring came up, but the ground seemed to come up with it, dirt tumbling from the area around the ring. Then they saw wood, and an opening beneath.

"A door!" Denis exclaimed. "Pull it all the way back!"

"If there's anything down there," Vincent said at once, "It's mine! I found it!"

Ignoring this claim, the other children pulled the door back. Down below, they saw a series of steps leading into the earth and into absolute darkness. They could barely see the bottom.

"Well, who's going for a look?" Sasha asked.

"Not me!" Denis said. "There might be snakes down there!"

"How about you, Vincent?" Sasha asked. "You said what's down there is yours. Well, go get it."

Vincent just stared at her, and Sasha laughed.

"I forgot, you're afraid of the dark."

"I am NOT!" the boy yelled. "I just got a sore foot, is all. But you, you're so brave and smart, why don't you go down there yourself, Sasha?" He grinned. "I'll give you a third of everything you find."

"Half," Sasha said pleasantly.

"All right, all right. And I hope it *is* snakes!"

Shrugging this off, Sasha walked over to the trapdoor and began climbing down. Rapidly she disappeared into the darkness, and into silence. The other children, surrounding the opening, listened intently, but they could hear no sound. Finally, after what seemed like a very long time, Sasha reappeared.

"What's there?" Vincent demanded.

"Nothing I could see," Sasha replied offhandedly. "At the bottom there's a tunnel, that goes a ways back and comes to an empty room. That's all. Just an empty room."

A chorus of disappointment greeted her report. She waved her hands.

"But that doesn't mean we can't use it for something," she insisted. "Probably the people who built the room are long gone, and the Frenchmen have forgotten it."

"Who wants an old dark room?" Denis said.

"We might, if we were ever trying to hide from someone." Sasha paused to let that sink in. "Let's not tell anyone about this. We might have something valuable here, at least to us."

There was general, if grudging agreement to her proposal. Eventually the children put the trapdoor back in place, smoothed earth over it, and carefully hid the iron ring in a clump of dirt and grasses. Then they remembered that Vincent was "it," and took off in various directions.

Sasha was well satisfied. No one would know about the discovery, and none of the others was likely to go exploring. She wanted to do some of that herself. She hadn't exactly told the others the truth. There was a tunnel down there, all right, but it seemed to go on and on forever. She hadn't found the end of it. But one day she would.

"A good day for sailing, Captain," Henri Aubrisson said with a smile. "And by the look of it, more such days to come. I hope to see weather like this when it comes time to go home to France."

Captain Jean Tremblay grunted in response. He wasn't interested in idle chit-chat. Especially not with a man like Henri Aubrisson. Aubrisson interpreted this grunt as grudging agreement. A man like Jean Tremblay, a man of the sea, was never an optimist when it came to the weather. Things happened too abruptly and they happened constantly. Even the naval officers who called at the island were in agreement. One officer had once told Aubrisson, "Neither the Dutch nor the English can make a coward out of me, but the sea can."

As the captain of the *Durance* stood beside him on the loading dock, Aubrisson turned his mind to other things. This was a most welcome state of affairs, but it called for caution. Tremblay's ship had not been anchored for more than a day before the caravan arrived on the coast opposite the island. Aubrisson had been busy in three-way negotiations ever since, as he and Tremblay selected cargo.

Ivory, gum arabic, and a respectable number of slaves now weighed down the ship's hold. And there was gold, too, although a great deal of it remained on the island. Aubrisson was thankful that he and Desjardins were of one mind when it came to gold and personal profits. The two men stored their share in the depths of the fort under tight guard.

"Time to go," Captain Tremblay said abruptly. Aubrisson nodded and from his pockets drew several sealed items that he had been saving until the last moment, as was the custom. They were letters bound home for France, letters from himself, Lieutenant Desjardins, and a few select others. Tremblay, receiving the massive packet, nodded without another word and stuffed them into his own coat pocket, where they made a considerable bulge. He proceeded up the gangplank and took a stand on the guardrail, where he watched as the sailors cast off the lines.

He was not alone in watching this operation. Most of the island's permanent population had turned out to watch the ship depart. They were women and children for the most part. Men were intermittent inhabitants. They went where work drew them, some on ships, some on company business on the mainland. But those who happened to be on the island were all along the shoreline, for this was after all a major event, one of the few events that interrupted the drudgery of everyday life.

At this point, Aubrisson was startled to hear the Captain's voice raised from the deck.

"Helene-Marie! Are you there?"

As if in answer, the young mulatto woman who was the garrison commander's occasional cook stepped forward from the crowd. She did so a bit hesitantly, looking up in question at the figure on the high deck. Suddenly, the Captain raised his hand and tossed something through the air. It was an accurate throw, for the young woman caught it easily, then stared down at what was in her hand in some kind of wonderment.

"*Au 'voir*," Tremblay called. There was a light mockery in

his voice. "Be good until we meet again."

With that the Captain turned away and marched in his slow, rolling, sea-legged fashion to the quarterdeck of the ship. Aubrisson, out of the corner of his eye, saw the people of the island close in on the young mulatto woman to inspect her prize, which was somehow cause for exclamations. Aubrisson had a feeling he knew what it was. He had seen the glint of gold as the object passed through the air. Probably a coin, a "Louie" or a "Joe," as the natives called them, named respectively after the portraits they bore: Louis XIV of France and the late King Joao of Portugal.

Finally, as the ship moved away, Aubrisson himself turned away from the harbor. There was a slight smile on his face. Always gold. It was well to remember what he was here for.

Mama-Lise, the Nurse Mother of the creche, was haughty in her anger. She was a large woman and well respected. Hence, her anger was revered.

"You asked him for it! Don't tell me you didn't, Helene-Marie. And you know better! *Merde*! You know better!"

"No, Mama-Lise, I did not ask for it," Helene-Marie replied softly, turning the ring around and around on her finger as if she still didn't believe its presence was real. "I did...admire it, and the other ones the Captain wears."

"That's the same as asking for it under the circumstances. You let a child put that idea into your head, woman. Yes, you, Sasha, I mean you. Don't bother denying it."

Sasha, who had been standing back among the crowd now stepped forward. Another child might have been sent scampering by the sound of her name uttered in that particular tone, but Sasha simply looked up at Mama-Lise and spoke.

"Why shouldn't she have something, if he gives it to her?"

"Impudent brat," the old woman growled. "You know what I'm going to do with you? When Hadithe Zakale, the teller of tales, comes back here to visit, then when he goes on his travels again I am going to send you with him."

Helene-Marie studied Sasha's reaction to this. It was not un-expected, though perhaps a surprise to the Nurse Mother, that there was only a shrug in response. The teller of tales had stayed on the island long enough to make a memory of himself, but Mama-Lise had twisted that memory somewhat to make him a bit of a boogey-man. The threat of his return was designed to frighten ill-mannered children into mending their ways.

Sasha had been a newborn infant when the teller of tales de-parted, and it had been seven years since then. But if she had any fear of this mysterious personage, she didn't show it. A brave girl, Helene-Marie reflected. Perhaps bravery and the boldness that went with it were more important in life than they sometimes seemed.

Her thoughts wandered back to the gold bauble on her hand.

Chapter Three

The white man's flushed, puffy face wasn't suited to give his angry words the proper effect. He stuttered, and he hissed, and he kicked at the sand and stones on the beach. All of this action was accompanied by wild emphatic gestures, typical enough of French expression to be unremarkable in most circumstances. Only now, with the gestures accompanying incoherent words, the effect was almost comic.

Jean-Baptiste, the *laptot*, or free sailor, didn't laugh, however. If he had raised his head, he would have shown a face like a mask, expressionless and unaffected. But he didn't raise his head. He merely stood by the shore with his hands clasped behind his back and his chin sunk onto his chest until the white man's tirade had subsided. When it did, *M'sieu* Danton, the Chief Factor of the Senegal Company, turned on his heel, spat in disgust, and marched away from the shore. A gesture flung back as he departed indicated that the unloading of the small company skiff was to resume.

"Eh, Batees! Give us a hand! You're only the skipper when

we're on the water!"

Now Jean-Baptiste did smile, for it was only old Gilbert speaking, and Gilbert was his friend. He'd have reacted much differently if those words had come from another member of the crew, particularly if they'd been spoken by the fumbling Wolof tribesman whose failure to obey orders had caused the company skiff to run aground. The damaged skiff was the cause of *M'sieu* Danton's anger.

But the Wolof would not have spoken. The Wolof knew no French, and besides, he was making himself very busy with the water kegs.

Raising one of the kegs himself, Jean-Baptiste shouldered the load and carried it up from the shore to the waiting watercart. As he reached the top of the rise, a sea-breeze wafted over from the windward side of the island to the west. It was sharp and strong and it caused Jean-Baptiste a pang of longing to pull it into his lungs.

It did not matter, really, that *M'sieu* Danton had berated him, for the company factor knew as well as Jean-Baptiste what had actually happened and where the fault lay. The display was for show. The Wolof would not crew on the water boat again, and that would be enough. But what Jean-Baptiste waited for was the day when he himself would no longer be bound to the waterboat. Not even as "captain," a position which gave him much responsibility and very little authority.

Jean-Baptiste was a *laptot*, a sailor, a man of the sea. And like all *laptots* , he was mulatto, born of mixed mothers and European fathers. He, like most, busied himself with the menial jobs on the island. Even as a captain he was little more than a slave. African men on the island, even free mulatto men, were treated as second-class citizens. It was the women who had all the power: the mulatto women, the *signarés*. Jean-Baptiste sounded the word with disgust. The *signarés* were merely whores who catered to the white men, exchanged their bodies for gold trinkets. The longer Jean-Baptiste stayed on the island, the more the situation disgusted him. One day he would leave this place; he would be the captain of a real ship. Then he would truly be free. In the meantime, he had to eat. So, he would do as the company factor asked. He would skipper the water skiff, he would watch in disgust as the *signarés* delivered their evening meals. Life would go on as before. A small hut, meager rations, tedious days...

It was surprising how much of an effect a soundless breeze could have on a man when a torrent of words had no effect at all. But it had started Jean-Baptiste to brooding, and later, in the hut he shared with Gilbert, the brooding continued.

They had made a meal in an single old iron pot, as was their custom; a stew this night, light on meat but heavy on a variety of vegetables. Now while old Gilbert snored in one corner of the room, Jean-Baptiste lay awake in the darkness, the roll of the sea echoing in his mind.

He could easily remember a time when he had not been a sailor. He had after all been fifteen when he first went to sea, and he was barely thirty now. Still, the latter half of his life had been far more memorable than the first half. Growing up as a free African in the French colony at Saint-Louis, he'd had the fortune to be the son of one of the Governor's household servants. He'd been able to get a place on a ship when he reached the right age. Hauling and throwing lines, caulking the innumerable holes that appeared in wooden craft passing through salt water, bailing when closing those holes proved impossible. It was a hard life, but he didn't have any trouble getting to sleep when it came his turn to do so. He found the food good. After all, the ships on which he sailed were the kind of coastal craft that ranged up and down West Africa, and there were always markets wherever they called. There was wine too, and there were women in the ports.

Jean-Baptiste, thinking of the women, grunted aloud in disgust. In any port, but not on this miserable island. Oh, there might be plenty of wine, but it was locked up in the factor's warehouse and in the military storehouses. And as for women, they might as well have been locked away too, for all the chance a free African lacking gold had of approaching them.

No, they saved themselves for white ship captains and others who could pay the freight. It had not, he recalled, always been that way. It was true only of the last three or four years. But somehow

29

these island women had learned that they could get away with charging for their favors; and now, though they might still live in mud huts, they sparkled with fortunes when they walked to church.

Next to the modest hut he and Gilbert occupied, there was the home of a mulatto woman. She had two children of her own and an older girl she was raising as foster-mother. He could hear faint noises from that neighboring hut, and he recalled vividly how he had made the same noises with her a few years back. He could even more vividly recall how he had been snubbed by her on this latest return to the island; snubbed because he had no trinkets to offer.

Not only had the woman snubbed him this time, but the older girl who lived with her, the one called Sasha, had openly mocked him in the village for not having any money. She had called him a macaque, a monkey. Had she been older...

"Batees?" a quiet old voice suddenly interrupted his thoughts. "You are ready to sail again, no?"

It startled Jean-Baptiste to realize that old Gilbert was still awake, and instantly he apologized for keeping the old man up. Gilbert merely laughed.

"No matter. But perhaps I have some good news for you. There is a ship coming."

"There's always a ship coming, Gilbert. Telling when it will get here is another matter."

"This one will be here in two, perhaps three days. A cargo vessel from the South, loaded already with gum and other things, not a slaver."

Jean-Baptiste hesitated. "Did you see this in the fire, Gilbert, or hear it on the wind?"

Gilbert chuckled. "I am as civilized as you now, Batees and no longer believe in those things. No, I heard this not on the wind but in the Factor's conversation with the Lieutenant at the fort. They are preparing to make some sort of deal with the ship captain called Leclerc. They say he's a shrewd man, hard to negotiate with. But they are resourceful. They'll find something he wants. They always do."

Jean-Baptiste snorted. "Leclerc? They can deal with him at

any time they wish. Just get him a woman, the younger the better. Especially if there are no slaves on board, he will be in the market for that, I can tell you." He paused, thinking things over. " But he isn't a bad sort. I've sailed with him before. And *mon Dieu* ! I will sail with him again. Yes, I am ready, perhaps more than you can guess."

"Oh, I can guess, Batees. You're a young man, and used to the sea. This is no place for a young man at all, much less so for one who is a *laptot*."

For a while the two were silent, but eventually Jean-Baptiste spoke again.

"What is it about this place, old one? It's different from other ports I've seen. And it didn't used to be, not until a few years ago. I can't put my finger on the difference, however."

Another silence slipped by, until Gilbert answered.

"No permanence, Batees. This isn't really a home for anyone. People wouldn't live here at all except for the ships that call. There's little here to sustain life. If the Factor didn't have a garden, there would be no crops here at all. And the people aren't under any rule except for the soldiers and the company. They have no ancestral ties to each other. Half of them don't know who their parents were or which tribe claimed them. "But," he added with sudden emphasis, "these are not things for your concern. Get some sleep, and dream of the sea. Who knows? They might even take you all the way to France, this trip."

Jean-Baptiste chuckled, rolled over on his side and tried to do as Gilbert bade him. It would be pleasant indeed to visit French soil, yes, and having heard so many stories of that fabled land, to find out whether they were true, or merely storytellers' lies, like so many others. But it would be good to get off the island in any case. And there was a parting gesture he would like to make. Especially knowing Claude Leclerc as he did, yes, it would be a useful and a satisfying gesture as well.

Jean-Baptiste didn't know it, but he had come much closer to serious trouble than he'd thought. Not because Eugene Danton was a vindictive man, not because the Company Factor was unaware of the reason for the damage to the water skiff, but because Danton was a bitter and frightened man these days, a man looking for a target. The only thing that saved Jean-Baptiste from a lashing was the fact that he was one of the only Africans on the island capable of coordinating the water skiff.

Danton, in turn, was of course unaware of Jean-Baptiste's feelings about the island. If they had been able to talk they would perhaps have found much common ground. Eugene Danton detested the island and everything about it. Each day seemed as if it might be his last.

He was in his late forties, a much older man than his predecessor. Danton shuddered at the thought of Henri Aubrisson. Such a young man, vital, and yet he was not strong enough to overcome the fever. The only remainder of the young factor was a small whitewashed cross in the island cemetery: Henri Aubrisson, 1660-1690.

The personal wealth Aubrisson had hoped to take home with him to France had been discovered after his death, and dutifully reported to the Senegal Company. Danton had reported and returned a full half of it to the company's accounts. As for the other half, well, it was quite satisfying to have such an amount on one's own account.

Fever was not the danger Danton feared, however. His fear was rooted in the deep financial trouble the Senegal Company faced. There was talk of absorbing the company into the sounder French East India Company. That would mean the dispatch of a new factor and inevitably, a hostile investigation of the old factor. He would be forced to take the blame for the financial troubles, and that was unacceptable to Danton. He had only been factor for three years. He'd be damned if he were going to take the fall for men like Aubrisson. If only the company could hold out until next year. Danton could finish his rotation, return to France with honor, and live comfortably on the private account.

It was another kind of trouble that brought Danton back to

his senses. A ship was coming, not one of the company's own, but a licensed free trader.

Normally that would mean a major opportunity both for the Company and Danton himself. Trade negotiations, both company-based and private could take place, profits could be discussed..... but this ship appeared to already have a full cargo. To make matters worse, right now Danton himself was short of the kind of trade goods that would appeal to an independent operator like Captain Leclerc. Still, he had to find some way to work a trade. He had to come up with something to draw away part of Leclerc's cargo cheaply, so that the acquisition could be laden aboard one of the company's own ships later on, at very heavy profit.

A heavy rustle of skirts up the stairs of his office building was followed by a knock at the door. Danton knew that a summons had been answered with the usual tardiness.

"So!" he called out. "Is that you, Elise? Where were you an hour ago?"

Unperturbed, the old Nurse Mother of the island's creche hefted her bulk through the doorway, and, without waiting for an invitation, sat down in the chair nearest the door. Fortunately, it was the strongest of Danton's chairs. Even so, the Factor winced.

"We have visitors coming," he told her, cautiously eyeing the legs of the chair. The old woman simply nodded her head, as if she had already known it. This of course was not possible, Danton thought, irked by her smug mannerism.

"One ship. Many sailors," he continued. "They can catch as catch can, in the usual fashion. There are however three ship's officers for whom arrangements must be made, and, of course, the Captain, for whom we must make special arrangements."

He pretended to study a paper in front of him, sitting quietly at his desk for a moment. Then he looked up.

"This ship is the *Hereaux*. The captain is Leclerc. You are aware of his tastes and preferences."

"*Oui*," the old woman responded in her guttural French. "I will pass the word."

"One moment. Captain Leclerc was perhaps not altogether

33

pleased with his companionship on his last visit. I think it was Arsene? Yes, Arsene. We cannot have a repeat. We need someone younger."

The old woman shrugged. "How young? Arsene is sixteen."

"So let us send him Helene-Marie's foster daughter. Sasha is her name, isn't it?"

"Her? *M'sieu le Factor*, she is barely starting to fill out."

"So much the better, for Leclerc."

The old woman sighed. "I would think the captain would be better off with another, perhaps Desiree, she is fourteen...."

"You have heard me, Elise?"

"*Oui, Monsieur*, I have heard you."

"Good. You may go, and attend to the arrangements. The ship will be here tomorrow night."

As soon as the old woman left, Danton checked out the chair she had used to make sure it could be used again. It had suffered no apparent structural damage, so he went back behind his desk to review his warehouse accounts. No doubt there was a dearth of things to trade. There was bound to be something hidden away that would appeal to Captain Leclerc, if he was in the right frame of mind.

The right frame of mind. Danton couldn't believe he had almost missed that detail. Luckily the *laptot*, Batees, had been around earlier and had reminded him of Leclerc's specific tastes. In fact, it had been Batees who suggested Sasha. Of course, Batees wasn't doing this to be helpful to the Factor. He wanted a favor in return, a position aboard Leclerc's ship.

Danton could sympathize with that. He would arrange it.

Despite the heat and stress, despite the heavy sweat that ran down his brow and back, Jean-Baptiste was a very happy man. His hands were chafed from pulling lines, but they would get used to it again. How long that took was unimportant. He was going to sea!

It had all happened so quickly. He was still trying to convince himself that the change was real. He had been called shortly after the ship docked. Danton, the Chief Factor told him to report to the first mate, the Captain being ashore already on other business.

The first mate had turned out to be an old sea dog named Lascelles, short of stature and short of temper, but a man with whom Jean-Baptiste had sailed on other vessels.

He knew others aboard the ship, too. There were several other free sailors out of the Senegal River colony of Saint-Louis. He had plunged immediately into the exchange of news and rumors. This had meant a great deal to Jean-Baptiste, for it seemed much more news than rumor that a momentous event lay before him: this ship was bound for France!

The ship was indeed fully laden, but it had taken on one vital necessity already, water. It was the captain's intention to bypass Saint-Louis itself and not make landfall again until he reached the Moroccan coasts. Then instead of unloading there, as most company ships did, he would press on to the French Mediterranean port of Marseilles.

Jean-Baptiste guessed the Captain had a personal interest staked in reaching France as soon as possible. He also guessed that it might have something to do with several large boxes packed deep in the hold and guarded by two large French marines. Whatever the reason for the Captain's haste, it hadn't prevented him from staying on the island long enough to make some sort of a deal. While the large boxes hadn't been touched, some cargo had been taken off, and other cargo taken on. There might be more, too, Stevedores stood waiting in the heat on shore, just in case there was to be another exchange.

Jean-Baptiste found this curious, but not compelling. There was no lack of things for him to do aboard ship, it never being the sailor's lot to sit unoccupied like a stevedore might. He put his mind to his work, and left speculation.

Fully expecting to spend a few more hours chafing his hands on the lines they were unreeling and testing, Jean-Baptiste was surprised to hear a loud commotion on shore. Captain Leclerc was racing, if that was the word for a man of his limited agility, for the gangplank. Danton, the factor, was following making a plea of some kind. But the Captain ignored him and trundled himself up the plank.

"More cargo, sir?" Lascelles asked quickly.

"No!" the captain shouted. "Get us out of this godforsaken place! *Merde* ! Move it!"

With that, the Captain swept past the first mate, not taking his usual place on the quarterdeck, but going directly to his cabin. Lascelles seemed puzzled, but, after all, he had his orders and soon began giving orders of his own. The gangplank came up, the lines were cast off, and the vessel was poled away from the shore.

Jean-Baptiste quickly made his way aft, intent on finding something to do there. He didn't know what had gone wrong, but it was something to do with one of the *signarés*. Two things he had seen: livid scratches on the Captain's face and Danton's angry gaze as he scoured the decks for someone.

With luck, the *laptot* thought, it would be a distant day before he set foot on the island again. Perhaps never would be the best luck of all.

In the hut of Mama-Lise, Helene-Marie knelt nervously before the old Nurse Mother's cushion-seats and asked her question.

"Mama-Lise, what have they done with Sasha? And what will they do to her?"

"What have the whites done?" the old woman grunted. "They've locked her up in the fort. For the moment, that is. As for what they will do to her in the time to come, what do you think will happen? Here we have a young girl who goes to a captain's bed, yes the bed of a French ship captain, and she kicks him in the parts and then bashes him on the skull so that he is knocked unconscious. They find these two in the morning, and the girl is calmly sitting on the bed, the man lying moaning on the floor. I say again, what do you think they will do?"

"Mama-Lise, you cannot let them hang her!"

"Why not? It would be a simple solution, not only for her but for the rest of us, is it not so?"

"But..."

The old woman waved her into silence with a hand.

"Enough. I don't mean to worry you. After all, you did warn me that she wouldn't go willingly with this man. You told me she hadn't been with a man before. This latter part I did not believe at the time, and still doubt. But while your warnings were heeded, mine were not, at least not where such things count. Well, we must deal with it as it happened. They are indeed very angry, but they have left her punishment.... to me."

A great sigh escaped Helene-Marie, but it gave way to a new wariness.

"I know that you dislike her..."

"Dislike her? I am outraged. Who is she, to do such a thing and endanger all of us? She is stubborn, foolish, selfish, calculating. She thinks herself a special person. She must be taught otherwise. She must be taught that there's a reason for the way things are done, and that they are not to be changed, those ways, simply because she would like things done another way."

The old woman rose from her cushions, at which Helene-Marie also got to her feet.

"I don't dislike her," the old woman continued. "Not exactly, and you will not have any further conversation with me on this point. But this I will say. She and her ways are a threat to all of us, Helene-Marie. Deep in your heart you must realize this. So I ask you to hold your peace, and not complain of the punishment I inflict.."

"Will it be.... permanent?"

"In pain or damage, no. In effect, I should hope so. But..."

"Yes, Mama-Lise?"

"It will not be easy, either." She turned abruptly, stepping aside from the door to signal that this talk was finished. Helene-Marie abruptly found herself outside, walking quickly through the village. When she realized that she was going somewhere other than her hut, when her conscious mind took over again, she was already halfway to the upper fort.

Just in front of the imposing upper works of the island, the rising land leveled off and actually dipped before resuming its climb to the top. The effect was the creation of a slight hill, not long enough to be called a ridge. It was here that Helene-Marie often came as a child, after having bad dreams. She only came to the place occasionally these days, to look at the land and the sea and the great dark continent beyond.

After a while, she remembered she had a meal to fix and two children of her own to care for, so she came down again, through the hill and back to the village. On the way, she had to pass through the cemetery which she didn't like to do. She hurried through it quickly, stopping only once to cross herself at the grave of the priest called Father Charles. He had been a good man, a good priest. She couldn't bring herself to fear his ghost.

Briefly she wondered why he had died so quickly and why he had never been replaced. But if there were any secret to this, it lay in the mind of *M'sieu* Aubrisson, blank now, and in its own grave not far away.

She did not stop in passing that one.

Mama-Lise would never explain the reasoning that led her to choose the particular punishment she inflicted on young Sasha. It may have been that the reasoning was ingrown, like a toenail, convoluted and tortuous. It may have been that the reasoning was fairly simple and direct. It may even have been that there was no reasoning involved at all. It was a time and a place for instinct more than reason, and much that was accomplished came about as the result of little formal thought at all.

But if its purpose was that it be remembered, it was successful, this punishment of Sasha.

For the young girl, the new day now began before dawn. In the darkness she would be shaken out of her sleep, out of her bed, and steered down to the sandy beach near the quay. There she would be received in utter silence by the half-dozen men of the water run, who would take her aboard the water skiff, and across to the main-land shore.

Every morning they made the same excursion. They made landfall near the mouth of a small stream, which emptied its waters into the bay. They had to be there when the tide was out. Otherwise the mouth of the stream would be foul with salt water rushing in from the sea rather than sweet with fresh water rushing out from the stream.

Once in position, they began the tedious, arduous work of filling the kegs that slaked the island's daily thirst.

Sasha was in charge of the smaller kegs, the ones that went to island families in the village. She could lift these even when they were full, although it cost her considerable effort. She had lifted these on occasion at home, but now she was doing it again and again and again, until a wearing numbness overcame her arms and her knees.

She filled each keg and loaded it into the skiff. There were thirty-five of them. All of this was accomplished before sunup, a necessity because of the tide.

Then it was time to board the skiff again. The boat-marshal was not Batees, however, and was not particularly skilled for the work at hand. Quite often the voyage, a rough one at best, was much rougher than it should have been. Sasha had never heard of *mal-de-mer*, seasickness, but if it had been described to her now, she would have recognized it well. Often she arrived at the island shore retch-ing, which in view of her largely empty stomach, was not especially pleasant.

Once the return landfall had been accomplished, the men loaded the larger kegs on the company carts. Sasha did not join this work. She had her own to do. On the shore she lined up her thirty-five small kegs. Then, one at a time, she began the process of deliver-ing them to the village homes. Up and back she trudged, up and back, up and back again, until the sun was high overhead and she was almost faint with weakness.

Finally she delivered the last one, to the same destination as the first. Mama-Lise, in virtue of her special position and responsibilities, received both the first and the last kegs to come into the village.

Mama-Lise kept the first keg in a cool place, for drinking water. She used the second for a variety of domestic purposes, including a daily washing of her face and hands. Like all the islanders, she could go to the far side of the island, facing the mainland. If the time and tide were right, she could wade into the bay and bathe in water that was only lightly salt. It was almost the same as bathing in fresh water, an unheard-of luxury for the islanders, one reserved for the whites who had rights to the feeble well.

But Mama-Lise was large and aging; she didn't make that trip often.

Sasha would watch Mama-Lise's daily ritual from a squatting position. Then, when she was finished, the old woman would go to a cupboard in the back of her hut and produce a small bowl. She would fill this bowl from the drinking keg, and hand it to Sasha. After the first few days, the young girl had learned to sip and savor the liquid, rather than gulp and swallow.

There was always the temptation, however, to drink the entire bowlful at once. Often this would be the first water Sasha had tasted since filling the kegs and the last she would taste until nightfall.

This went on for three months. In all that time, few spoke to her; and she herself could speak to no one except in answer, and then only in a few words. This part of the punishment might well have been a blessing, for given the circumstances, she could not speak without pain. It was worst of all in the last minutes before she received the first bowl of water in the afternoon, watching Mama-Lise bathe slowly and casually in the thatched hut.

This was Sasha's punishment.

In time she grew almost used to it, and in some ways the last few weeks were better. For one thing, the factor finally did as the water skiff crew themselves had suggested. He gave command of the run to the old carpenter, Gilbert, who not only proved himself a canny seaman, but a humane one as well. She was bound to obey his orders, of course, when they were on the gulf. So, when one morning he produced a flask and gruffly told her, "Drink," she did as she was bidden, and kept quiet about it.

Yet in some ways these last few weeks were the worst of all, for now she had an occasional kindness to contrast with her normal treatment, and it sapped her spirit. There were times when she thought of running, but even in desperation she never really considered it. Where would she go, and how would she get there?

As for hiding, there was always that; there was a trap-door and a tunnel on a long low ridge by the lee shore, forgotten by her childhood companions, but well-remembered by Sasha. She had explored it several times with a lone candle for a torch. It led far down into the earth, and at the end was a set of steps similar to the ones on the shore, leading up to a wooden trap that she could not pull down; it had to open upwards.

But she had a good sense of direction and distance, and knew where it had to open, into the white men's fort, the lower fort, Fort Saint-Francois.

That way lay no escape. And as for hiding, she couldn't hide forever. No, there was only one thing to do; keep taking her punishment until it was done with.

And yes, one thing more...

She would remember it well.

Chapter Four

He didn't know where he was or how long he had been there. He barely remembered who he was. The time he'd spent under the earth in fear and darkness had leached more than his body. But he did remember what he was and why he was there, and that sufficed to keep him alert and alive.

The bad nights of his childhood seemed like nothing now. Neither war, nor wounds, nor the shaking of the earth beneath him had ever prepared him for what he had endured in the last few months.

Still, it would be all right. He no longer felt the shackles on his hands and feet. He no longer cringed in terror at the sudden unexpected fall of the lash. And if the next visit brought both a threat and a hope, he would be ready, as always, to go either way.

Arsene gazed sadly at the broken crock. She had no sense of

guilt over its loss, only disappointment. She might never have heard the proverb about the pitcher that went once too often to the well, but she would have recognized its truth.

A few days earlier, sitting on the low ridge by the fort with a few of her friends, she had seen a large Portuguese vessel on the verge of mooring fall victim to a sudden gust of wind. Instead of drawing up neatly alongside the dock, it had smashed into it, crushing two shoremen and disfiguring a third. Misfortune was to be expected. Only its degree was ever a sufficient case for surprise.

She gathered up the pieces of the broken crock and walked away from the well. It might, after all, be mendable. There were only four pieces; lines cleanly broken, no shattered debris. If not, she would simply locate and appropriate another crock at an opportune moment in the fort's kitchen. And if there was no opportune moment she would simply go thirsty for a while. It was late June on the island. The rainy season would come within two weeks.

"Arsene! You are all right?"

The girl's head jerked up. Had she not recognized the voice, she would have recognized the speaker from her choice of words. No one else had ever asked her such a question.

"But of course," she replied "It was the crock that fell, not me."

"It seems to be a clean break. You will mend it."

This was not a question but a statement. Arsene regarded the other girl with a sidelong glance. As always, she had mixed feelings. There was no question in her mind that her companion was the best friend she had in the world, but everything else about her made Arsene wary, if not uncomfortable.

They were walking together now, back toward the village. For a while there was silence between them. Then abruptly Sasha spoke.

"Arsene, I need your help."

A few paces later, Arsene responded.

"Yes, I will help. What is it?"

"Tonight," Sasha replied. "Meet me at the Chapel. I'll tell you about it then."

They walked on in silence a while, and then as easily as she had appeared, Sasha vanished down one of the narrow village streets. Arsene continued on with her broken crockery back to the hut she shared with three other women roughly her age, none of them with family, all of them old enough to look out for themselves.

It was not for Arsene to judge her own life, whether it was good or bad. But she knew there was something missing. Of all people she knew, only Sasha had ever come close to providing that missing thing, whatever it was.

Which was why she would be there.

The chapel, cleaned and swept once a week by Mama-Lise and old Gilbert, looked as though it were ready for Mass. The service, however, had not been held for several years. The last priest to visit had been an elderly Portuguese man whose ship was returning from Goa. He stayed for only a few days.

There was always the chance of a French visitor from Saint-Louis, but for some reason those plans always seemed to evaporate as quickly as the rainfall. It was becoming increasingly obvious that no one intended to appoint a successor to Father Charles any time soon.

Meanwhile the only sign of continuing devotion was the rack of small candles by the Mary altar. Usually about a third of them were lit at any given time, as they were now.

Silently, saying to herself the words she had been taught, Arsene lit one of the candles and sat down to wait. She didn't have to wait long, for it was almost dusk, and as twilight arrived in earnest, so did Sasha. Arsene noticed that she carried a package under one arm and a small deep basket in the other. She didn't question this secrecy, but merely followed Sasha outside.

As the two girls passed the altar, Sasha paused and picked up one of the candles. Carefully she placed it in the bottom of the basket.

"Will we need light, then, to see where we're going?" Arsene finally asked.

"We'll need it when we get there," Sasha replied, not offering any more information.

The light was fading fast, and of course the candle in its deep basket was of little help. Sasha, however, moved quickly and confidently in the dark. Born on the island, she knew its every turn. Arsene followed without question. Finally, the two reached the entrance to the old hideaway. There, Sasha stopped, and after setting down the basket, took out the candle and opened the package. For the first time Arsene saw that it contained food. Her eyes grew wide as she began to understand the secrecy.

"Who is down there, Sasha? Who is she and who is she hiding from?"

Sasha smiled, her teeth shining in the twilight.

"Very good, Arsene. But it's not a she, but a he, and he's hiding from the white traders."

"A slave?" Arsene was astounded. "But Sasha, the penalty for helping an escaped slave..."

"Isn't pleasant, and I would not incur it," Sasha finished for her. "But really I'm helping us, not him. He found this place on his own. He came out of the shadows several nights ago when I had come down here by myself.... for the usual reasons."

Arsene nodded. Sasha often wandered away from the village. Sometimes she came here, as Arsene herself sometimes did, if she were with a trusted companion. Only Sasha would come alone.

"No more questions now," Sasha said abruptly, reaching down to sweep aside the mound of dirt that hid the metal ring on the trapdoor. "Watch for me until I come back up."

Arsene watched her go down the ladder into the darkness, holding the candle and food in one hand, and the rungs of the ladder with the other.

He waited until the woman was settled, her package and candle down. Then he stepped out of the shadows into the passageway.

The smell of the food overpowered him, and he ate, not so

much like a man, but like a hungry wolf, savaging the meat and vegetables like the innards of a kill.

When he was finished he nodded in thanks. Then he spoke, in his native tongue.

"I want to go to the mainland now," he said.

Sasha shrugged. "I've told you I will help you, but you'll only have a chance on a moonless night."

"And the new moon is days yet away, yes, I know. But your rains, I have heard they come shortly after the longest day. How am I to cross so much water in a storm?"

"Much more easily for not being seen."

The man accepted his fate silently, squatting down on his haunches. After a while, he asked: "What now then?"

"Tell me again," Sasha said, "About the Wolof queen and the Portuguese."

The man sighed. He knew the tale, but he was not a storyteller and it didn't appeal to him. Nevertheless he talked for fifteen minutes or so. After all, he must earn his supper.

Later, after he had finished and the young woman had left him, he rummaged through the food package again, looking for scraps he might have missed. But, there was none.

As he stood up, a queasy feeling assaulted his stomach. He sat down at once and waited a while before rising again. The feeling was still there when he did.

He had to wonder whether he could make it, until the moon and the rains came.

There was a banquet in the fort the next night, in honor of a visiting captain on the eve of his departure for America with a cargo of slaves and spices. As often happened, most of the island's younger women wound up serving the company in one fashion or another. To Arsene's relief, she and Sasha were given tasks connected with serving the food. This didn't prevent the occasional pinch from the men, however, as she and her companion distributed the courses.

If anyone there knew of an escaped slave on the island, there was no sign of it. Arsene had to accept the incredible as fact, that he had not only gotten away, but managed to do so in a way he would not be missed. There were of course hundreds of slaves, but usually the alarm was quick to sound when one turned up missing. Arsene could only assume he had missed the accounting process, or that someone who suffered too heavily from responsibility was not about to acknowledge the loss.

Back in the village afterwards, Arsene found herself too restless to sleep. Not knowing what to do, she went out and wandered, until she saw a light burning in the hut Sasha shared with Helene-Marie. This hut she entered without thinking to knock. Helene-Marie was asleep in one corner, but in another Sasha was preparing some food. Arsene's eyes widened as she saw Sasha grind up some crystals and mix them in with the meal. Then she mixed in a strong-tasting herb as well.

Suddenly, Sasha's eyes came up and she saw Arsene. The girl, not willing to meet Sasha's eyes, wanted to run, but eventually she held her ground and looked straight at her friend's calm smile.

"You are perplexed, Arsene, or so it seems. Well, is it not obvious what I am doing?"

"Of course," Arsene said promptly. "You are poisoning him...."

"Correction," Sasha said easily. "I have been poisoning him in small doses, from the start. You understand... I certainly can't help him to escape. Even on a moonless night they'd be sure to find him."

"Then why not have the soldiers come and take him?"

"Because I would have to show them our hideaway, or else he might reveal it on capture, hoping to ease his lot."

Arsene understood. Yes, they must keep the secret of that hideaway. But she was not at all sure it was worth the price of a man's life, even if he were only an escaped slave. After all, she'd had her lessons; she was no heathen. Still, Sasha seemed to have no remorse. She seemed sure.

"It's a heavy decision," Arsene said at last.

"Not that heavy, and it's a decision I had to make."

"You act," breathed Arsene, "as if you ruled here!"

Sasha shrugged. "Perhaps some day I shall. But certainly not if I am weak in the knees when it comes to something like this. But you don't have to help me, Arsene. You need not come with me any more, if it strains your conscience. But...you must keep the secret."

Arsene stared into her friend's cold, black eyes. *Mon Dieu*, she thought. Such a she-devil, and yet she's only fifteen!

The last day before the rainy season was a bright one; calm, with a good solid breeze.

On a rise above the harbor, where a visiting storyteller had once sat contemplating the strangeness of the island and its people, two young women now sat with their faces staring at the lower door of the fort. It was a narrow thing, and tightly guarded. Not far from the foot of it cauldrons smoked and the smell of hot iron rose from braziers.

"There he is," Arsene said quickly at one of the first black faces to appear from the passage. She and Sasha both watched as the man, his face expressionless, was pinioned in the embrace of two much larger Africans. Then another rose from a brazier, bearing a long rod with hot metal at the end. Even from where they sat, they could hear the sizzle as the branding iron dug into the slave's left arm.

The man made no sound. Indeed, he was like all the rest who followed. After some cold water had been thrown on the brand, he moved off down the short steps to the gangplank, to disappear inside the slave ship. Like the rest, he was chained at the ankles and the arms.

"Yes," Sasha said after a while. "It's the only thing that makes sense. He knew he couldn't get away, so he sneaked back the way he sneaked off. Look, he hasn't been beaten. Even if he had turned himself in voluntarily, they would have punished him. "

Arsene glanced at Sasha with a twinkle of relief in her eyes. Their mystery had been solved.

It had been three days since the slave had disappeared from the tunnel. At first the young women had assumed he had made it safely to the mainland; that he had swum the three miles without waiting for the new moon. The night before, however, Arsene, on an errand for the Chief Factor, had spotted the slave in the shadows of one of the barracks. Quickly, she got word of it to Sasha.

"But how did he sneak out in the first place?" Arsene asked.

Sasha's face was a mask of indifference, her shrug expressive even for her. Arsene couldn't know that Sasha already knew the man's secret route, having discovered it with a bit of searching. It was a secret she was determined to keep to herself, at all costs, against the day it might be needed.

"The main point is that our secret is safe. He won't risk telling anyone of the tunnel now.

With that, Sasha turned away. "Come, we must prepare for the banquet."

Arsene, determined to put the event out of her mind as Sasha had, quickly followed. "I suppose our purpose will be the same as last time?"

"Of course," Sasha reassured her. Then her gaze was bold. "Do you think Danton or Mama-Lise will set us aside for any other purpose, given our records?"

Arsene, despite herself, laughed.

"You are no more reluctant than I am, given the right circumstances."

"No, of course not. But the circumstances must be right, as you have said. They're right when I'm not a gift, but a prize. And I will have my due."

Arsene nodded timidly. She learned never to question Sasha when she carried that tone.

"Come!" Sasha cried, grabbing Arsene's arm. "We must

hurry! We would not want to be late for the last banquet!"

Arsene understood. There was one more ship leaving the island tomorrow. This last load would empty out the slave barracks. After that the summer rains would hinder the approach to the island. It was not without reason that the islanders greeted the approach of the rainy season as the approach of a holiday.

Chapter Five

"West of where the caravans meet, and off the shore by the mouth of the great river called the Smashing One, there rises an island...."

So the storyteller began and continued, weaving formal words and phrases around a new kernel of tale. It was indeed a new tale in a sense, for it had been many years since he had first told the Ashanti people about the strange island off the western coast. The tale had taken on many changes since then. But, like always, the Ashanti people were always eager to hear the tale of the island where white men ruled; the island where black men were kept in chains; the island where a new mother chose death over a life of shackles. Hadithe Zakale shuddered as his thought crept back to the months he had spent on Gorée, the women of Gorée....Whatever the subject matter, the storyteller always made it a point not to become lost in his own tales. He forced the thoughts from his mind and concentrated on the story at hand.

"Still," Hadithe Zakale thought to himself, "It's a hard place to forget."

Startled by a hand on his shoulder, the storyteller quickly turned to see Kwame-Uhru standing behind him. He wore a look of concern on his face.

"It's late and you have had a full day, my honored guest," the old chief said quietly. "Nevertheless, if I may impose upon you, will you walk with me a ways to the stream and back? For there is something I would ask, and something I would tell you."

"Of course, honored Kwame," the teller of tales replied, and with that the two men walked away from the village.

The old chief didn't speak until they had reached the stream, and then he sat down on the riverbank, indicating to Hadithe Zakale that he should also sit, beside him on his right in the place of honor.

"There are tellers of tales," the old chief began, "and there are tellers of tales. Your boast is that you can weave a tale to suit the occasion, is it not?"

Hadithe Zakale smiled. "It is mine, and that of all others who follow the craft."

"I remember many years ago I asked you about a place I had seen in a dream; a place, my friend, you said you had seen; a place where the women and white men ruled. If you had never seen such a place as I described, you would have invented it?

The teller of tales chuckled for answer, which drew a response in kind from the High Chief.

"Ah, that was a good answer. Were I asked, in my turn, whether I truly dreamed of such a place, I would give the same." Then his voice lowered several tones. "But you, teller of tales, *have* been there."

"Yes," the storyteller replied quietly. "But it has been a long time."

"But you have been there? This island exists?"

The storyteller cast the High Chief a measuring glance, a bold thing under normal conditions, but understandable under the circumstances. The teller of tales was intrigued by Kwame-Uhru's bluntness.

"I ask this because of more recent information that causes me concern. You have not heard that the King has suffered a great defeat?"

Hadithe Zakale stared at the High Chief in absolute silence. Such an admission was unheard-of. The old man held up a hand.

"I am not disloyal, far from it, but we have lost many captives, and we lost them to the Dinka. Obviously the Dinka are taking them westward to sell to the white ship captains. I don't know how many, or how long the journey will take. Obviously it will take longer to move a line of captives than it would take for a lone man to make a journey."

He paused, and peered through the deep night into the eyes of the teller of tales.

"By now you must be thinking I am about to ask you to go for me, as a scout. I am not about to do so, Hadithe Zakale, for you are only a teller of tales. What I want is information. The latest I have heard from the West is that the rule of the women on that island is stronger than it ever was... that they are beginning to become traders themselves, in gold and tusks and yes, slaves too. Can this be so? And can Ashanti deal with them, deal in terms of bargains?"

"It has been a long time, Kwame-Uhru. All I can tell you is what I remember and what I have heard." The storyteller didn't want to embellish this story. The High Chief signaled him to go on.

"It is true. The women, the *signarés*, are very powerful. They are ruled by one called Mama-Lise. But the island has now been taken over by the French East India Company. A man named Bruie is to replace Danton any day now. I have heard little about him. Who knows what we can expect."

The High Chief was silent for a moment and then he shifted his eyes to meet Hadithe Zakale's placid stare. Several thousand lives are at stake, not to mention the prestige of Ashanti and the honor of the Great King."

Hadithe Zakale thought this over and nodded. Kwame-Uhru had not asked him to go. Nor had he mentioned any reward that would come of such a journey; such talk would have been insulting to the storyteller. Still, the idea of visiting the island intrigued him. So many changes had taken place in his twenty year absence. He wondered if....Anyway, he was heading in that general direction, and could make a detour.

"I am going northwest," he said aloud. "I could guide your man as far as the island, and perhaps help him in other ways. Beyond that, as you have said, I am only a teller of tales."

Eagerness crept into the voice of the old High Chief.

"Ashanti does not forget its helpers," he said. "You expect a token from me for this visit; it will be more, and perhaps more useful, than others of its kind. Let us walk back now, and we can discuss this further at a time when neither of us is spent from a day's hard effort."

So saying, he got up, and began walking, Hadithe Zakale with him, mulling over his reasons once again to see if they justified the commitment he had just so casually made. Usually he liked to think things over, but the idea of the island had come upon him suddenly. He wondered why.

There was nothing there; no water, no crops. Only ships, and white men, and off in the distance, fish as big as houses, and an old woman who was nothing more than a nurse-mother to the people.

And an odd-looking teen girl of mixed blood and tribe, who had thought him an old man then. She must be an old woman herself now.

Hadithe Zakale shook his head as if to clear it. Why had that come to mind? He would have to think about it, and think about what relationship it would bear...to the story.

After all, he was a teller of tales, and whatever he did always related to the story he would be able to tell as a result.

Chapter Six

The day was a bright one, the coastline and the sea itself visible for miles in any chosen direction. The small trading packet flying the flag of France and the ensign of the French East India Company had all of its canvas aloft to catch the slight but steady breeze off the African coast. Sailing slightly off the wind, it was making excellent progress, and what could have been a two days' sail would be over in less than one.

The man standing by the starboard railing on the ship's quarterdeck was well aware of this good fortune. He also knew that the new arrangements he had made during his brief tenure were already turning the fortunes of the company around, filling warehouses in the settlement of Saint-Louis with cargo and the coffers in Paris with gold. And furthermore, he knew that winding its inevitably slow way toward the coast was a cargo the like of which neither the company nor its predecessor had ever seen, at least for size and value.

But all this knowledge did not lighten the scowl on the man's face. Nor did it make him readier with a kind word for anyone who happened to approach him. Andre Bruie was a hard man to please. If things were going well, they could be going better; and unless things were absolutely perfect, a situation demanded action and adjustment.

Andre Bruie, governor of the French Senegal Colony in all but name, was not thinking the thoughts of a satisfied man. The situation in Saint-Louis might be approaching his standard of perfection, but he was on his way to another place, the island of Gorée. The situation there was far from adequate, much less perfection.

In his mind he recited a litany of damnation, finding space for admirals and their relatives, greedy factors, ship captains who thought with their privy parts rather than with their brains, and tribeless half-breeds who imagined that they could beat the company at its own game.

They were in sight of the island now, and Bruie could make out the hill on which the upper fort stood. The lower one soon came into view. Some of the other passengers on the packet might be distracted by a whale's spout in the distance out to sea, but Bruie kept his eyes on the island. Studying the forts carefully, he made a mental memorandum: he must check with Lieutenant Drouin about the state of the defenses.

A random thought intruded. It was a thought that might have amused another man; it merely surprised Bruie. In all his litany of damnation, he had hardly spared a thought for the English or the Dutch, who most certainly deserved a share.

As the ship rounded the southern tip of the island, and the harbor came into view, Bruie saw that there was one other vessel in the vicinity. Without thinking, he drew out his spyglass to check it out. But it was only the waterboat, the small skiff making its daily run back from the rivermouth to the island. The only surprising thing was that this time it carried passengers, two of them. Both were Africans, one dressed as a messenger of some kind, and the other carrying a drum. Bruie grunted. If he knew enough of Africa to recognize a messenger, he also knew enough to recognize a wandering storyteller.

Another memo went into his mental notebook: Inquire as to who is entitled to ride in the company skiff, and what fare they must pay. Then whatever the policy is, change it, in the Company's interest.

With that thought, he dismissed the water skiff from his mind and returned to inspecting the lower fort, now looming in front of him.

"It is good to have you visit again, teller of tales," Mama-Lise said. "But who is this who comes with you, and why do you bring him?"

Hadithe Zakale bowed his head slightly and smiled. Respect for age was automatic in Africa, and while Mama-Lise had been an aging woman twenty years ago, she was a very old woman now. Still, she had an air of authority. He couldn't help but admire her.

Had she been a man, even the Ashanti messenger would have displayed the tokens of respect, but he was unused to the island, and despite Hadithe Zakale's explanations, he still had not really accepted the fact that women ruled there.

Before the storyteller could answer, Mama-Lise interrupted to indicate that they should sit. They were on the small rise near the children's creche where a large blanket had been spread and baskets full of fruits and nuts placed around it at intervals. Mama-Lise had been at the shore to welcome the waterboat, forewarned of what it contained.

Taking the proper time, as was customary, Hadithe Zakale didn't answer the old woman's question at once. Instead, he paused long enough to crack and eat a handful of nuts. His companion did likewise. Only then did the storyteller give his answer.

"Honored mother, this is the messenger called Sokolo, who serves the King of the Ashanti. It was his mission to come here, and he would have come eventually in any case, but I was asked to show him the quicker way, since I was also coming here."

"So," the old woman said, "you do not bring him, he brings

57

himself. And what is your purpose, young man?"

The Ashanti called Sokolo was not quick to answer either. However, Hadithe Zakale thought to himself, this was for reasons other than simple courtesy. Finally, after dispatching a piece of reddish fruit, the Ashanti spoke.

"Honored lady, my message is from the ruler of Ashanti to the ruler of this island. I find myself in an awkward position, as regards its delivery."

Mama-Lise chuckled. "You are well-spoken, young man, as befits one who speaks for a high king. But perhaps I can clarify matters for you. There is no one ruler on this island, unless it be the white man called Bruie, and he arrived just today. When he goes back to his settlement at the mouth of the Senegal, then there is the white man called Drouin, who is chief of the soldiers in the forts. There are three ships in the harbor; their captains are called Champlain, Sauvage and Maupassant. There is a fourth ship whose captain, Tousaint, is absent. Each of these men is sovereign over his own ship, and answers to no one here for what goes on aboard it, or what goes aboard it."

"We, our humble selves, who inhabit this island, are not permitted to have a chief of our own. If we *were* permitted to have one, you would find no man to take the job. Better to sign on as a sailor, as most of them do. As for myself, I am but the mistress of the children's creche. It is true that I speak for most of the women here, but by no means all."

The storyteller found himself called to alert by those last five words. There was an odd tone to them. Exasperation, perhaps? If so, Mama-Lise hid it well... better than Sokolo did in his response.

"Honored lady, this is beyond my understanding! How can such a situation continue?"

Mama-Lise shrugged. "I don't know, but it has continued for many years...with some changes of course. But I do not wish to add to your confusion, Messenger Sokolo. I merely want to let you know where the power lies, so you can determine for yourself the proper destination for your message. Myself, I cannot advise you without knowing the message itself, and it would be presumptuous of me to ask, in view of the circumstances." She spat aside. "No doubt one or two of my younger colleagues would be that presumptuous, but not all young people are as polite as you are."

If anything, this last exchange seemed to add to the Ashanti's confusion. But Hadithe Zakale was not concerned for him. Messengers such as Sokolo were well and thoroughly trained in a special kind of school before being allowed to carry so much as a routine demand for tribute to a remote village. There were times when boldness and decisiveness were required of them, as they might be of the Great Chief himself. Always the key was the same: do whatever advances the King's business. Methods were not normally questioned, only results.

"So be it," Sokolo said suddenly. "I find I cannot advance the King's business without revealing at least the nature of my message. So I will do so. It concerns the captives the Dinka took in the battle at the Twisted Falls. I have specific instructions regarding ransom."

Mama-Lise considered this information. "But in order to arrange ransom one must know who has title to the captives."

"That is true enough, honored lady."

"And still a difficult thing to determine."

"Still, honored lady?"

"At this precise moment, yes. As I understand the situation, a white shipmaster and his *signaré* have gone inland to arrange the purchase of these captives with one Abdullah al-Ghul, an Arab trader. He is one of several known to the Dinka and others to whom the Dinka consign their prisoners of war. That's all I know. We will know more when they arrive at the coast. But as of today? Today I couldn't tell you who holds the captives."

Sokolo the messenger considered that. Then, almost as an afterthought, he asked another question.

"Honored lady, what is a *signaré*?"

"That..." Mama-Lise paused. "That is the word for the shipmaster's island wife, young man. It is from the Portuguese, as I recall. One of the few things they left us." She smiled at Hadithe Zakale. Then she picked a piece of fruit out of the basket, and only when she had finished eating it did she speak again.

"At one time," she said, "the white shipmasters and traders waited here on the island, or at points on the coast, for the Arabs to bring down the slave cargo. But the route of the slave is a long one. From time to time they may be bought and sold to other traders on the route. Of course with each sale the price goes up, as is natural. With each mile there is an added cost. The whites realized it might be to their advantage to go inland, and catch the slavetraders early."

She paused, shifting her considerable bulk on the blanket. "They couldn't go without guides. And our island girls, who speak many tongues, but have no tribal ties, make excellent guides."

"Our *signarés* do not, however, come cheap. They have a contract; it amounts to a temporary marriage. Danton, the last factor of the old company, helped us draw it up just before he left and the new man took over. Of course our island girls made changes, and suggested a few ideas to make it more binding, but the point is that it suits the purposes of both the white shipmaster and the girl, and therefore it works."

"A powerful idea," Hadithe Zakale said, rather doubtfully. "Your idea, Mama-Lise?"

The old woman spat aside again. "Hardly mine, teller of tales. Do you remember the woman who drowned herself, those many years ago when you were last here?"

"Yes, I remember well."

"She left a girl-child. You remember her too?"

"Yes. A woman grown by now, I imagine."

"Indeed. She is twenty now, but much older than her years... and a source of more trouble, I often think, than she is worth. There are even times when I wish her mother... but never mind. The ideas are hers, and many of the other young women follow her. There is much gold, also much trouble, and no doubt there will be a great deal more of each before this tale is in shape, Hadithe Zakale. It is very early in the day, though, thankfully, late in mine."

She turned again to the Ashanti messenger. "Sokolo of Ashanti, you are welcome here as a guest of the island, a thing that I can make you even with my humble power. Accept this welcome, and I shall do my best to assist you in conveying your message to the right person, or persons, as the case may be. If I can do no more than that, it's because, as you see, the situation permits no more to be done."

Sokolo hesitated, but not long enough to sample more of the fruit or nuts. Instead he sighed and nodded his head.

"I thank you, honored lady, on behalf of my king, the Ruler of Ashanti. And I accept your hospitality, so generously offered, reminding you that the Ashanti do not forget their friends."

"REVILLE!" a voice suddenly barked loudly in French. Mama-Lise alone of the three on the hill understood the command to get up. The two men would have understood enough from the tone of it even if they had not drawn conclusions from the appearance of a squad of armed soldiers. There suddenly emerged a ring around their meeting-place.

Quietly, and with a natural dignity that did not speak of any obeisance, the two men got up. With more haste, and yet more difficulty, the old woman did the same. She glanced about the circle and finally spoke to the one man of the surrounding French who was not in a military uniform.

"*Monsieur* Bruie," she muttered. "What is all this? We are doing no harm here."

"I will be the judge of that," the grim-faced Frenchman replied. "I take it these macaques do not speak French. Well, I shall teach them respect for those who do! And I shall know their business, old woman, before the sun gets much lower in the sky."

He turned to the man next to him, who commanded the squad.

"Sergeant, take these two to the proper place in Fort Saint-Francois, and give them the usual ration and the usual restraint. Get me one who speaks these African tongues for the interrogation."

"I can translate for them," Mama-Lise interrupted. "They are..."

"They are none of your affair!" Andre Bruie shouted. "By heaven, I see I must teach you something, too! Get to your nursery, old woman, and cease meddling in affairs that don't concern you. Or else it will be much the worse for you. I have had enough of you half-breeds and your arrogance. Entirely enough!"

61

As quickly as she could, for the sake of her bulk and her remaining dignity, Mama-Lise exited the circle of soldiers. On her way, she caught the eye of the teller of tales. There was in her look both apology and warning. He answered with a shrug of dismissal, and she was gone.

In turn, he caught the eye of the Ashanti messenger, to warn him to postpone any conversation.

As they were led away down the hill toward the fort, Hadithe Zakale quickly considered his own position and that of his companion. He didn't like the prospects. Their respective standings, as a storyteller and a King's Messenger, made them almost inviolate anywhere in Africa... anywhere, that is, except where the whites were in control. It was a delicate situation, and in order to extricate himself and Sokolo from it, he would have to use much thought.

He did not, however, despair. For he had two advantages of which his captors were unaware. He knew the ways of men and he also, despite Bruie's assumption, knew the language of the French.

"So, captain, you come to me with a great bargain, and give me the terms on which it is to be made! No wonder the natives forget themselves, if they have Frenchmen such as you to show them the way!"

Captain Charles Tousaint, master of the tradeship *Saint-Marie*, stared levelly into the glowering eyes of the young man before him. He measured his words carefully, as carefully as he had already measured the man himself, making allowances for youth, and drive, and objectives.

"I have more than a passing acquaintance with your regulations, *Monsieur* Bruie. I have followed them to the letter, as carefully as I expect my crew to follow my own orders. If you have particulars to set before me, do so. Otherwise we are wasting time that would best be devoted to business."

The glowering brow of Andre Bruie barely flickered. Even so Tousaint knew he had scored.

"You keep to the letter, captain, but you violate the spirit. You and I know very well that the arrangements between you and your black woman, which permit you such bold adventures as going inland to pick up slave cargo, are not what the company had in mind when the rules were written. I am putting you on notice. As far as my powers go, they will be used to enforce the spirit as well as the letter of the rules."

The captain chuckled. "At the cost of cargo? I think not!"

"I will get the cargo, Captain Tousaint, and I will do so without prejudicing the company's interest."

Captain Tousaint shrugged. "One must make decisions and one must take responsibility for decisions, is it not so? I am content with my own performance. You, I trust, will make certain that you and the Directors are content with yours. Tell me how you wish to handle the matter of these twelve hundred Africans. I hardly think you wish me to pitch them into the sea!"

"I want them processed carefully, for maximum return. You are well aware that this island cannot accommodate all of them at once. A little matter of water, not to speak of food, or had you forgotten?"

"You can handle half of that problem easily," Tousaint replied. "And I will only make it necessary for you to keep a third of the slaves here. My ship can take four hundred, and after proper arrangements are made with Captain Devereaux of the *Saint-Michel*, you can load and dispatch another four hundred. This will leave you with only four hundred to hold on the island, till the next ship comes."

"Twelve hundred count, is that what you have?" Bruie ignored the Captain's drift and ostentatiously glanced at a piece of paper before him. "I was informed that the count should be closer to three thousand."

"Interesting," the captain murmured. "What source would that be?"

"That is none of your affair."

"Did you train in Spain, *Monsieur* Bruie?"

The Chief Factor stared at him. "What do you imply?"

Tousaint, master of the expressive French shrug as he was, used it again. He had dealt with factors before. They had to be put in their place, true, but it was best to make sure they were put in it before they realized what was happening to them. Especially the young, the eager, the greedy and the bureaucratic. *Monsieur* Andre Bruie was clearly all of these.

"Perhaps, Captain, we won't need your ships at all."

Captain Tousaint studied Bruie carefully. His face was a nonchalant mask.

"Why is that?"

"Because you may think you know Africa, Captain, but you do not know it as a company trader does. You have your captives; you can no longer feed them, or water them, without my aid. You have named your price, which you presume the company will gladly pay. You also assume the company will pay you further charges to take them to the Americas. Well, halve your price and forget taking them across. I myself will arrange the details from here."

"Read your regulations," the captain said quietly. "I have the stated privilege of transporting the cargo I bring in. And the privilege of assigning such to a brother captain."

"That is if they are to be transported. I shall sell them here. They shall not cross the ocean."

"Indeed! And at a profit for the company? The local tribes don't want them, certainly not as many as twelve hundred. And they could hardly pay the price even if they did, even by barter, let alone in gold."

"I need not inform you of my arrangements. No, Captain, as the English might say, you have purchased a pig in a sack, and now you find out what its true worth is. You have until tonight to accept my offer. I don't think you will want it to decrease as you contemplate how to feed and water these Africans."

Andre Bruie rose abruptly and, with a vigorous nod, indicated to Captain Tousaint that he was dismissed. The older man got up more slowly, but just as deliberately. He was a full head taller than Bruie, but they would measure the same on a scale, for the Captain was lean and wiry from seafaring.

"You shall have your answer," he murmured, "in the morning, *Monsieur* Bruie. Not a moment before. Read your regulations."
Abruptly he turned and left, not waiting for a response.

"It's lucky for that milk-skinned swine that Ashanti is far from this island," Sokolo said bitterly as he hefted the heavy chains binding him to the dungeon wall. They were long enough to allow him some movement, but their length added to the weight and made movement difficult.

"It is no matter," Hadithe Zakale replied. "We have gone over this situation many times. One must have patience and confidence. Surely the King will appreciate your difficulties, when the time comes for reward."

"If I return," Sokolo said. "One cannot trust a man whose eyes are like those of a fish. He tells me through his interpreters that he will accept the offer of ransom, but he suggests arrangements that would put it in his power to take the ransom money and still hold the captives. I cannot even discuss terms with such a person. Besides, he doesn't have the prisoners in his hands."

"Not as yet. But they must be nearing the coast, if they're not yet at it. I detect a slight impatience in his discussions with you."

"Yes. Obviously he knows my mission is ransom, and he is unhappy that I don't acknowledge it and come to terms. But, I am charged to deal with the actual holder of the captives. Think you I have done right?"

"I would think so," the teller of tales replied. "Perhaps in more ways than one. As I have told you, some of the things he has stopped his interpreter from translating are... most interesting."

Sokolo sighed and leaned back against the wall, trying to get comfortable. His eyes flickered in the storyteller's direction. He watched the older man carefully for a long time before speaking again.

"You bear this privation well, *m'zee* ," he said at last, using the respectful title of Elder. "Yet this is at least as humiliating for you as it is for me, and it must be harder for one who is no longer as young as he used to be."

Hadithe Zakale smiled, searching his memory for a story.

A noise in the hall indicated the approach of dinner. Hadithe Zakale ended his search and prepared to make the painful effort to retrieve the food. But, to his surprise, the food did not appear through the slit in the door. Instead, the door opened and the slight figure of a woman appeared. In her hands she carried a basket of food. It was not the usual ration, but a much larger and more varied meal. Fruits, nuts, vegetables and fish filled the basket.

Behind the woman was the usual guard, whose face they seldom saw. He was bearing a jug of water, which he now set down. After speaking a gruff word or two to the woman, he went back outside and closed the door.

"This is good of you, Helene-Marie," Hadithe Zakale said, his voice and eyes full of warmth. "But you take a great risk."

"Risk!" the woman scoffed. "I die of shame that I cannot do more. Your guard is one I know well. Besides, I bring a message, not so much for you as for the honored messenger here. Will you speak to him for me, Hadithe Zakale? For I do not have the standing to speak to a messenger of the King of Ashanti, and I am not sure that even if I did, I would know the proper words and courtesies."

"That will not be necessary," Sokolo spoke up at once. "You have brought us food at a great risk to yourself, and this is no time for deference. Speak without fear. I welcome your words."

"My message then, is this. Shortly you will meet the man who has title to the captives. When you do, do not offer ransom for more than a dozen or so. Say you have come to ransom nobles only. Otherwise the man who has imprisoned you will soon own the captives, and you will be in deep danger of losing them all."

"How can this be? And whence the message?"

"I cannot tell you how this can be, sir, but the message is from the white captain called Tousaint and from Sasha, his *signaré*. It is she who has formed this plan."

Sokolo shook his head in puzzlement. "A woman?"

"This woman, yes," Helene-Marie said. She straightened up. "I raised her Believe me, she knows what she is doing."

In the silence, Hadithe Zakale spoke, with a chuckle.

"Well enough, Helene-Marie. From what I have heard, I believe you completely."

"This is *not* acceptable, Lieutenant Drouin, and you and I are going to have to do something about it." Lieutenant Marcel Drouin, commander of the forts on the island, studied Andre Bruie carefully. He had known factors before, here and in other French colonial outposts, but nothing in his past experience seemed relevant at the moment. He had the advantage of knowing a confrontation was about to occur, but it had been impossible for him to decipher exactly what this particular Chief Factor really wanted.

"I am at your service, of course," the Lieutenant said with more than a tinge of formality. Still, he tried to keep any hint of irony out of his voice.

Bruie gestured toward the window of the Factor's office, the crowded and cluttered cubbyhole that had served the needs of island administration for nearly twenty years.

"More space," the Chief Factor said abruptly. Then, as Drouin's mind began to race over the possibilities of relocating the office, Bruie ticked off additional points. "A stone building, Drouin. I would prefer to have it ready in a fortnight. And I'm sure you will agree with me that until such time as it is ready, I will be using your own command post. You will vacate it immediately and arrange to have these materials moved in."

Drouin opened his mouth, but no words came out. Finally two did.

"*Oui, Monsieur.*"

He was almost ready to rise, but Bruie interrupted him.

"Then we shall see to the forts, next," he said. "They are in no condition to withstand the bombardment of a modern warship of even the smallest size. Even a third-rater would overpower you. Refitting the forts will, in addition, provide useful employment for the undesirables on the island until such time as we are able to get rid of them."

"The forts certainly can stand improvement," Drouin replied. "Although, as you know, it isn't their condition that makes us vulnerable. It's our location, lack of supplies, especially water..."

"I know all about that," Bruie said impatiently. "I am not impressed by the argument. All that is necessary is additional storage."

Drouin knew enough to drop the matter there. It was no use discussing military matters, let alone naval ones, with a company factor. Many careers had been damaged in such arguments. Instead he shifted the discussion.

"These undesirables you mention," he said. "I am not sure I understand which ones you mean. There are any number of men among the *laptots* who were born to cause trouble, but for the most part they are only here between ships. They spend most of their lives as shipmasters' problems."

"*Laptots* do not concern me," Bruie replied. "The undesirables I mean are these damned women who seem to think they own the island. Put them on notice, Drouin. We are not the Portuguese. They seem to have failed to notice this."

Drouin allowed himself the drift of an eyebrow upward. "They are, of course, something of a strain, *M'sieu*, at times. But I have been told they serve an economic need."

"I will be the judge of that," Bruie replied. "Again, we are not Portuguese. Nor am I a soft French factor, like their Eugene Danton. Their economic contribution will be to reinforce the fort. If they are strong enough to walk around with these heavy burdens of gold that I see constantly, why, they can carry burdens of stone too. Is it not so?"

Abruptly the Chief Factor got up and walked to the door of the cubbyhole, indicating that the interview was at an end. Drouin rose up swiftly in the military fashion, suppressed a salute, and walked out. He was a few steps down the hall when Bruie called after him.

"One more thing, Drouin. Keep an eye on that damned *griot.* You know who I mean, that storyteller. If he strays from the village, I want to know about it."

"I understand," Drouin replied. "Perhaps it would have been better not to release him? We can always..."

"No! I don't want him in the dungeon. Did you not know, Drouin, that the macaque speaks French? I'm sure he's been feeding information to the Ashanti, which is why the Ashanti is being difficult. Well, he'll get no more help from that source. Tomorrow morning, when my new office is ready, I intend to bring the Ashanti to it. I will also bring in the captain, Tousaint, and that slut he's been relying on to do his business for him. They'll all learn at once that a new day has dawned on this godforsaken island!"

Drouin nodded and hastened away. He was glad to be out of the Chief Factor's presence. But even out in the open air, on the parade ground of the lower fort, he felt a sense of oppression. It was as if the small room still enclosed him.

As he often did, he took in all the activity in the fort without really making a conscious effort to do so. There was nothing out of the ordinary: no slouch, slack, or failure of discipline. He had at least been given a good command, an excellent one, really, for a colonial outpost.

The soldiers were few in number, but they were well prepared for their task, as long as that task didn't change suddenly, back and forth and back again, at the whim of a person who didn't understand their need for stability.

After all, it was a colonial garrison under his command, not a Guards Regiment. And it was used to the slow pace of the tropics, not the bustling speed of Paris. Would this be recognized?

Drouin's sense of oppression faded slowly. Time would tell if the manifest energy of Andre Bruie would be good or bad for Drouin's command... and Drouin himself.

Chapter Seven

Andre Bruie prided himself on being a thorough man, and for once he was satisfied with his own performance. In the short time since taking over Lieutenant Drouin's headquarters room at the lower fort, he had arranged that room to his satisfaction. The jumble of books, papers, maps and memorabilia he had inherited from Eugene Danton now sat in logical order on shelves along one wall. The really important papers were filed in drawers in the large desk at the center of the room. Behind the desk was a large and comfortable chair, and behind that, at the south end of the room, a single window let in light in a slightly distorted fashion, the glass being somewhat warped and uneven. Still, it suited Bruie's purpose. He wouldn't have to look at the bright background and the distorted glass... his visitors would, and that would unsettle them.

They would be more unsettled by the hardbacked chairs that faced the desk. Bruie had made several calculated moves in anticipation of the day's meeting. Those chairs would do for Tousaint and Drouin. As for the Africans, they would sit too, on three-legged stools drawn up against the back wall. He would have made them sit on the floor, but that, he felt, might have been more comfortable for them.

In the office of Andre Bruie there would be room for several people, but only one man's pride.

He was pleased with his arrangements. And from his point of view, the meeting had started well. Tousaint and Drouin shifted uncomfortably in the hardbacked chairs as Bruie read them a long policy statement. It was carefully worded, of course, reminding them of their respective responsibilities to the company.

Against the back wall sat the two island women called Helene-Marie and Sasha, looking perhaps more composed than the two white men, but not taking any part in the discussion. Between them sat the storyteller, and there was one more stool on the right for the Ashanti, when it came time to bring him in.

He was well aware that these five people, in particular, had lines of communication open between them; they had traded information behind his back more than once. Tousaint would look to anyone for a possible way to escape his predicament. Drouin, a typical colonial officer, would do the same in order to secure his position. The storyteller and the women also had their own purposes. Bruie was sure of that. Nevertheless, he had decided to show them they couldn't prevail against him, even five together.

"So there you have it," Bruie said at last, finishing his long statement. "Do I make myself understood?" Hearing no oral response, he reached into his desk and drew out a large sheet of paper, already filled out except for signatures. "Here you are, Captain Tousaint. A contract for the purchase of twelve hundred Africans. Let's get this part over with. The day is wasting."

Tousaint took the contract, squinted at the crabbed writing, and read it through. He set the paper back on Bruie's desk.

"A slight error of fact, *Monsieur* Bruie. This is not a contract; it is merely a bill of sale. There are no terms for the transport or the transport fees."

"That is correct. You will also note that the bill of sale, as you call it, stipulates two-thirds of the price you originally expected to receive, rather than a mere half. Further delay, *Monsieur*, may make me regret my generosity."

"You realize of course that you cannot assign transport to any other ship in harbor at the moment, if I am not involved and do not give my consent?"

"Of course. Including the ship now arriving, Leclerc's. I'm not concerned, for I shall make other arrangements."

"And you will be responsible for feeding and watering the Africans until such time as you can make these arrangements?"

"Yes, of course. Well?"

Captain Tousaint let a long sigh escape him. Then he smiled.

"You're a hard man, *Monsieur* Bruie. I see that I'm beaten. Well, there are other days, and perhaps other kinds of cargo. I will accept your terms."

With a casual gesture, Tousaint took the bill of sale in hand again, reached across Bruie's desk and took a quill pen from an inkwell. He signed the document with a flourish and then, reaching into a small box next to the inkwell, took out a few pinches of sand and sprinkled them over the signature. Moments later, he blew the sand away and handed the paper back to Bruie.

Bruie nodded, deeply satisfied. Even full of arrogance, he was surprised that it had gone so easily. He knew ships' captains; there should have been at least a trace of bluster. Then again, perhaps the captain knew he was going to have to take these terms, and didn't want to embarrass himself further. Bruie put the contract away in his desk.

"Now," he said, "to another matter. Drouin, you've told me that this Ashanti messenger requires a translator. You've also told me that he will have none of mine. You've suggested I use one of these people on the stools."

"It would seem most... ah... expeditious."

"Expeditious! You amaze me, Lieutenant, with such words!"

Bruie glanced at the two copper-skinned women. He may have to deal with the African messenger, but he'd be damned if he would let these women take part in any of the negotiations. Triumphantly, he eyed the storyteller.

"What will be your fee, *griot* ?"

Hadithe Zakale rose slowly from his stool and faced the factor.

"You are addressing me, *Monsieur* ?"

"Who else?" Bruie barked. "Are there other *griots* standing behind you?"

"No, *Monsieur*, but then I myself am not a *griot*. *Griots* are always local people, who sing a man's praises or mock another for a fee. They speak of ancestry in farfetched ways, for good or for ill. I myself am a traveling teller of tales. As to fees, I can accept none. It's up to those who ask of me to determine the value of my work. I shall translate the words. You will judge for yourself what this is worth."

Bruie was irritated, although he tried to conceal it. Obviously there was still room for more pride than his own in this office! After a long and searching look at Hadithe Zakale, in which he detected perhaps arrogance but insufficient evidence of insolence, he nodded. He turned to Drouin.

"Have your men bring in the Ashanti."

Drouin went to the door, opened it, and gave a command down the hall. Resuming his place, he waited with the others until a shuffle of feet indicated the arrival. Two armed guards brought in Sokolo, unchained, still rubbing his wrists to rid himself of cramps and poor circulation.

The guards took stations on either side of the door, while Sokolo advanced and stood staring at Andre Bruie. There was no way for anyone to read his face, except perhaps Hadithe Zakale, and the storyteller was not about to translate what he read there now.

"Tell him to sit," Bruie said to the storyteller, waving a hand at the vacant stool.

Hadithe Zakale translated this information. At this point Sokolo glanced at the stool, and spoke several words to the storyteller in a raised voice. His obvious agitation amused Bruie.

"Well? Has he a problem?"

"He asks," Hadithe Zakale replied slowly, "if you mock him."

"Ah! So the stool is not good enough for him, eh?"

"*Au contraire,*" the storyteller replied. "It is too good."

Bruie just stared at him for a moment.

"Explain."

"He is a messenger of the King of Ashanti. Among the Kumasi Ashanti, a stool is for high chiefs and royalty. It is their, how do you say it, emblem of sovereignty? To them it is as a throne is to you French. Would you, *Monsieur*, sit on the throne of King Louis?"

Bruie hesitated, but only for a moment.

"Tell him, then, that we sought to honor him, not insult him."

Hadithe Zakale relayed this information, and Sokolo responded with a flurry of words that soon ceased. Then, calmly, he added two more words.

"Well?"

"He thanks you for the honor, *Monsieur* Bruie, but he prefers to stand.

"Then let him stand. All right." He turned to Tousaint. "Now perhaps I shall embarrass you, Captain. I am well aware of the message you and your woman relayed to this man. The ruse you set up has been discovered. This is no matter now, for if nobles were all he wanted, he would still ransom them, for a far greater price than I have contracted to pay you. I don't believe he came merely to seek nobles."

He pulled the contract out of his desk. "Here, storyteller. Tell him this is my title to the slaves. And ask him now if it's true that he's only here to ransom men of noble birth?"

Many words were exchanged between the messenger and Hadithe Zakale, and some time passed before the storyteller turned back to Bruie.

"As to your question, *Monsieur*, he replies that the tale about his being here to ransom nobles is not true."

Bruie smiled thinly, permitting himself an amused glance at the reaction of Tousaint. There was a certain discomfort to observe. The African woman called Helene-Marie seemed equally unhappy. But, oddly enough, there was no change at all in the expression on the face of the young woman called Sasha.

"So I thought. Now let us... "

74

"He says," Hadithe Zakale continued quietly, "That he has come to ransom only one man."

Bruie got up suddenly.

"What? What's that?"

"Only one man. A prince, the son of the Ashanti chief."

Angrily, Bruie rounded on Tousaint.

"Another one of your tricks?"

"I don't think it's a trick," the storyteller said quickly. "I was amazed when I first heard of this ransom effort, *Monsieur* Bruie, for I have traveled widely and know something of the Ashanti's ways. They do not usually ransom men who have been defeated in battle. In their eyes a defeated warrior deserves his fate. Usually they are reluctant even to exchange prisoners with an enemy. I knew there had to be a special case involved here, but of course, Sokolo could speak the full truth of his mission only to the one actually possessing the captives."

"So!" Bruie snorted. He stared at Sokolo for a long time. Then he recovered himself.

"Let it be so. That one man will cost him as much as twelve hundred, then. Small price to pay for a king's son, is it not so?"

Again, Sokolo and the storyteller exchanged words.

"He says he will discuss a price," Hadithe Zakale related, "when he has seen the man he seeks with his own eyes."

"I do not bargain," Bruie snarled narrowing his eyes. But then a look of amusement came over his face. What did it really matter? Let this messenger see his Ashanti prince. Let him see him bound in chains.

"Very well," he said signaling one of the guards. "I'll send a man to fetch him. But I can't tell an Ashanti prince from an Ashanti serf, I don't mind saying, so this messenger had better describe him."

Again there was an exchange of words, and again Hadithe Zakale used fewer French words to translate Sokolo's message.

"He says you can tell a prince by what he wears, but since the Prince is probably not in his original clothes, he will be identifiable by tattoos. As with all Ashanti royalty, he has special ones."

"Yes, I know savage customs. Describe them."

Hadithe Zakale described the tattoo patterns, while Bruie busily scribbled some notes on a small scrap of paper. At the end of the narrative, he handed the paper to Drouin.

"Here, Lieutenant. Take the water skiff and its crew, and go get this man at once."

"I fear I cannot," Drouin replied." Anticipating an increased need for water, I sent the skiff off to fetch more."

"So!" Bruie said, admiring himself for not losing his temper. "And how long..."

He was interrupted by three clear sounds that reverberated through the fort: A bell, rung once, and then twice in quick succession.

"What's this?" Drouin muttered. "Another ship? Were you expecting another ship, Tousaint?"

Bruie held up a hand. "Never mind. I see the water will be needed. Well done, Drouin. As for the Ashanti, we'll just have to wait."

"You might as well wait forever," Tousaint said quietly.

Bruie whirled on him. "What do you mean by that?"

"The man the Ashanti describes, I have seen him. I have not seen him for some time. While we were negotiating with the Arab called al-Ghul, several captives tried to escape. Three were shot, one captured. The one captured was the one with the tattoos."

"So?"

"Al-Ghul decided to make an example of him. He had him impaled in front of the others. I wondered why they set up such a wail, for one man in twelve hundred."

"Stop translating!" Bruie ordered.

"Why not?" Tousaint said. "If you think this is a trick, go and see for yourself. You won't find him in the caffle. He's dead."

Bruie drummed his fingers on his desk. Hadithe Zakale spoke quietly to the messenger, whose expression didn't change. He merely bowed his head, and as quickly raised it, speaking a few words.

"Well?" Bruie demanded.

"He says he shall tell the King his son died well, and that his mission here is at an end."

"*Foutez le bete*," Bruie muttered. He was silent for a few moments. "So be it. Tousaint, I read your face. You think the tables are turned. Well, we shall see. You can take your captives to America, then, at the usual rates. But I've still made a good price for the company."

"That's true," Tousaint replied. "But, you didn't make transportation a part of my contract. Which means I am free to negotiate my own terms for their passage." He chuckled. "Shall I tell you those terms, *Monsieur* Bruie?"

The cold eyes of the Chief Factor of Senegal lit up with a savage fury. But before he could speak, a woman's voice intervened.

"May I speak?" Sasha asked.

Bruie studied her. Not knowing exactly why, he nodded consent. It might have been because she seemed to be the calmest person in the room.

"*M'sieu*, you have been distracted by the presence of Sokolo the Ashanti and by your own thoughts. But you're a man of business. Such games you and my captain play, these last few days... forgive me, but they have been those of boys testing each other, not men respecting each other. Now, put an end to it and be men. Tear up the sales contract, and agree on the original terms. I am sure the captain will accept them. And leave thoughts of change for deeper consideration. I am young, sir, and I know full well that change is needed. But it must be considered in light of all the facts."

Bruie's jaw dropped. He had never had a woman address him this way before, let alone an African one. And she spoke perfect French.

"I will not be trifled with," he muttered.

"No one trifles with you, *Monsieur*. I merely suggest that it would be expedient for business, if it were done this way."

Tousaint chuckled. "She has a head on her shoulders, as well as a body below them, is it not so? If you agree, *Monsieur* Bruie, I shall agree as well."

Without speaking, Bruie quickly drew out another document. This time it was a pre-written, standard company contract. He filled in some blanks, blotted the writing and handed it to Tousaint. Tousaint read it carefully, signed it, and blotted it in his turn. Finally Bruie added his own signature. When he had finished shaking the sand off, he returned the document to his desk, and seemed to be somewhat recovered as he did so.

"All right, that's settled. Woman, there will indeed be change. I see, however, that I do need to study the matter more thoroughly. But certain things cannot be permitted....you!"

He suddenly spoke over Sasha's shoulder, "Helene-Marie! You have bribed a guard and carried messages to men I had incarcerated. There is no excuse for your conduct. Yes, I know all about it. And you have until tonight to leave this island, on pain of death if you ever return."

Bruie had expected the shock on Helene-Marie's face. What he hadn't expected was the composed face of Sasha. Before he could ponder the fact, however, there was a loud knock on the door and exclamations of deep agitation.

"Go away!" Bruie commanded loudly. "Wait until I am finished!"

"Lieutenant," a muffled voice spoke on nevertheless, "The ship!"

"Later," Drouin called "I heard the bell, Talbot."

"It's a *warship*, sir!"

Drouin bounded to the door unbidden, then flung it open.

"A warship! What flag?"

"None, sir."

"Pirates!" the Lieutenant exclaimed. "Worse than the Brits! What size, Talbot? How many guns?"

"A fourth-rater, sir. Thirty-two guns."

"Puny," Bruie scoffed. "Surely your forts can deal with that, Lieutenant?"

"Of course, sir. But it need not come in range of our fort guns to harm us fatally."

Suddenly, Lieutenant Drouin's face got very red. "Talbot, is the water skiff back?"

"They are coming back, sir, but it seems without a full load."

Drouin shook his head. "That will be the last of the water for a while, Chief Factor. Without water..."

Bruie raised a hand to end Drouin's sentence.

"You don't need to spell it out for me, Lieutenant Drouin. I understand the implications."

Then before Bruie could speak again, a great roar reverberated through the room.

"Three guns, Drouin said thoughtfully. And not aimed at the fort. You see, *Monsieur*...it begins."

Chapter Eight

Before nightfall there was a considerable change in the office of Andre Bruie. The rough seats and stools were replaced by comfortable chairs, five in all, with one of the wooden hard-backed chairs remaining to stand beside the Chief Factor's desk with a cushion on it. A large and detailed map of the island and vicinity covered most of the desk, a map held down by a variety of instruments. Other maps and certain reference books lay close at hand, and when the conference began, the hard-backed chair was filled with a company clerk. His rapidly moving pen scratched out every word spoken.

It was a difficult task for the clerk, for the four ships' captains who'd been invited were quite voluble and fluent. The language they used required some sanitizing. Pochette, the clerk, looked up at Andre Bruie from time to time for help, but the Chief Factor merely shrugged. Bruie let them talk. He knew they had to blow off steam before cooling down enough to deal rationally with the situation.

Devereaux and Tousaint stressed the need to load cargo. Champlain, whose holds were already crammed, stressed the need for his own ship to get away from the island. Leclerc, the most recent arrival, stressed no specific needs, but roundly criticized the changes that had taken place on the island since his last visit.

When each man had had his say, and a brief silence had taken hold of the room, Bruie seized control of the discussion. He turned to Lieutenant Drouin.

"How long can we hold out?" he asked.

"With mild adjustments, two or three days," the Lieutenant responded promptly. "With hard measures, four or five."

"Not even a week?"

"*Monsieur*, we were lucky the water skiff made it back. Four or five is better than nothing." Then, sensing Bruie's irritation, Drouin added, "With desperate measures and unusual good luck, perhaps a week."

"Well, we can study your desperate measures, but what do you mean by 'luck'?"

"Rain."

"It's not the rainy season."

"I am aware of that, *Monsieur*."

Bruie drew back in his chair, slapping his desk in frustration.

In his mind he rapidly reviewed the situation. The pirate ship, one must assume it to be a pirate ship, lay anchor just off the southern coast of the mainland, just out of the range of the fort's guns. It blocked all traffic from this island to the mainland, and obviously intended to enforce that blockade, for it had fired two three-round salvos on the little water skiff. One shot had decapitated an African on the skiff and another had grazed the hull; two other men had panicked and jumped overboard, to be lost to the sea and the sharks. Fortunately, the remaining men, under the old African called Gilbert, had managed to get the boat safely to shore.

But now the pirate ship was silent, silent and waiting.

"They haven't even sent us demands," Bruie muttered. "We don't know what they want."

"Of course we do," Captain Champlain said. "They want us to send someone to them, asking for terms. I'm sure they're well aware of our situation."

"I think we can take that for granted. But perhaps they are not yet aware of a prize they could take without forcing us to surrender: the slave-caffle on the mainland."

"That's unlikely to appeal to them," Tousaint replied. "Pirates have been known to dabble in the slave-trade, but most pirate ships aren't built to carry very many slaves. And they would have security problems if they did."

"Still," Bruie observed, "they could go ashore, take over the caffle and threaten to destroy it. Or... recruit."

"I think not. My men still guard the slaves, and they are well armed. The caffle is also in a secure place. My people have signalled me that all is under control."

Bruie shook his head, still disbelieving.

"Damn it all, there are four ships in this harbor. Each of you has guns, is it not so?"

"Not enough to be a match for that ship," Leclerc said at once. "Not even all of us together. It would be foolhardy."

"Even if your choice lay between surrender and starvation?"

"It would still be foolhardy," Leclerc said again, this time more sternly.

Bruie raised a hand. "I only suggest a possibility. You could try."

" *Merde*," Leclerc snorted. "I hardly have enough powder to fire a salute."

At this, Bruie rounded on Lieutenant Drouin and demanded to know how much black gunpowder the forts possessed. Drouin gave him the details, up to the moment; munitions were his special study, as well as his responsibility.

"But," he said at the end of his recital, "I agree with Captain Leclerc. It would be foolhardy. The pirate ship would have a better chance against our forts than the ships would have against him."

Bruie mulled it over. "But you refer to twenty empty kegs, Drouin. What do you keep those around for? They can't be used to transport water."

"No, sir. But we may find some use for them, if only to take on more powder from a passing ship. On this island one must not discard anything out of hand. Things are too hard to replace."

Bruie nodded. He was all in favor of thrift. But he did not make any further mention of it. There was a time to discuss details, but this was not it. It was time for decision.

"Enough," he said. "We can't sit around. We will send someone to the pirates. I will send one man in a boat. Leclerc, you will provide the man. Send the one who used to live here. What's his name? Batees? I will not risk a white man on such a mission. We will send a ship's boat. You, Tousaint, will provide the boat."

With that he stood up, nodding his head for emphasis, and ended the conference.

There was a moon that night, but it was barely visible; a thin sliver of a crescent that provided only the palest of highlights. It was hardly enough for a man to see his own footsteps, let alone his surroundings, unless he was accustomed to total darkness.

Hadithe Zakale, however, was such a man, and for him the light was more than sufficient to wander the island. He knew what he sought. There was a high point on the hill, a short distance away from the upper fort.

His thoughts wandered back to Sasha. What a remarkable woman she was, the way she had dominated Bruie. So much power for one so young. Again he thought back to the day he had watched her mother fling herself into the sea. Ah, yes, the woman who chose to live freely, or not at all. What fire she had, what spirit! Sasha was so much like her. And yet, Sasha had so much more.

The storyteller shuddered, recalling the haunting visit he had had with her the night before. She had come to him, stepped out from the shadows, decked in golden baubles. It was the first time he had seen her in twenty years and he had been amazed by her stength and beauty.

She had said she wanted to discuss the details of the meeting between Sokolo and Bruie. Hadithe Zakale trembled as he remembered the fire in her eyes, the wickedness. Now, for the first time, the teller of tales truly understood the nature of her visit. She had not come to help Sokolo, but to help her captain, Captain Tousaint. She had manipulated the situation to suit her own needs. She was indeed very cunning.

The teller of tales forced his attention to the moon. For a long time he stood there, watching the stars and listening for the night sounds that he remembered coming across from the mainland. They were there, but like the moonlight, they were faint. He couldn't account for it, unless the human presence of the slave caffle and the near menace of the pirate ship had somehow made even the animals sense it was time to hesitate or hide.

Using his ears, he became slowly aware of another human presence nearby. Moments later, he saw a figure in a dark-colored cloak approaching. He could tell two things from a distance: one, it was a woman, and two, she was wandering with no specific destination. As he focused his eyes more closely, he recognized her, and decided to call out before she was upon him.

"Good evening, Helene-Marie."

She cried out at the sound of her name, and turned to run, but he called after her to identify himself and assure her he meant no harm. She halted, hesitated, and then with some sort of odd sound in her throat, turned to face him.

"You frightened me, teller of tales. How could you find your way up here on a night like this?"

"I have night eyes." He paused. "And you?"

"Me? I have lived here as long as I can remember. Were I blind, I could find my way around."

Hadithe Zakale nodded in agreement. Then, in almost a whisper, he said: "I came up to see the stars, and to hear Africa. I see the stars, but Africa I hear but faintly."

"I hear it well enough," said Helene-Marie, shuddering. "That's why I came here, to get away from it."

"Get away? I don't understand."

"From my dreams. There are dreams that I have, and when

they will come I don't know. On such nights I wander the island, rather than attempt to sleep."

"They must be evil dreams indeed, to trouble you so. Does the man Bruie frighten you, with his threat to send you off the island? He may change his mind."

"His kind rarely does that, Hadithe Zakale." She gestured at the peak of the rise, near where they were standing. "Will you sit? I would like to do so, but only if you do so as well."

Hadithe Zakale laughed, and sat. Helene-Marie did the same, facing him. She took a tuft of the sparse grass from the hillside and crumbled the clod that held it together, letting the shoots flutter away.

"I will go like that," she said. "Wherever chance takes me."

"You have no one? You are of Africa, and yet also of the sea."

"I am neither. I am of the island. No one is bound to me."

Hadithe Zakale hesitated, briefly.

"But you have had children. Are they not grown by now, or close to it?"

"They would be, had they lived. Andre was drowned as a small boy, and Jeanne died of a fever six years ago."

"But what of Sasha? Is she not your daughter?"

"Sasha? Yes, I have Sasha. Or perhaps she has me. I don't know. She frightens me, Hadithe Zakale, almost as much as Bruie does... although I try not to show it."

"Ah. Well, she's a strong young woman, a leader. Perhaps one day she will wind up ruling this island, when Mama-Lise goes."

"Are you blind?" she choked out, so upset as to forget herself. "She rules now! All the younger women follow her, imitate her, react to things as she shows the way. Mama-Lise is but a shadow of authority, and I fear even that will end soon... very soon. And then life here will be entirely as Sasha envisions it. And before that happens, I would rather be gone myself, even in exile. I fear leaving, Hadithe Zakale, but I fear my dreams more."

"You dream... of her? I still do not understand."

"No, not of her," Helene-Marie replied. "Shall I tell you what I dream, Hadithe Zakale? Perhaps you would believe it. Perhaps

85

not. I will tell you anyway. I dream of moans and groans and clanking chains, and long lines of men getting on ships; endless lines, going away never to return. They stagger through my dreams until I wake up in a cold sweat. I am sick to death of the dream, and when I see the reality each day, I get sick too. It's evil. And Sasha and her friends will make it worse."

For a while after this, Hadithe Zakale was silent. His mind raced in search of adjustment. He hadn't realized, hadn't even suspected, what was troubling Helene-Marie. He wasn't sure he grasped it even now.

"But surely this is none of your doing," he said at last. "What these men suffer, others have decided to put them through, In a great many cases, I'm sure they've brought what they suffer on themselves. You're not responsible for it."

"Am I not? I serve those who arrange these things. I make it easier for them to get done what they seek to do. I give them food, give them water, give them myself when that is what they seek. How can I escape the evil itself?"

"And you would rather wander far away, alone, than to do it any longer?"

"I fear I must."

"It's a lonely life, wandering."

"You seem content."

"I? I am a tale-teller, at home anywhere and nowhere. People welcome me, seek me out, so I am not lonely often. But on long trips, I must confess, the silence has often closed in on me and troubled me."

He stretched out his legs, which were getting cramped. "I did not realize that myself until recently, but I acknowledge it now. These past few months I've had a traveling companion, and I shall miss Sokolo the Ashanti when we part company, as we must."

Helene-Marie just stared at him, eyes very large. There seemed to be a tear in her eye, at least there may have been. It was difficult to tell in the faint moonlight. Hadithe Zakale started to say something else, but she turned away from him. After a moment she spoke again.

"You never ask for one of us. You never have."

"So that's it," he said with a smile. "What am I, Helene-Marie? Am I a ship's captain, or an Ashanti prince, or a *laptot* ?"

"You know very well that you are a teller of tales."

"Yes, I tell stories. And those who hear them always judge for themselves what they are worth. Sometimes people give me food, as you do here, and a place to sleep. Other places give me the same, and more; trinkets, remembrances, nothing of any great value except to me. And some places, unless I refuse, offer me not only a bed, but someone to share it with."

He coughed. "I do not often refuse."

"I'm sorry...that we haven't offered..."

"You people always wait until you are asked for something. Maybe it comes from too much living around these white traders. Maybe they are such swine with a woman, that a woman wouldn't go with one of them unless asked. I don't claim to know."

"No one would think that of you," she said quickly.

"No. But... they wait to be asked." He sighed. "Shall I tell you, Helene-Marie, which of the island women I would prefer? Or can you guess?"

Helene-Marie turned to face him, and abruptly dropped her eyes.

"She is very beautiful," she said softly. "I know I've said that I fear her, but I can tell you do not. And unlike many of us, she at least has no fear of offering herself to a man, if it suits her purposes or her inclinations. I think she would be honored. If you won't ask her, perhaps you would allow me to tell her that an offer would be...suitable."

Hadithe Zakale laughed.

"Ah, Helene-Marie! You are right. Sasha *is* a beautiful woman. I would hardly think of driving such a one away from me. But for a man like myself, she lacks...seasoning. She is at once too hot and too cold, too quick and too slow, there is no medium about her. Give her a few years. Myself, I think I would prefer someone a little older. Someone old enough to know the world, yet young enough to stir its fires...and young enough to respect me as an elder." He chuckled. "Are you able to see the matter more clearly now, Helene-Marie?"

She stared at him. Her mouth didn't drop open, but her lips did part at last, and words came out in a small voice.

"You can't possibly mean...?"

There was no answer. For a few more moments she stared at the teller of tales. Then, slowly, she stood up, and Hadithe Zakale rose at the same time. They stood facing each other for another long moment. Which of them moved first, it would have been almost impossible to tell. Anyone watching would have thought that they reached for each other at the same time.

But it was a dark night, and there was no one around to see.

At daybreak, Bruie was at the harbor, supervising the launch of the ship's boat and giving detailed instructions to Leclerc's *laptot*, an African called Batees. This accomplished, he toured the forts and the Village, checking the inventory of food, water, fuel and other provisions. At last he did the same aboard the four ships in the harbor.

Bruie was a driver, and no man on the island knew it better than Denis Pochette, the junior clerk of the company. He was a young man, barely started on his career, who was neither tall nor muscular, nor brave, nor well connected. He had but one thing going for him, and that was an ability to write rapidly in a fair hand. By late afternoon on the second day, he felt even that slipping from him. He had been writing constantly all his waking hours, taking first the minutes of the conference and then accompanying Bruie on his inspection tours.

Relief from this duty came to Pochette only when Bruie noticed that some of the clerk's notes were becoming less than precise. Bruie cursed Pochette for carelessness, called in another clerk to replace him, and at once proceeded to round up the captains and Lieutenant Drouin for another conference.

While this was going on, Pochette deposited the last of his

88

memoranda with the other papers in his own clerical cubbyhole, and went off to take a nap. A few hours later he dutifully reported back to the Chief Factor's office.

"Is your hand recovered? I hope it is, for your sake and mine." He gestured to the stack of papers on one side of his desk. "At least you are legible. Where did they teach Janvier to write, in some English monastery?"

Janvier was the clerk who had taken over for Pochette, and he was, of course, not the best of hand-writers. Pochette merely shrugged. It was not his place to criticize a fellow clerk, even if invited to do so.

"Take these notes," Bruie said, "decipher them as best you can, and give me something I can READ! I want it by morning! I have other things to do besides supervise clerks!"

Hastily, Pochette pulled the papers together and left the Chief Factor swearing softly to himself. The clerk returned to his own cubbyhole and lit the night-lamp. It was a poor light and Janvier's writing was indeed atrocious. But Pochette could understand that. Janvier had been writing very quickly, and the subject matter was unsettling; the demands of a pirate.

Suddenly Pochette saw a motion in the darkness away from his desk. For a moment he disregarded it as a trick of the flickering lamp. Then he looked up and stared. There was a woman standing in front of him, in a white dress that barely hid her body.

"How long have you been here?" he demanded in a petulant tone, meaning to sound severe.

"A while," Sasha replied. "I came to see you."

"I am sure of that!" he scoffed. "I have had nothing to do with you women since I got here."

"Out of dislike, or different inclinations? Or fear?"

He caught his breath. "What do you want?"

"Words," Sasha said. "Words that I need to hear. I cannot read your language very well, but you can tell me what I need to know. It's all there in your papers."

"Do you think you can come in here and get me to betray Company secrets?"

"Yes," she said.

And so saying, she pulled a tie-knot on her shoulder; the dress dropped away. Pochette was left staring at what for him was an incredible sight...an impossible body...swathed in clear coppery skin. He kept staring until she spoke again.

"You need not read everything. I need only to know of a few matters. After that, well, a man takes his opportunities, or perhaps they are gone forever. Who knows what the morrow may bring?"

Pochette gripped the paper he was holding in both hands, as if it threatened to escape from him and fly away. But he didn't take his eyes off the woman, and as he stared, a hunger stronger than the belly's demand for food rose up inside him.

"Where shall I begin?" he asked in a low voice.

Chapter Nine

"It's good of you to visit me, Batees," old Gilbert said, puffing heartily on the thick cigar Jean-Baptiste had brought him.

"Even you by yourself, after so many years, would have been very welcome here. But this tobacco is better than any I have ever tasted. It must come from over the broad sea, in the lands of legend."

"Real enough lands," Jean-Baptiste responded. "I have seen them. It's been many years since Leclerc chose to come this way, but he hasn't been idle." He paused to puff on his own cigar.

The two men were in Gilbert's hut, where he lived alone now, a tribute to his rapidly advancing years. There had in fact been no one to share the old man's hut since Batees had left. Gilbert was a man of few needs. For the most part , he was content with the occasional bottle of wine that came his way, with a wink, from the Lieutenant at the fort. He would have offered some of this to Batees, if there had been any left. Sadly, the younger man had been too late.

"So you've had many adventures," Gilbert said after a while. "Distant lands...France too?"

"France, too," Jean-Baptiste said through a harsh laugh. "Give me the sea."

Gilbert was surprised. "It's not true what they say about France?"

"Oh, very true, very true. There's also a lot that is true that isn't mentioned."

"Then there are indeed towers twice as high as our hill fort, and people in the thousands and thousands in a single city?"

"Yes indeed. Thousands of people crammed together, running to and fro, buying, selling, eating, drinking. But what goes in must come out, no? They don't tell you about that. There are streams in those towns that flow with nothing but shit. The horses shit on the streets. Everywhere the smell is enough to knock a man down. I suppose if I were born a Frenchman, I'd be used to it, and able to put up with it. But I'm used to better things."

"I imagine the bilge of a ship smells little better."

"Of course not, maybe worse. But at sea, we rid ourselves of it quickly and leave it far behind." He paused to take another drag off the cigar. "And their women, they are worse bitches than the ones you have here."

"How so?"

"Money, always money. Money for dogs I would not spit at if I hadn't been long at sea. And even then, the ones that don't think they're too good for a sailor, think they are too good for an African. The hell with them!" He laughed again, this time more easily.

"No, let me have another taste of the lands they call the Americas. In those ports, a sailor really can live like a king, and have the best of it. It's true the Spanish own most of it, but for now, they welcome our trade. And they have things like these cigars. A city called Havana is where they're made." He laughed again. "Also they have women who do *not* smell like shit, and don't seem to think I do, either."

"Many adventures," Gilbert murmured, thinking to himself. "But that's you, I'm sure, wherever you go. And did you not just have a small adventure here by our island?"

With his cigar, Jean-Baptiste made an elegant gesture of dismissal.

"Not much of an adventure," he said. "But perhaps it's not complete yet, either. Are you curious, then? Shall I tell you about it?"

"If you feel like doing so, and no one has sworn you to secrecy."

"Hah! So much for their oaths, if they'd tried to impose them. No, I have no problem talking. I had the honor to give *Monsieur* Bruie a full report."

"So. They're pirates?"

"*Oui, vraiment*. Yes indeed. Lately come from the Americas themselves, just long enough for the Spaniards to lose track of them. When their trail's cold, they'll go back and resume their habits. They operate normally out of a small island in a stretch of sea between the continents, a sea called the Caribbean."

"They told you this?"

"Oh, yes, very openly. I talked to one who said he was their Captain."

"What country?"

"None. And all. The Captain says he's an Englishman, but I wouldn't know. I did notice Spaniards, Portuguese, even a Malay or two in the crew. There was an American native, and there were a few Africans, including a Fan." He chuckled. "All different, all alike. Two or three weapons on each man: knives, swords, a couple of huge pistols. They're a mean looking bunch. One or two of them might even give me trouble in a fight."

"I see. Well, what did they want?"

"A long list. You could boil it down to food and supplies."

"Not gold?"

"Not even mentioned."

Gilbert was silent for a moment.

"Then they, too, are starving. The Factor might be able to wait them out."

"Perhaps, but he won't. Like all but a few of the whites I have met, this Bruie is gutless. He gave in at once, offered to exchange the supplies for permission to make another water run."

93

Gilbert sat up from his half-reverie.

"Eh? Batees, you should have told me! I must get some sleep if I'm to go for water in the morning."

"Yes, yes, you will go. But when you land, Gilbert, think twice before you come back."

Gilbert stared at him. "You think they'll cross Bruie, and fire on the skiff?"

Jean-Baptiste shrugged. "Who knows? But whether they do or not, think, Gilbert! You're not getting any younger; why not look for a little adventure yourself? You are good with wood and tools, and the pirate ship cries out for a carpenter."

Gilbert stared off into the night, and after a while, spoke again.

"Is that what you have in mind for yourself, Batees? You are a very bold man, but this..."

"Is nothing important," Jean-Baptiste finished. "Tomorrow I will take the supplies to the ship, and you and the water crew will fetch water. And what each of us does after he leaves the island in the morning is for each of us to consider. Is it not so?"

Gilbert nodded slowly. "It may not be easy," he grumbled. "If I know Bruie, he'll have my crew packing and loading those supplies overnight. They'll be exhausted."

"Not in the least," Jean-Baptiste responded. He laughed. "I have saved your men that trouble. Bruie was indeed going to do as you feared, but I suggested perhaps it was time the women around here did some useful work. He was quite pleased with the idea. So now, while we men sleep, this island's precious *signarés* break their backs packing and loading the ship's boat. Does that not please you?"

"You still bear that old grudge, eh? Well, I can't say I blame you, Batees. I know the women never treated you well. Ah well, many things still make me curious. If I didn't have to sleep, there would be many more questions But I will leave it at one."

"Which is?"

"You mentioned one thing about those French towns that still puzzles me. Perhaps you can explain that word you used."

"Eh? What's that?"

"What are *horses*?"

The sun rises quickly in the tropics, but it had yet to catch Andre Bruie asleep. In fact, once again he was at his desk even before the first light appeared in the sky. He had dispatched a considerable amount of paperwork before the first rays began to filter through his distorted window-glass. Shortly thereafter, he was surprised to hear a knock at his door.

There stood Sasha, reporting as ordered at first light.

She wasn't wearing her white dress this time, but a golden-colored one, and to her modest display of bracelets she had added a gold necklace and some other trinkets. Bruie looked at her skeptically, but not because of the gold.

"You look surprisingly fresh for a woman who has worked through the night."

For an answer she held out her hands. There were blisters on them, and some fingers bled from small cuts.

"And you washed," he said. "Where did you get the water?"

"I washed in the sea, *Monsieur*, at a place where the water is only mildly salty. And I put some oil on my skin afterward. I hope it will pass. I don't seek to offend you."

Bruie nodded. "It is all done then?"

"Yes. All the goods and supplies are packed, and the kegs are nailed shut in case they happen to be bounced around on the sea. And the kegs are now aboard the ship's boat."

"*Bien.*" He paused, staring wonderingly at the impassive face.

"It was a good idea," he said reluctantly, "to think of using those empty powder kegs to carry the supplies. Much more prudent than laying the goods loose in the boat...and certainly better than risking our water-kegs for the purpose. But how did you, Sasha, know we had that many empty powder kegs?"

"I can't say, really," she replied. "Things get talked about around the fort. I just recalled that it had been mentioned."

A thin smile crossed Bruie's face.

"You have a good ear. Is it good enough to have heard who came into my garden area, and stole a chicken out of my private coop? One of the men, or one of your island brats?"

"A chicken, sir?"

"Yes, a chicken. Lays eggs, or at least this one used to....a bird!"

"I understand what it is, *Monsieur*. But why blame the children?"

"It turned up missing shortly after one of your creche-breaks. So I ask you..."

"I know the men have been compiling their rations for a stew. The food goes much further that way," she said thoughtfully. "But I, at least, have not tasted chicken in it."

"You? I understood only the males were involved in that."

"That's true, but a male can bring a woman a bowl of it, if he chooses." She smiled. "One or two usually do."

Bruie wanted to pound the desk with his fist, but he restrained himself. Finally he said, "You must know, Sasha, that I can't tolerate the way you and your women operate here. It just cannot be allowed."

"It would seem, *Monsieur*, that we fill a need. Many needs. We can be sent away, truly, but then who would do our work? Would you buy slaves to perform it?"

"Possibly. Slaves would be under better control."

"Too much control, *Monsieur*, for them to, as you say, operate. Slaves cannot do our work."

He stared at her, totally exasperated.

"Are you people," he asked at last, "even Christians?"

Sasha's raised eyebrows registered a mild surprise. *"Oui, Monsieur*, of course. We have all been Christians here since the time of the Portuguese, and none of what you call heresy has touched our island. Have you not seen our church?"

"Church? Your chapel I have seen, but I haven't seen anyone tending it."

"We haven't had a priest here in several years," she informed him. "It seems that saving souls is one thing, but keeping them is another, is it not so? But we follow it as best we can, and there are always candles being lit, which you would have seen if you'd been by the chapel at night. Perhaps one day they will send us another priest, and he can teach us better ways."

Bruie shuddered. It was on the tip of his tongue to say that a priest would be less welcome than... but he cut off the thought, and deflected the conversation.

"It might be difficult, after your last one succumbed to this climate, to find another willing to take up the post."

"Ah, that was too bad. Father Charles was a good man. As for the climate, well, it seems odd that he was so healthy for so long, and then gone so quickly." She smiled. "It was just a little while after your predecessor, *M'sieu* Danton, found out that he was teaching us to read."

Bruie stared at her. But this was not something he wanted to get into. Instead he stood up.

"Enough. It's time to see the boat off, and get the skiff over for more water. We must guard against treachery from these pirates." He hesitated. Then he let out a short barking laugh. "Yes, you can come and watch, if you like. Come with me."

He strode out of the office, Sasha following behind. Once she was out of his sight he all but forgot her, for his mind was racing to other things.

It was a gamble to give the pirates supplies, of course, but the island had enough of what had been demanded, and the island needed the water desperately. Besides, he thought, as he approached the edge of the fort compound, a French warship might indeed appear. Better chance of that, than of rain!

Jean-Baptiste, breathing in and out with a careful rhythm,

97

lifted and sank the oars in time with his breathing. He was quite pleased with himself. Even in the rough waters he was able to handle the boat fully weighted down with supplies. Such was his strength. Bruie would be impressed.

Jean-Baptiste laughed out loud as he thought of Bruie. What good was Bruie's praise now? He wouldn't be there to receive it. No, he was determined. He would sail aboard another kind of ship, one with no flag, and he would prosper at it, too. His companions would be jackals, but that was no matter; he would learn from them, until it came time to show them that they had taken on an African lion.

And after that...

A sudden breeze caught the surface of the water and threw it over him as spray. It was only a momentary distraction. He didn't even break his stride at the oars. This was the calm part of the bay's waters, and it was relatively shallow. A ship entering this part of the channel had to watch its soundings with care. The pirate ship had certainly done so, which spoke of good seamanship and not a little knowledge of the coastline.

Jean-Baptiste was too concerned with himself to take any interest in the goods he was carrying. They were in kegs, and the kegs were covered with a thick canvas tarpaulin to guard against the least chance of soaking. *Monsieur* Bruie was indeed a thorough man.

As he approached the pirate ship, Jean-Baptiste stole a brief glance at the waters to the east. He wondered idly if old Gilbert would take the hint and join him. Among jackals, he could use a friend. Even he, Jean-Baptiste, could not guard himself at all times. Besides, he rather liked Gilbert.

Well, if Gilbert did, he did. The choice was his. A friend could be useful, but at the bottom a man had to be able to survive on his own. Jean-Baptiste was quite sure that he would do so.

"That you, Batees?" a thickly accented voice called out. The rower looked up at the ship. It was the Portuguese who had called, the one who seemed to be second in command. Or maybe he was the third. Jean-Baptiste couldn't remember. It was no matter.

"Coming 'longside," Jean-Baptiste called out.

"You have got what we wanted, eh?"

Jean-Baptiste just laughed, and drew the oars out of the water, fastening them securely in the oarlocks. When he looked up from this task, a rope line snaked down to him. He grabbed it, secured the boat, and accepted another line. A thicker line came down at last, and Jean-Baptiste knew what that was for. He would tie it one at a time around each of the kegs, so they could be hauled aboard.

"Now show us, Batees," called the Portuguese. "What do you have for us under that sea-rag?"

With a loud laugh, Jean-Baptiste flung up the near side of the tarpaulin. As he did so, an unexpected flicker of light caught his eye.

If Jean-Baptiste had had time, he might have recognized the source of light as one of the little votive candles from the island's chapel, sunk in a glass jar. He might also have noticed the cord that was wrapped around it and tied to the tarp. And he might even have recognized the nature of the dark powder sprinkled between the edge of the tarp and the kegs, waiting to catch the spilled candle's flame.

But he didn't have time.

From the shore of the island it seemed as if a flash of bright light swept the pirate ship, suddenly transforming it into a monstrous vessel several times larger than it had been. Then the wreckage fell, and all that could be seen on shore were flaming chunks of wood dissolving into shapeless clouds of smoke. The cloud was still rising when the noise of the explosion reverberated across the shore.

For a moment all the motion was at sea. The people on the shore stood as if riveted to the rock and sand. It was Lieutenant Drouin who found his voice first, and then only spoke two words in a whisper.

"*Mon Dieu*," he said.

For once Andre Bruie echoed a subordinate's words. But, being what he was, he went on from there.

"My God, indeed! The pirate's magazine has exploded!"

99

"That, too," Drouin replied.

"What do you mean by 'that, too'?" Bruie demanded with instant irritation.

"*Monsieur* Bruie, I do not contradict you, but there were two explosions. Yes, the ship's magazine went. But, just a moment before, the ship's boat went first."

"The ship's boat! But how..."

"I don't know," Drouin replied quietly. "One may conjecture, of course."

His eyes fell on Sasha. Bruie, following his glance, rested his eyes as well on the imperturbable woman who faced them.

"Let me guess," Bruie said at last, sarcasm edging his voice. "Your women dutifully loaded the kegs full of supplies, but then at the last, they got confused, and by mistake loaded the ship's boat with twenty kegs of black powder."

Sasha bowed her head, ever so slightly, but never took her eyes off the factor's face.

"I wouldn't insult your intelligence with such a story, *Monsieur*. We were not confused. This was my plan. I beg you, if there is blame, let none of it fall on the other women, for they only did as I told them."

"But Batees..." Captain Leclerc suddenly burst out, unable to hide his rage any longer.

"Batees was a brave man," Sasha said at once, "a very brave man, willing to do anything to help his Captain and his shipmates."

Leclerc tried to say something in reply, but strangled on the words, and bowed aside choking.

This left Bruie and Drouin staring at Sasha, and they did so for a long time in silence.

"I suppose that's how it will be reported," Drouin said at last. "Unless you, *Monsieur* Bruie, wish to report my negligence as well. I accept full responsibility. It was I who took my men away and left these women to their task."

Bruie waved a hand. "Spare me, both of you, your assumption of responsibility. You know very well it was planned." He paused. "By all of us, for the sake of this island and of His Majesty

Louis the Fourteenth, the Most Christian King of France."

The people on the shore stared in awe at Andre Bruie. He grew rapidly impatient under those stares.

"Well? What other explanation can there be? Can you offer better, Lieutenant? Or you, Captain Leclerc? I think not! Even I can recognize a trap once it's sprung." He glared at Sasha. "But I'm also a man who resents being manipulated and deceived, for whatever purpose."

"I understand, *Monsieur*," Sasha said. "But it is said of you, as you have often said of yourself, that you judge a man by results. Can you do otherwise of a woman?"

Again he stared at her. After a while he said, "The noon hour is a while away yet. Go about your business, Sasha, whatever it is. Then come to my office when the sun is highest in the sky. There are things we must discuss."

Saying this, he turned from her as if forgetting her presence, and addressed the white men gathered around him.

"As for you, officers, captains, you must come with me at once. The crisis has been resolved, the situation has changed, and we must move rapidly to change with it, to recover what we have lost in time and wealth, and move on from there."

He turned on his heel and strode away, the other whites following.

Sasha said nothing more until the whites were out of hearing.

"Arsene," she called at last. A young woman detached herself from the crowd of onlookers and approached her closely.

"Yes, Sasha?"

"I will be with the Chief Factor this noon, and then away for a while on errands. When night falls, you and the others meet me at the far end of the village."

The young woman studied Sasha's face for a moment; like her, betraying no traces of emotion.

"It will be tonight, then?"

Sasha nodded.

"Tonight."

101

The waxing moon was pale and narrow, but little fuller than it had been the night before. It still was not much to see by, but Mama-Lise had no trouble finding the place she sought; she had after all been on the island longer than any.

It was a spot on the hill dominated by the upper fort, not far from the place where a storyteller and an island woman had met the night before.

It was more difficult for her, with her bulk, to carry with her the things she needed: the sticks, and the rocks, and the other things she hoped would make things right and proper.

She had always heard that old people remembered the near past dimly, and their childhood with extreme clarity, but that must have been a fable. Her childhood memories were what she wanted now, and she couldn't find them; not enough to inform her, or direct her, with any certainty.

Perhaps if there were still a priest on the island, she might have gone to him and laid her fears before him, calling on the Christian God to help her through. But this she doubted in her heart. Long ago when the slavers had brought her here and left her as not quite suitable, she had been taken in and the Portuguese had made a Christian of her. But their God was a God of the daylight, of hope and brightness. She couldn't believe he would let himself be bothered with the things of the darkness and the night.

The old woman suppressed a shudder. She had been right; oh, yes, she had been right. Something had warned her of what was to come, and that warning had forced her to make a small theft from the Chief Factor's possessions. How desperate she felt when she had taken it.

Well, it had to be done. The sacrifice had to be made. Only one God, the strongest one of them all, could help her now. Of course, it must be a life or death situation to invoke the Great God of her faraway homeland; but she was quite sure the circumstances fit that.

If only she were close enough...

Suddenly she broke off thinking, stiffening her spine and her thoughts. The gods gave strength, but only where some of it already existed.

With an interrupted squawk, the chicken died in her hands, its neck wrung in one sudden move.

"Damballah!" she cried. "Forgive me coming to you this way, not knowing the right words, not knowing the right deeds. Take this life I offer, and keep evil from me, that I may have peace in my last days."

There was silence all around; no change in the stars, no change in the sky. Dully, Mama-Lise tried to remember if there was even supposed to be a sign. A shooting star? She couldn't remember.

Then, out of the night, a light appeared. It wasn't from the sky, it was a light on the earth. Someone had lit a torch within a few feet of her. The old woman scrambled to her feet. Many figures stood around her in the darkness. She couldn't tell who they were immediately.

"What evil do you fear, Mama-Lise?" a voice asked quietly.

Mama-Lise stood still. She recognized the voice, and now, as the old eyes grew accustomed to the bright light, she recognized the face, too.

A small sigh escaped her. No one but she could have heard it. Yet, with that sigh, it seemed as if a burden had left her, a burden of fear. What must be, must be. If Damballah had given her that much courage to face the end, then perhaps that was enough. She wouldn't go down whimpering, or begging.

"So, Sasha," Mama-Lise said in a harsh tone, "you have come at last. And you, Arsene, Paulette, Henriette, Desiree...yes, I know you all. Am I too much, even now, for one alone? Well, go ahead. Be about your business, as you would have it."

"You think our business is to harm you, Mama-Lise?" Sasha asked.

"Hah!" The old woman spat. "Don't play with me, Sasha. You killed Batees, who only hurt you from a distance. What will you do with me, who harmed you with my own hands?"

The torch flickered against the starlit sky.

"Yes," Sasha said. "I killed Batees. But can you understand why?"

"I think I do."

"I fear you do not. Batees cared very little for whom he harmed, or to what extent he harmed, as long as the harm served him. He asked for what he got."

"So! You are a great judge of what people deserve?"

"I did not judge him, Mama-Lise. But when there came to me a way to preserve my own people at the sacrifice of an outsider, I had no qualms. It was necessary; he had no standing to complain."

Mama-Lise peered at Sasha through the torchlight. The old woman was, after all, African, more African than Sasha. With that came all of the African's uncompromising, unsentimental sense of justice. Yes, this she could understand.

"But what of me?" she asked after a moment, some of the harshness gone from her voice.

"You were hard on me, Mama-Lise. But then, I imagine I was a difficult child. I can't complain of the way you treated me."

The old woman faltered for a moment, then recovered.

"If that is so," she said at last, "then why are you all here?"

"To tell you that they have chosen me to lead them, and that now they follow me, instead of you."

Mama-Lise snorted. "That's no great surprise."

"Perhaps not. But now it is done openly. Bruie confirms it now, for what his confirmation is worth. Another's would be better."

"Another's? Whose?"

"Yours."

"Mine?"

"Yes, Mama-Lise. Yours. You have raised us, and we respect that. Still, we are no longer children. We go different ways. Set aside the burden you don't need to carry. Give us the chance to do as we think best. Keep the creche, and give the children your time and your thought and your care. They need it, we don't."

Sasha laughed lightly. "Though you may doubt it at the moment, we all feel this is true."

Then, in the torchlight, she took a step forward and knelt down in front of the old woman.

"As for myself, Mama-Lise, I would rather have your blessing than your curse."

Mama-Lise stood over Sasha, her mind a racing with confused thoughts. She remembered the prayer she had made to Damballah, and thought again. Perhaps he did more than I asked, if in a different way.

From her hand she took a small ring, the only token she possessed. Holding it in one hand, she took Sasha's right hand in the other.

"I shall care for the children," she said, "as long as I am able. But you, Sasha, must now care not only for them, but for the rest of us as well. Night and day we must be in your thoughts. Our welfare must come before yours. When it comes to our safety, you mustn't even think of yourself at all. Do you accept this burden?"

"Yes."

"Then it's yours," Mama-Lise said, slipping the ring on her finger.

The rains had long been delayed, or they were coming, and even a man not familiar with Africa of the northern tropics could have known that simply by looking at the western sky.

For a brief while, it wouldn't be necessary for the islanders to worry about water; there were great cisterns standing ready to catch the rain and dispense it. But, on the eve of the rains, there was yet one task left for the water skiff. It was to act as a passenger ferry.

There were three passengers. One got aboard quickly, without a backward glance; fitting actions for a King's Messenger taking the first transportation back home. The other two lingered on the shore a while, deep in conversation with a woman in a white dress decorated with many golden baubles.

"You may still stay," Sasha said earnestly. "And you may come back whenever you wish. Bruie does not insist on this punishment any longer."

"I know," Helene-Marie said. "And we have been through this many times, Sasha. It is I who chooses to go, and I go willingly. I have offered to be Hadithe Zakale's companion, and he has accepted."

Sasha shook her head, but a smile crossed her face.

"I suppose it must be so, then." Then an uncharacteristic laugh escaped Sasha. After a moment Sasha became very earnest again.

"She isn't all I have, Hadithe Zakale, for I have my own people now, and must think of them. But she's the only mother I have ever known. Protect her."

"As long as she's with me," the teller of tales said quietly, "she need fear only what I fear."

Sasha stared at him. "But you... fear nothing."

"Oh, Sasha, you are still so young and still see with a child's eyes. It's true, I need fear very little, but everyone fears something."

Sasha still stared at him in disbelief. Then she took something from her dress. "I have something for you. This for you, Hadithe Zakale, though not from me, comes through me."

She handed him a small disc on a chain. Both were made of the same metal.

"Gold?" The teller of tales was surprised. "I don't usually carry gold."

"It's a very slight burden. Do you remember telling *Monsieur* Bruie that he must himself decide what he should give you, when you translated for the Ashanti?"

"Yes, I remember, but I'm surprised that he did."

Sasha's laugh was light this time.

"He has a very strong mind and uses it well," she replied. "I will never like him, really, nor he me...it would greatly surprise us both I'm sure, were it otherwise...but I respect him, and I believe he now respects me. No matter."

"This is a coin, Hadithe Zakale, a Louie as they call it, a gold

106

piece with the image of the King of France. *Monsieur* Bruie says that when you look at it, you should remember who sits on the French throne, and it's not a Chief Factor."

"So," the teller of tales said with a smile. "He begins to understand things like the memento?"

"He does. I will teach him more. And perhaps he will teach me some things...but enough. And this is for you, Helene-Marie," she said suddenly, holding out a small ring. "Yes, I know, I have long worn it. It would please me if you would do so, from now on."

Hadithe Zakale saw that Helene-Marie's hand trembled as she accepted the token, a small ring that appeared to be made of iron. Being what he was, he asked what it meant.

"When the mother who bore me died," Sasha explained, "the sharks got most of her. But a part was washed ashore. When I was old enough to understand its importance, Helene-Marie gave this to me. Well, my mother wore it once, and now my mother shall wear it again."

Helene-Marie was still staring at the ring when Sasha took it out of her hand, and put it on a finger. Suddenly Sasha embraced her, and then held her away, turning with a simple, "Good-bye."

And then Sasha was gone, before either Hadithe Zakale or Helene-Marie could say another word; gone back among the bevy of *signarés* waiting on the shore.

Moments later the storyteller and his companion were in the water skiff, sitting next to the Ashanti as the waves leapt up and the island faded behind.

Hadithe Zakale noticed eventually that Helene-Marie was glancing back over her shoulder at the harbor.

"It goes," he said softly. "And then it's gone."

"I know," she replied. "I was thinking of the ships. As we leave they're moving more men aboard those ships. I didn't want that to be my last thought of the island, but it seems that I must carry it that way."

"But not in your dreams." the storyteller said quickly.

She laughed, this time almost as lightly as Sasha did.

"No, I don't think so." She gazed up at the storyteller. "But if

I do, at least from now on, I can hope that someone will wake me."

Chapter Ten

From one of the many pigeonholes at the back of his desk, Andre Bruie drew out a rolled page of parchment. He unrolled it, smoothed it somewhat, and handed it across to the young man who sat before him in one of the Chief Factor's hard-backed, wooden chairs.

The young man, recognizing the document, made a gesture of impatience.

"But sir," he said, "as I've told you, I've already received a copy of the company's general rules and policies. I was most careful to study it on the voyage, so I could begin performing my duties at once in the proper fashion."

"Quite commendable," Bruie grunted. "It speaks well of you. But this document is somewhat different. I gather you haven't been acquainted with the special adjustments peculiar to this post. This copy includes those adjustments."

The young man read, a puzzled frown spreading across his heavy eyebrows as he did so. Finally, he lowered the parchment to his lap.

"This is somewhat different, indeed," he said. "In fact it's much different. Not just for what it says, but for what it implies. I wonder why they didn't give me the proper information in Paris."

"Oh, to be sure, they did," Bruie responded. "A new employee should always begin by studying the general policies of the company. He should keep them in mind as an ideal for achievement. But as a guide to a particular station, to the practical performance of duty, you will find that they don't always suit the company's ultimate interests." He permitted himself a small smile. "It's a lesson all of us have had to learn, some at greater cost than others. You are fortunate. I offer it to you free of charge."

The young man regarded him carefully. "Thank you, *M'sieu* Bruie."

"Don't mention it. Now, as I promised you, we shall have a tour of the fort. I might suggest, however, a change in clothes. It's liable to be somewhat dirty. Less formal wear, less subject to damage or soil, might be appropriate."

The young man nodded. "I can see that conditions here are somewhat at variance with what I expected. Unfortunately, I didn't bring much with me in the way of what you call less formal wear."

"That's understandable, *M'sieu* de Gennes. You will, of course, be expected to dress well on many occasions, as a company representative. But for routine wear in this climate...well, I'm sure that our storehouses have proper clothing in your size. As you see, I find it prudent to wear such clothing myself, on routine occasions."

He scribbled a quick note on a small scrap of paper. "Take this to Brassard, the quartermaster. He will fit you properly and then we can begin."

As if reluctantly, the young man rose, bowed formally, and retreated out the door of Andre Bruie's office. The Chief Factor of Senegal fell back to his interminable paperwork, but after a short while he found himself with his chair turned around, facing the window, looking out over the bright scene in the harbor and thinking very, very dark thoughts.

He sighed, muttering an obscenity softly to himself. It was of course, no real fault of the young man. No doubt he was admirably fitted for certain tasks. Nor did the fault lie with Andre Bruie himself, for he had been most explicit concerning what he had in mind for the man who filled the post of Assistant Chief Factor, Senegal. Very explicit indeed! The fault lay rather with the directors or their agents, those mysterious people with tenuous connections who shaped the policies and personnel of the company.

Here he was, Chief Factor of France's most important commercial station on the African coast, with responsibilities that should have kept him at a desk in Saint-Louis, spending half of his time on Gorée, and the other half playing war-admiral and coast guard as well. He was on the verge of securing for France a commercial monopoly on the gum arabic trade up the Senegal River. He had finally eliminated residual Portuguese influence along the Little Coast stretching down toward the Gambia, and at the mouth of the Gambia itself he had secured a small foothold and commercial presence in the Dinka village of Albreda.

Yet all this list of solid accomplishment could crumple up like paper, and preventing that crumpling required him to be in not two, but three places at once.

The reason wasn't internal weakness. No, it was external, what Bruie spoke of as *mal d'angleterre*, the English disease. In this case, the English disease was the English presence at James Island. Like Gorée, James Island was not very defensible and depended on the presence of armed ships. The English, however, had warships. Bruie worried they would eventually use them against Albreda, and maybe even Gorée herself.

Fortunately, they couldn't do what the pirate ship had done several years before. After that incident, Bruie insisted that a warship be stationed at the island. It was the *Princesse*, a ship of sixty-four guns.

The ship was a solution, but it was also a source of problems. For one thing, the captain of the *Princesse* was a degenerate drunk who could only be kept to his duty by Bruie's actual presence aboard the vessel. For another, there were constant demands on the warship, as the result of illegal English commercial encroachment.

111

From where he sat, overlooking the harbor, Andre Bruie could see a huge bustle of activity. There were three French commercial vessels resting at anchor along with the *Princesse*. There was also a vessel at the quay, taking on cargo. And off to one side, resting empty and silent, were three commercial vessels with no flags flying and hardly a man aboard. Once they had flown the English flag, but they had made the mistake of flying it along the *Petit-Cote*, the Little Coast, which was a French preserve. So they had been seized, and a prize court had awarded them to France. But what to do with them was apparently a puzzle for the directors in Paris. So, they sat lifeless in Gorèe's harbor.

And now, not to Bruie's surprise but to his deep dismay, the English at James Island had a regular warship of their own, the *Rochester*. It also mounted sixty-four guns and could be considered a threat to France's holds.

The prospect of such a development had been stressed in Bruie's long and carefully written letter to the directors, pleading for an Assistant Chief Factor. The Assistant could then handle the affairs on Gorée. He could defend Albreda and patrol the Little Coast. Bruie had also requested a replacement for the Captain of the *Princesse*. He knew naval politics well, though, and wasn't overly optimistic.

What he needed was a strong, experienced executive with a talent for adapting to ever-changing conditions. Instead, they had sent him this ninny, this green Parisian dandy, with a child's faith in rules and not even the sense to bring tropical clothes.

Perhaps, Bruie mused, their sending Maurice de Gennes to him was meant as a compliment. Perhaps this was the directors' way of telling Andre Bruie that he was held in the highest regard in Paris, and that they were confident he could make a silk purse even out of this egregious sow's ear.

Still, given the circumstances, he would have preferred a more appropriate token of the directors' esteem.

Footsteps down the hall alerted Bruie to the impending return of his new assistant. With a further sigh, he rose, went to the door, and opened it. It would be best to get to this part quickly, and quickly through it. He had work to do, and it was work of primary importance, casting great shadows over his prospects for attending the evening's entertainment at the *Pavilion Pierreux*..

"Perhaps you've heard," Bruie said casually as they descended the steps of the lower fort's subterranean vaults, "of *M'sieu* Torrington, the famous English pirate?"

"Yes, I have," came the reply. "He was the fellow who tried to take this island, several years ago. The only survivor of his ship."

"Close to that. Actually there were a few others, but quite frankly, we let them drown. Their captain was the one we saved, to send back to an Admiralty court. The court convicted him, of course, and sent him back here to be hanged. At the last moment, however, they changed the sentence to perpetual imprisonment."

"I remember that," de Gennes replied. "I thought it odd at the time, to show such clemency." He paused. "He isn't... still in here?"

"Oh yes, but of course, he's still here. You will see him shortly. But dismiss all thought of the Admiralty's clemency from your mind. As you can already see, this isn't the place one would wish to spend any portion of one's life, let alone the rest of it."

Amused, Bruie sensed de Gennes repressing a shudder. It was, of course, understandable. The darkness, the thick air that seemed to close in on the torch, the strange repellent smells, and above all the dampness; these could affect even a man with a strong mind and stomach. Bruie himself seldom went beneath the fort.

Bruie reached to the left and pushed open a wooden door. The slave who had accompanied them thrust the torch inside, providing a vague light to the small room.

"General stores," Bruie commented. "Odds and ends, materials no longer needed for the moment, materials that wound up here for no apparent reason...those things now useless to us." He reached into a box and drew forth a handful of strangely assorted baubles:

113

beads, small brass castings, plain metal rings.

"Pretty, eh?" he laughed abruptly. "I understand the Dutch once bought an island much bigger than this from the American natives, with nothing more than the likes of these." He threw the trinkets back into the box. "But Africa is much closer to Europe, and Africans have known white men longer. They know what we can produce. They don't want baubles like these anymore. "

Bruie pulled the door shut and they walked down the passageway past several other wooden doors of the same type, somewhat warped and dilapidated from the damp.

"The same sort of thing in these, de Gennes. I can tell you're wondering why we don't clean out all of this stuff, and burn it."

"It does seems strange to keep it."

"We keep it, de Gennes, because one never knows when something may suddenly become useful. The cost of shipping something from France is considerable, eh? Those charges have already been paid. It would simply not be prudent to send for more of something, if it were already here. Every Factor is what the English, damn them, call a 'pack rat'. It's the force of necessity."

"But if the natives don't want any of this stuff ..."

"They may some day, or someone else might. But they do, of course, demand other things... European cloth, for example."

" And guns, if they can get them."

"The circumstances must justify that, de Gennes. We have arrangements with the native kings of Cayor, of Sine, and of other places along the Little Coast. I have some...discretion in the matter. Otherwise it's a question for the directors in Paris. But even more than guns they want... ah, here we are."

Bruie reached into his pocket and took out a large key, for the door he now approached was locked. He opened it, revealing barrels stacked upon each other. Opening one barrel, he took out a handful of a dark brown substance, sniffed it, and handed it to de Gennes.

"Tobacco?" de Gennes murmured.

"Indeed. The leaf that burns. It's taking Africa by storm as it took England and our homeland." He drew a small pouch from his pocket, took the tobacco from de Gennes and put it inside. "I rarely indulge, but a good pipe is pleasing from time to time. However, these are special company stores, not trade goods. They keep better underground over the long haul, as long as the kegs are kept tightly sealed. Robert, will you, please?"

The slave went at once to the keg and resealed it with an iron tool. When he had done this, and Bruie had locked the door again, the Chief Factor handed the slave the pouch he had filled with tobacco.

"For coming with us," he said.

"*Merci, m'sieu,*" the slave replied. His enthusiasm was real.

"This one speaks French, then?" de Gennes asked as they walked further down the dark passages.

"Most of the permanent population on this island speaks French, de Gennes. In fact, they generally speak better French here than you would hear in Saint-Louis. Of course, when we go to the Pavilion tonight, you'll hear it for yourself. Our hostesses would shame the Parisians."

De Gennes came to a halt.

"Do you mean to tell me that we're to be entertained, as if in a salon, by African women?"

"Um, mulattoes, really, for the most part. What did you think, de Gennes, when I told you of the Pavilion and its parties? You know there are no French women on this island."

"...But it seems somewhat improper. The rules, after all, say that..."

"The rules? I showed you the rules, de Gennes...the rules that count. They aren't what you learned, so learn better. The women you meet tonight, the ones called *signarés*, are the key to the prosperity of the whole Senegal enterprise. They have the connections. So, if the rules don't provide for them, then the rules must at least give them room to do what they do best."

As he spoke, they came to the end of the passageway, and another staircase. It was a steep one that quickly took them to a much lower level. The air was a bit thicker. Bruie was not bothered by it, but de Gennes seemed stifled.

They now came to a door that was not only locked, but barred

115

as well. Bruie had to use two keys to open it. The torch revealed a jumble of thick iron chains. In front of these was a much more slender chain, longer, with a round attachment at one end. Bruie reached behind the slender chain and pulled forth one of the heavy ones.

"Lift this, de Gennes. It's heavy, no? Examine it."

De Gennes did as he was told. "Heavy, yes. Good workmanship. What are they used for?"

"They are wall-irons, de Gennes. Very good for holding a man to a wall, or immobilizing his legs and hands. We have no use for them now. We have a new system that makes it possible to make use of the slave while he's here, rather than keeping him immobile against a wall." Bruie reached down and lifted the slender chain.

"This is a *collard*, de Gennes. Can you guess its function?"

De Gennes examined the slender chain, checked the round flat strip at the end. "This is the kind that you put on slaves working in the quarry, or on the docks? Around the neck?"

"Yes, of course. It keeps them restrained. We attach the other end to a huge stone that takes ten men to lift. There are only six collards to a stone, so the slaves won't go anywhere far. But their arms and legs are free, and so they can work in a restricted area." He fingered the rounded end, showed the mechanism of bolt and lock at the back. "This device is the key. It takes a tool to open it, so the slave can't get loose simply by fingering it." He chuckled. "And who do you think invented this?"

"One of the soldiers, tired of guarding slaves, no doubt."

"*Au contraire*. It was invented by a *signaré* on this island."

De Gennes was astounded. "But what possible reason...? "

"Could she have for helping us?" Bruie finished. "She wanted me to let her build a stone house with slave labor. I told her she could have the men to do it, if she could secure them and still give them room to work. Then I laughed and dismissed the idea. She came back with this, within a week."

"But I haven't seen a smithy on the island."

"There are ironworkers in Sine," he replied.

De Gennes muttered something under his breath, and Bruie laughed.

"Keep your mind on the big picture, de Gennes. But never take your eye off the small thing, because it may be important too. Yes, *Pavilion Pierreux,* the Stone House, was built as a result of this invention, built for the senior *signaré* on the island. Now it serves her, and also serves some of our purposes as well. Never underestimate the African, de Gennes, or the mulatto... or indeed anyone you chance to meet here."

De Gennes was silent for a moment.

"What's left for us to see?" he asked quietly, at last.

"Hm? Oh yes, Torrington, the English pirate. Let's step down aways, to the place where those unlit torches are sitting."

The slave who had accompanied them suddenly began to tremble.

"*Monsieur* Bruie...?"

"Yes, yes, Robert, I understand. Just come with us as far as those other torches. We will bear our own light from there, and you can wait for us."

"*Merci, monsieu,*" the slave said with obvious relief.

They went forward, and Andre Bruie himself lit one of the spare torches. Leaving Robert behind, they went down a long corridor, around a bend, and finally came to a barred door at the end.

"Torrington's cell?" de Gennes asked.

"Indeed," Bruie replied. "There's no need to worry, by the way, when I open the door. He's still chained to the wall with one of those old-style restraints. I say this not to reassure you, of course, but to remind you that we do follow regulations."

"I hear no noise," de Gennes said as they came up to the door. "Surely he must have heard us. I would think he would at least rattle his chains when human beings came his way!"

"Well, I'm not at all surprised," Bruie said dryly.

This time it took three keys to unlock the door. Without further ceremony, Bruie threw open the door and stuck the torch inside. The room was small; the torch lit it all.

Maurice de Gennes gasped in horror at the small pile of bones, topped by a nearly toothless skull, that sat amid the heavy iron chains.

"*Mon Dieu, m'sieur!*"

"What did you expect?" Bruie demanded roughly. "A living man, after three years down here? Begin to use your head, *M'sieu* de Gennes, and learn to recognize what's in front of you." Bruie set the torch in a sconce just inside the door, folded his arms, and leaned up against the side of the doorway.

"The common fate of us all, eh? Nothing you might not see in the catacombs of Paris, my young friend. He was, after all, sent here for the rest of his life, so this conclusion shouldn't be that much of a surprise."

"How did he die?" de Gennes asked in a small voice.

"Of starvation." Bruie replied. "He refused to eat from the moment he was put in this cell. Didn't even drink. To the very end he kept demanding that one of the guards have the decency to kill him. But of course my hands were tied; the law of France had spoken. I couldn't touch him."

Bruie stepped on a small bug that threatened to leave the cell. "When he died, and it was only six months after he came here, we shut up the cell and left the rot to do its work. Not that there was much work for the rot to do. He was pretty well shriveled up by the time he breathed his last."

Suddenly, from the young man's throat there came a growl.

"Enough, *Monsieur* ! I understand your point. I've known contempt before, enough to know when I'm being treated with it. I'm as aware as you are that I have much to learn. I came prepared to learn. I must tell you, though, no one ever taught me anything by rubbing my nose in shit!"

Bruie, eyes in their fish setting, stared at the young man for a moment. Then a trace of a smile crossed his mouth, and something faintly resembling a chuckle came from it.

"Well now! A man at last. This I can deal with, *M'sieu* de Gennes. No, no, you are not a dog. But, in this business you really are a puppy, and my first task is to make you realize it. Has that been done? I think so. Well then, let's go back to the light. I fancy you may not find the party at the Pavilion enjoyable...in light of our recent discovery?"

The young face was supple. Bruie noted it, noted how quickly de Gennes tried on several different expressions, finally settling on one that seemed to suit the occasion. It was resigned, a trifle amused, giving deference, yes, but only the minimum. Well, it sufficed.

"I shall find it fascinating, I'm sure," de Gennes said quietly. "And I shall keep my eyes open, and my mind on the larger picture. I'm here, whether or not either of us likes it, and since I am determined to make the best of it, who knows? I may surprise us both."

Bruie laughed, and drew the door of the cell shut, locking it with the three keys.

Back in his office, Bruie found that the pile of paperwork hadn't changed, but his company had. Instead of de Gennes, there was Lieutenant Drouin sitting in the hardbacked chair, idly jotting his way through a few pages of his commonplace book. He looked up when Bruie entered, rose formally and correctly, and as formally, bowed.

"*M'sieu le factor*," he said, "I wish to speak with you."

Bruie was behind his desk by now, and seated. A faint hint of exasperation crossed his face as he replied.

"Marcel!"

"Yes, sir?"

"*Must* you go through this *pas-de-guerre* every damned time you come into this office? I'm a man of business. Get things out and get them done...but you know my mind."

Lieutenant Drouin chuckled. It was a soft chuckle, very unlike Bruie's.

"That's better. Now what does the Lieutenant need with the Chief Factor?"

"Old Gilbert wants to see us both."

"Ah."

Bruie put down the document he had taken up, after at least pretending to stare at it for a moment. He eyed Drouin with a very

119

cautious gaze.

"His business?"

"Important to him, obviously. Shall I bring him in?"

"Of course."

Drouin rose, casually enough, and opened the door to call an order down the hall. In a few moments they were joined by old Gilbert, who came carefully into the room, supported now by a cane. His steps, however, were as precise as they had ever been. He sat down in a padded chair, which, without asking, Drouin had meantime retrieved from its usual hiding place.

When the old man entered, there were two cigars on the table, one of which Bruie offered to him without a word. The old man accepted gracefully, lit the cigar, and took a few puffs before speaking.

"The English ship is coming," he said quietly.

"Ah," Bruie said, not showing any surprise. "How soon? Word by drums, or man?"

"Drums. But late. The ship may well be here tomorrow, before noon."

Bruie picked up the second cigar, reached across the desk and handed it to Gilbert, who stuffed it into the front pocket of his tattered storehouse shirt.

"Of course, you've told no one else? Sasha, or your men?"

Gilbert slowly shook his head. "Although it seems I must, in the end. The men especially... I must at least prepare them, if we are to make a special water run before the ship comes."

"No immediate need for that, Gilbert. We have the cisterns. Do not interrupt your pattern. As for Sasha, I'll tell her myself tonight. But Gilbert ..."

"Oui, Monsieur?"

"Don't be greatly concerned. This, I think, will end in smoke and clouds, not powder-bursts."

Gilbert eyed him carefully.

"Truly?"

"Truly, in my judgment. But be ready if I do need to call on you."

"*Oui, Monsieur.*"

With that, the old man rose and left as slowly and as silently as he had come. Bruie and Drouin remained in the room, just as silent, until the footsteps had long ceased echoing down the hall.

"We really ought to get him off the waterboat," Bruie said at last. "He's earned a quiet sunset, eh?"

"The boat's his life," Drouin replied. "And no one expects him to pull an oar. He's not the kind who becomes a pensioner."

"True, I suppose. Well! It seems we must prepare for the English disease to manifest itself in our waters. Do you think this is a serious incursion?"

"No, no, I didn't lie to Gilbert. I think it's a demonstration of strength, an attempt to surprise us and shake us up a bit. After all, they have no way of knowing for certain that we are aware of the presence of their new warship along these coasts. And the ship comes alone, Marcel. If they wanted to take this island, knowing the *Princesse* was in harbor, they'd at least have the intelligence to bring along their armed merchantmen as well."

Drouin laughed. It was a hearty, unrestrained sound.

"Did I amuse you that much?" Bruie asked in a sour tone.

"But of course," Drouin replied. "I look at you, Andre, and I think of how much you have learned in these brief years...how much further you have come than any of us. You rule the French part of the coast. You have learned to supply a fort, to keep an island occupied, to deal with native kings, to fight a ship and to keep a peace. Not bad for a man who came on like *M'sieu* de Gennes only a few short years ago."

Bruie stared at Drouin, anger clouding his face. He let the anger dissipate before he spoke.

"Really, Marcel? Was I ever that bad?"

Drouin chuckled. "No...not quite. But close."

"Close?"

"Close."

Bruie stared at him for a long time. Then his snort burst forth.

"Well so be it, then! Perhaps there's hope for us, in that case.

For France, for the company, for ourselves....even for *Monsieur* de Gennes..." He paused, and spat aside from the desk. "The damned pup!"

Drouin was still smiling.

"Did you get him to stand up to you? Sounds like you did."

"Hm? Oh, yes, yes, of course. I had to kick him rather hard, but the kick did register in the end. I'm not so sure how he will react to our *signarés,* though. I'll have to have a word with Sasha beforehand. The least I can do is ask her not to corrupt him before I'm through making him."

Drouin stood up, bowed formally, and made to take his leave. But before he reached the door, he stopped, turned and smiled.

"Someday," he said, "We really must turn Sasha loose on the English."

Bruie considered that. After a while, smiling in his own turn, he shook his head.

"It would be deserved, of course. But it would be dishonorable of us to do that to an enemy...even the English."

Chapter Eleven

"Bourrique!" came the raucous screech, interrupting the many separate conversations going on in the great parlor of the Stone House. "Bourrique! Bourrique!"

Amused by the intrusion, but only daring to show a hint of amusement, Andre Bruie permitted himself a small smile. The rest of the company, however, dissolved in laughter. It took something highly unusual to unite the variety of people present at the Pavilion Pierreux this particular evening, but Bagatelle the parrot had just succeeded in doing so.

"Bourrique!" screeched the parrot one last time, and then fell to biting on one of its claws, firmly griping its high perch with the other. That perch itself was above the dais where Sasha sat, framed in her own alcove by two huge male slaves. Bruie noticed that even the slaves, who still had a very limited knowledge of French, were showing amusement to a faint degree. The rest of the company, ship captains, junior officers, company officials, *signarés* and would-be *signarés*, along with a few house servants, were still laughing openly.

"Naughty bird!" Sasha reproved. "With all the wonderful words you hear at my salon, did you *have* to pick up 'she-ass'? Who could have taught you that?"

A guttural laugh nearby answered her question, and an old shipcaptain, Janvier of the *St.-Bertrand*, bowed in mock apology.

"I accept the blame, Sasha," he said. "I don't know where your bird heard me speak it, but that's my word...almost my voice too. Why *Monsieur* Labine... " he waved a hand toward his first mate, on the other side of the big room "nearly dropped his wine-glass when Bagatelle spoke."

Soon the laughter died down and the conversations resumed. Most people were seated on the couches in the central part of the room. Some were on cushions near the edges. Still others were on the stone seats that dotted the alcoves in the walls. Bruie himself was an alcove occupant. With him, between the two high pillars that created the alcove, were Sorel, a shipcaptain; Sorel's *signaré*, Cecile, a young mulatto somewhat darker than Sasha; Genevieve, an even younger mulatto who was lighter in complexion and not yet bound to a man; and Maurice de Gennes, Bruie's new assistant.

Bruie still kept his eyes and attention loose enough to stay on the pulse of the Stone House. It was easy to do this from where he sat, for while the parlor room was large, it took only a relatively few people to fill it to the verge of crowding. So, he could casually debate prospects for a rapid expansion in the gum arabic trade with Sorel, while still keeping a fervent eye on de Gennes, who was becoming acquainted with the ladies.

Glancing around the Stone House, Bruie idly recalled the day Sasha had sketched it for him, and realized once again how close the reality had followed her idea. He'd had some difficulty in the beginning understanding what it was all about, but few things possessing inherent logic escaped Bruie's grasp for long. A great stone-pillared parlor, with quarters for servants at the back and quarters for Sasha at the side....

"So!" he had said. "Why should I let you build a palace...and give you slaves to do it in the bargain?"

"Because you and the company will also find it useful," Sasha had come back. "It is needed, and I am the only possible mistress for such a place."

Now, barely a year after its completion, Bruie had to admit that the Stone House was, if not an absolute necessity, a very desirable thing to have. It might not be necessary to his own relaxation, since the word was barely in Bruie's vocabulary, but it was surprising how events at the Stone House seemed to ease the transaction of business without ever seeming to affect that business directly. Perhaps the old alchemists, or the new natural philosophers, would speak of the place as a catalyst. Whatever its nature, it certainly worked.

And, glancing around him, still in faint amusement, Bruie made a further note: *signarés* made much better connections with captains and officials when they could entertain them in a place like this. Far removed, indeed, from the necessity of doing everything on their backs in mud huts and ship's cabins! It was refinement, certainly. It was almost... French.

Not quite, Bruie also noted. Although it was a parlor here, in Paris it would have been considered little more than an open porch with wide spaces between the surrounding pillars. Given the rains of France and the generally chilly climate of Europe, the Stone House would have been totally unacceptable. But here on the island of Gorée, where it so seldom rained, and breezes on and off shore kept the air moving, little more than shade was required for comfort. Even the occasional rain could be kept out by the brightly colored cloth curtains that hung on the pillars. They stood ready to pull together, to cut off the space between. Of course, they were not used for rain only, but for other purposes as well.

And a few torches, properly placed, could keep the parlor room of the Stone House bright all night long. Sasha had placed them properly, and prudently, so that they stood far from the curtains, but close to the intimate conversations.

A few moments later, there was another outburst from the parrot, but this time the word was neither new nor outrageous, so no one paid much attention. Bruie, however, found himself watching the parrot, an untethered bird which seemed quite content to occupy a high perch, and showed no desire to fly away.

Bruie wondered if it might be one of those colorful female parrots, so often found in Africa and so rare among European species. Usually among the European birds, the male was the one with the brilliant plumage. Bagatelle had the plumage all right... green, red, and yellow with a few specks of some color between blue and purple. If it was indeed a female bird it was certainly in the right company, for the *signarés* decorated the room with brilliant colors of their own.

They were all alike in that each one's clothing was made from a bolt or two of European cloth, or American or Indian cotton. But each one of the women strove for a different color scheme, a different way of draping the cloth, a different effect. Somehow, even when the patterns seemed distinctly European, the swatches took on an exotic cast when they were draped over a *signaré*. And then there were the thin silk scarves of different colors, several combined into a headdress that was something between a turban and the type of festooned conical hat European women had worn at court several centuries before. And perhaps all was not gold that glittered, but on a *signaré*, everything that glittered was indeed gold.

Had Bruie been nearsighted or otherwise dull of sight, which he was not, he still could have identified each of the women in the parlor by her colors. Even at a great distance, even if she had been separated a ways from her captain or her official, each *signaré* had a signature of her own. Of course, most of the women were not separated. They confined their men in the alcoves as if each was hosting her own separate salon, with the unassigned and uncommitted wandering between. It was all very sedate and civilized, but there were undercurrents.

Bruie's eyes fell on Desiree. He had heard the stories of the sock of sand she had stashed under her bed in the small hut she kept in the village. The sand in question had previously surrounded the last footprint left on the island by her departing captain, St. Ives, who had sailed for France with a rich cargo less than a month ago. According to *signaré* custom, she would be ready to accept a new captain, or a new company official into her favors as soon as the moon was new again. That new moon would arrive quickly.

Desiree had been passing among the guests on the cushions and the couches, but in so passing, she had paused several times to speak earnestly to *Monsieur* Davout, first mate of the ship *Marseillette*. He wasn't a captain, but his ship's cargo was a rich one, and he was known to be generous. He was also already assigned, the point being that his own *signaré* was indisposed this evening in her bed, purportedly due to the kind of belly-sickness that went with bad fish. And there were other things...

"*Monsieur*! If you please!"

A sudden flurry indicated the escape of the young mulatto Genevieve from the over-attentive grasp of *Monsieur* de Gennes. De Gennes, who was already much in the mood of the salon, and perhaps, just perhaps, a little tipsy, drew back with little remorse. The flush on his face and the devilish smile confirmed that he was not at all put out by the reprimand.

"You pardon, *ma'amselle*," he said with a slight bow. "I meant no harm."

"Then there was no offense," Genevieve replied lightly. "But do tell us more about your father's famous cousin. He was well known on this island, as you have learned."

Andre Bruie smiled at the young girl's skill. How delicately she had manipulated de Gennes' attention. How cleverly she had drawn him into his own arrogance. Already, de Gennes had regaled the company with several tales featuring his relationship to the Count de Gennes, the French admiral, who, during the recent hostilities between England and France, had sailed from Gorée to the Gambian station of James Island and forced the capitulation of the English governor, Hanbury, on the second shot.

It was quite a tale in itself, but perhaps more boldly told than it might have been had Maurice de Gennes remembered that Bruie had been on the island at that time. Whether he would be more or less bold in telling it, knowing the English were again on their way to the island, was of course an open question. But it, and some others, would be answered in due time.

Suddenly there was a stir. A name had been called in a strong, clear voice that didn't have to be raised to be heard. Out of the corner of his eye, Bruie saw the girl called Desiree scramble to her feet with a sudden nervous gesture, and scurry off in the direction of the dais where Sasha was seated. They met, several words were spoken, and then Sasha turned and walked off casually in the direction of her own apartments. After a moment's hesitation, Desiree followed quickly behind.

There was a brief hesitation in the party-babble, but the talk quickly resumed. Throughout all this, Bruie noticed that the two huge slaves who stood by Sasha's dais had remained immobile. They stood arms folded, eyes staring forward. In some ways they resembled a pair of Arabian genii. They were, after all, dressed in the same fashion; bare to the waist, legs covered with billowing pantaloons, heads wound with turbans. A scimitar at the side would have completed the picture, but, of course, they were not armed.

Bruie still had his doubts about them, but once again, Sasha had sold him the logic. Sasha had also given them their names, Samson and Hercule, once Bruie had bought them and concocted the covering paperwork. But the men knew they owed their lives not so much to Bruie, but to Sasha, and he hoped there would never be a conflict between those two loyalties.

So far there had been no such conflict and Bruie had to admit to himself, that it would have been a great waste for these two to have been destroyed. The men were kin to one another, some sort of cousin-relationship. They were from the east, from central Africa, where they had been members of a tribe of cattle-herders. Bruie himself wasn't even sure how they had managed to be captured by a slave caravan. He did know that they would have made first-class, very profitable slave material, if they hadn't arrived at the island each with a part of a foot missing. They had cut themselves, cut off pieces of themselves, in an attempt to escape.

Damaged goods that hadn't been cut out of the caffle at sale time! An unfortunate mistake, but there was a policy to cover it. That is, destroy the damaged goods. And, except for Sasha's intervention, that was exactly what would have happened. Bruie remembered that plea, and how it had been backed up by, of all people, the level-headed Captain Tousaint... Sasha's captain, on the eve of his departure.

"*Eh bien*, Andre," Tousaint had said over the inevitable wine. "Sasha has her salon now, and you see it's a good thing. But you have to have some of Drouin's men handy for the mildest gathering, and even still, someone is always getting out of hand. You know a sailor takes little thought of taking on a soldier, or vice versa! But these Africans... hah! Even crippled, you won't find one of the sailors, or the soldiers, looking to take them on."

Bruie recalled making some remark to the effect that if they were to guard a place that so resembled a harem, perhaps they should be fixed in the same fashion as the attendants at such places. But that had brought a laugh from Tousaint.

"You need not deprive them of those things. Rest assured they are in a safe grip!"

With a start, Bruie realized that he had done too much thinking, and had almost missed the hour when he was scheduled to meet Drouin back at the fort. There were preparations to be made. The Lieutenant was normally as much of a fixture at the Stone House as any Frenchman on the island, but even with Bruie's reassurance, he rejected the offer. He wasn't about to leave the fort with the English on the way.

With Sasha out of the main room, Bruie's absence might have been awkward. But he had a routine for such an occasion. He leaned over to Captain Sorel.

"How is your head, Captain?"

"My head? Just fine, *M'sieu*. I talk too much. When I talk, I don't drink too much wine."

"I must go for a while."

"Ah! I understand you." He smiled, sitting up from the cushions in the alcove. "I relieve you, then."

Bruie whistled softly in a certain pitch, and when he turned to the two giants by the dais, he saw their eyes resting intently on him. Without speaking, he clapped Sorel lightly on the shoulder. Samson and Hercule nodded almost in unison, very slightly. The message had passed, and so, for the moment, had command of the salon, should there be a problem.

Bruie, walking quickly outside in the warm air, found that his quick whistle had been addictive. He was actually whistling a tune as he went down the moonlit walk. Things were going well, all things considered. Let the English come, for all the good it would do them, or harm it would do them. The *Princesse* would be ready.

"We won't be easy for them, Andre," Lieutenant Drouin said with some satisfaction.

"I hardly thought we would be," the Chief Factor replied.

"But I'd still feel more comfortable if you had sent a message to Saint-Louis." He paused. "There is still time."

Bruie shook his head. "*You* might be more comfortable, Marcel, but Saint-Louis would be in an uproar. All they have there is Bretagne, who's a very good man, but also a very old one, and somewhat querulous. Which is why I asked for a real assistant. Well, this will certainly put the puppy to the proof."

Drouin sighed. "Give the boy time! He's only been here a few weeks."

"I give him time," Bruie said as he poured wine into Drouin's glass until the Lieutenant waved the bottle back. "I also give him rope. Tell me, does my memory begin to fail? Did the Comte de Gennes actually take James Island six years ago, with one shot from one ship?"

Drouin frowned, puzzled. Then the puzzlement left and the frown remained.

"You don't mean to tell me that's his story?"

"One of them. He's the idol of the moment. The women are eating up his tales. Not quite like they did for the tales of that mainland drum-carrier a few years back, but close." He smiled over his wine. "Some day, Lieutenant, you must show me a copy of the report you wrote on that matter. I'm sure you kept one."

"I most certainly did!" Drouin chuckled. "Not that I need to consult it. I may not be a storyteller, *M'sieu le Factor*, but I am, and

130

intend to remain, an officer. So, I cultivate my memory. Shall I quote you a portion?"

"Not really necessary. I, too, have a memory. But if you would be pleased to do it, why, go ahead."

"Ah. It would please me indeed. I do have regrets at missing your affair this evening. So let's see: salutations to superiors aside...."

"*Merde!*"

Drouin sat back in his chair, smacked his lips over the wine, and spoke in a conversational tone with some slight restraint.

"In relation to the capture of the island of St. James, in the mouth of the River Gambia, I have the following to report. On the first of July, Admiral the Comte de Gennes arrived in Gorée harbor in command of the sloop *St. Francois*, with three other sloops and two bomb vessels following his flag. He was provisioned here and we sought to provide him with information as well, concerning the English establishment in the Gambia mouth. We were able to provide him with a deserter from the English establishment, who had recently taken refuge on the island. The deserter reported to the Count, in my presence, that the island of St. James held a garrison of 65 whites, and that there were also half-castes and free Africans to a similar number, responsible for handling, in all, sixty to seventy guns in the fortifications.

"The deserter also told the Count that their water-cistern was not bombproof, that they had no more free water on their island than we at Gorée, and that their magazine was also vulnerable. He supplied the Count with locations, drawn on a rough map of sand. The Count then sailed from Gorée on the 19th of the month, and on the tenth of August returned here to report that he had appeared off James Island on the 22nd July, flying English colors. He then drew his own colors to the mast, surrounded the island with boats, cut off its communication with the mainland and commenced bombardment. A white flag, he reported, was shown after the second shot which landed near the magazine. The Count also reported that he had left men behind at the island to demolish the fortifications, spike the guns, and render the place harmless in detail."

Drouin let out a snort at this point, and drew himself another sip of wine.

"So much for that. As for the establishment of Albreda, and how our Sovereign Lord and King agreed to give back James Island two years later, well, you know as well as I."

"Indeed," Bruie replied. "So it was two shots, from six vessels. I did think the version I remembered was closer to the truth."

"Well, perhaps it changed in the family telling."

"Perhaps. But, *M'sieu* de Gennes went into great detail in describing the English deserter... oh, what was it? Oh, yes, de Gennes called him a beef-eating, Pope-hating, vicious and dreadful low-life Protestant! Subhuman, I think he said...really lower even than an African."

"*Mon Dieu!*" Drouin exclaimed. "O'Brien wasn't there with you, was he?"

"Of course not. He's on assignment, getting and keeping Captain Henri Picard drunk, so that at least we can have the *Princesse* ready, if not her skipper."

Drouin chuckled. "I fear O'Brien might remind de Gennes, rather forcefully, that there's a difference between being an English deserter and being a deserter from the English fleet. It would take a great deal to offend O'Brien; beef-eater, low-life and other things wouldn't do it. Calling him a Pope-hater, however, might. But insinuating that he was an Englishman... that, without question, would do the job."

"Well, I spared his feelings, then. And now unfortunately, night wends on toward morning...."

"Villon?"

"No, Bruie. I have to get back."

"Oh." Drouin considered, looking at his empty glass. "I too. But that could perhaps wait." He looked at the factor. "You still could go a pace beyond yourself, Andre. You don't enjoy Sasha's entertainment?"

"On the contrary, I enjoy it immensely. Perhaps not the same way others do."

"Truly. Well, at least let me get off a fresh tale for your amusement."

Bruie hesitated. Then he laughed.

"All right, Marcel. If it really is a fresh one."

"Fresh to me, and you've heard all of mine. It concerns... "

Drouin broke off, hearing, as Bruie himself did, footsteps in the hallway. They were light, and they were quick. Then there was a light, quick, but urgent rap at the door.

"Enter," said Bruie, gathering himself.

Through the door came Cecile, Captain Sorel's *signaré*, still in her colorful wrap, but with her silken scarves in disarray on her head. More than her panting, the disarray showed that she'd been running.

"What is it?"

"You are needed."

Bruie's patience was usually thick; now it was at its thinnest. "What now?"

"There has been an... incident."

Patience snapped. "Report! Completely, Cecile!"

"*M'sieu* de Gennes, he had to be restrained. My captain and Sasha both ask for you."

Bruie shoved back his chair and stood up, not even looking at Drouin as he strode out of the office. Cecile followed behind, her quick steps almost keeping pace with Bruie's purposeful stride.

"He did what?" Bruie yelled.

"He began...what is the word? Confiscating the girls' head-dresses. Ripping them off their heads, like a collector taking taxes... as it has been described to me."

Bruie found himself standing almost alone in the middle of the Stone House's grand porch, hands on hips, confronting five people who had remained to meet him. Even the alcoves were empty. By now there should have been curtains drawn across many, if not all of them. But, the people who would ordinarily have occupied those alcoves had, for the most part, discreetly gone away.

133

All that remained were the flickering torches, the slightly billowing, unshut curtains, Sasha, Sorel, Cecile, Samson and Hercule. And, at the edge of Sasha's own alcove, a deeply snoring Maurice de Gennes, flat on his back, and breathing hard. There was a very large bruise on the left side of his head. Bruie looked at him the way he had looked at the bug in Torrington's cell, just before crushing it.

"So!" he said after a moment. "Sorel, you challenged him; and he lifted his hand to strike you."

"He missed," the captain said shortly. "Another moment and I would have put him peacefully to sleep, but he stumbled away and started screaming his way through the middle of the room. I signalled to Samson and Hercule, and when they came toward him, he started to run at them, screaming all the louder. But he fell, and hit his head."

The fish-eye was out now, and it was resting on Cecile.

"You said he had to be restrained."

"It wasn't over," Sorel interrupted. "He got up, and started taking off his clothes... pissing them at the same time."

"And?"

"Samson and Hercule picked him up and put him on the cushion next to Sasha's alcove." The old captain sniffed. "It will have to be cleaned and aired, of course."

"How many saw this?"

"Few saw the whole of it. Most had already left."

Bruie, standing over the young Assistant Factor with some indescribable expressions crossing his face, felt a hand on his arm.

"A word, sir?" Sasha asked.

Bruie glanced at her. "You always want two words, Sasha, or more."

"Many words, you're right. But only two thoughts. First, Samson and Hercule. They must know they did right."

Bruie shook his head, but only to clear it. He stared into the eyes of the giant Africans, set his jaw, and nodded abruptly. The two large presences bowed, and left the room.

"And the second thought?" Bruie asked.

"Bring yourself to breakfast here, if you will, tomorrow."

Bruie shot her a glance.

"You know what is coming here in the morning."

"Breakfast will be ready before dawn," she said quietly. "I've asked Mama-Lise to prepare it."

Tired and angry as he was, Bruie found himself smiling.

"I'll be here, Sasha. You distress me."

"Distress you, sir? How?" Sasha asked innocently, but her eyes already anticipated the answer, with amusement.

"You can do everything but cook," he responded. "And damn it, when you can't do it, you find someone who can. All right. But much before dawn, Sasha; in fact at four turns of the hourglass, I shall be here."

"I shall be waiting," Sasha replied. "So will breakfast."

Chapter Twelve

To Sasha, life was a dance. Some watched while others took part; a very rare few did both, and an even fewer number could do both at once. She was, in her own mind, one of the very fewest.

It was with this in mind that she awaited Andre Bruie at breakfast the next day, while the sun warned of its pending rise in the eastern sky. There had been a few dances the night before, and one of the performers had perhaps slipped. But, Sasha was sure she hadn't seen the end of the performance in question. Bruie had essentially put her on notice that there must be another act to follow. There was even a bit of a plot to go with the moves and gyrations of the ballet.

"You usually watch the sunrise," Mama-Lise said with a grunt. She was sitting across from Sasha at a table drawn up into the *signaré's* private alcove. Breakfast was ready. Mama-Lise had but to signal the house servants how and where to serve it. They waited on Bruie, and in the meantime the old woman took her ease in the chair that would be his.

"I *am* watching the sunrise," Sasha responded after a moment. "Do my eyes seem to wander?"

"No, perhaps not. Perhaps it's the new order of things that the sun should rise in the south. I hadn't yet heard that, but your information is much better than mine these days."

Sasha laughed. "You still have your eyes, Mama-Lise. I'm just concerned that our leisurely breakfast not be disturbed by inconvenient visitors."

"Stupid English!" the old woman grunted. "I have seen them all, Sasha: the Portuguese, the Dutch, the English... the French. I've even seen something of the people called Italians and Swedes. Of them all, the English I prefer least."

Sasha studied her, her face expressionless. "And now I am to ask you why you dislike the English, skipping over the question of whether or not they're involved in whatever I'm watching... if I'm watching anything at all. I fear you are assuming some things, Mama-Lise."

It was the old woman's turn to laugh.

"Very good, Sasha. And wise of you to admit nothing, not even to me. But don't forget that I was keeping secrets when you didn't yet know the meaning of the word... or any words at all."

"I learned that early," Sasha responded. "Both the word 'secret' and the word 'discretion.'"

Sasha paused to sip a drink of mixed fruit juices, mainly apricot, from a cup on her side of the table. She was hardly surprised that Mama-Lise had figured out it was the English who were expected. On reflection, however, Sasha wasn't all that concerned. But she still kept up the front. After all, even the best of dancers must keep in practice.

"*Eh bien*, Sasha!" came a man's voice. "Am I intruding?"

Sasha smiled, stood up, and bowed all in one easy motion, at least as far as the eyes of Andre Bruie could tell.

"Welcome, *M'sieu le Factor*. Please be seated."

Bruie took the seat that Mama-Lise had been keeping warm for him, while the old woman busied herself giving orders to the house servants. The next few minutes were occupied with an elaborate island breakfast, hot dishes alternated with cold. By the time the last had been served, the orange ball of the sun was edging over the eastern horizon, poking its rays through the mainland forest.

Then the full light of day came flowing into the Stone House, striking the alcoves on the western side. Only three of these alcoves indicated, by closed curtains, that they were still occupied. From two of them, *signarés* emerged: Arsene, as always, Sasha noted, a late-comer; and Genevieve, who had yet to establish much of a reputation one way or the other. They gazed awkwardly for a moment at the group viewing them from the breakfast table. Then, regaining composure, they giggled and scurried away.

One alcove remained with a shut curtain, and from behind that curtain came a groan.

"*Monsieur* de Gennes, I presume?" Bruie said as he finished an after-meal drink of apricot nectar.

"Yes, of course. He'll take a while to recover, but I'm sure he'll do so. He is perhaps somewhat foolish, but at least he's not treacherous."

Bruie, at the last word, looked into Sasha's eyes.

"So," he mused, "the young man is not the problem you wanted to discuss this morning. You surprise me, Sasha."

"I'm sure that I don't surprise you entirely."

Bruie considered her remark. "Your girls are your problem, Sasha. I thought we both understood that."

"Desiree is no longer one of my girls, as you call them." Sasha responded promptly. "I have, shall we say, severed our relationship, and she's no longer welcome in this house. As for the reasons, I'm sure you were watching with your usual acumen last night. I don't need to go into details."

Bruie nodded. What Sasha had done was understandable under the circumstances. Desiree had tried to flout the rules, and had set herself out as bait for men already taken. This was one of the things Sasha's system was designed to avoid, and one of its greatest strengths from Bruie's point of view, though the company directors might not like it all that much. Sailors and soldiers might still brawl, as they always would, over gambling debts or insults or for no particular reason. But on this island, at least, they had ceased brawling over women.

Or had they? Bruie had a sudden thought, and at once realized the problem Sasha was facing. Or rather the one he was facing, now that Desiree was an independent operator.

"So," he mused. "You're telling me that it's up to me to control Desiree now."

"If anyone can," Sasha responded. "I've confessed my failure by dismissing her from my friendship. Of course, you should have little difficulty with her yourself. You represent authority. She might be somewhat reluctant to defy you."

"You're very encouraging," Bruie said with a tight smile. He called to mind a vision of an island girl promising complete compliance with his wishes, and then violating them at any and every turn...causing trouble without end, setting comrades against one another, scheming for revenge. Naturally, Sasha was the ultimate target, but others would become involved.

He realized, with a bitter feeling, that Sasha was indeed calling on his protection...certain of getting it, for his sake, if not for hers. Well, he thought to himself, this is what I get for allowing these women such a position of power. But, why complain? He procured goods, he procured slaves; now he procured women too. He was the pimp, and now he had to provide the protection.

"We are not whores, *Monsieur* Bruie," Sasha stated sharply, sensing his thoughts.

Bruie's eyes shot up. For an uncanny moment he had the feeling there was something to the superstitions that wafted out of the mainland; that people could indeed read minds. But the feeling passed. Back in France, the gypsies were not mind-readers. They were simply shrewd observers and accurate guessers, all that was really needed to give the appearance of mind-reading.

"I've never called you that," Bruie answered Sasha at last.

"I realize that, *Monsieur*. But you might be tempted to think it, if things like this were a constant occurrence."

"I trust they'll not become so, Sasha, and I'm sure you will do your best to prevent it. I shall offer whatever assistance seems appropriate."

"You might," Sasha smiled, "get us a priest."

Bruie stared at her for a moment, and then thought he saw the joke. He was actually grinning, and about to say something, when the bell on the upper fort rang once, and then twice in quick succession.

Instantly Bruie got up.

"Our visitors arrive," he said. "At least they didn't disturb our breakfast." He gestured toward the last of the curtained alcoves. "Send *Monsieur* de Gennes to me, when he is presentable.

I hope it's sometime today!"

The English ship, the *Rochester*, came to an anchored halt about half a mile off the south coast of Gorée. There appeared to be no immediate hostile intent, although all of the vessel's flags were flying.

Bruie spent little time in his office, pausing only to gather up some papers, a sword, and another item he kept carefully hidden in his desk. The sword was only for show, and he felt awkward belting it around his middle. The last time he had worn one was on his one visit to Versailles, where anyone who proved himself a gentleman could enter the Royal Presence and see the King in state. One proved himself a gentleman by wearing a sword.

But the other items were for more practical purposes. Out in the open air again, he descended the steps and pathway to the platform overlooking the harbor. There, waiting for him, were Lieutenant Drouin and his senior sergeants, along with officers representing each of the ship captains in harbor; the captains themselves were aboard their vessels, ready for action if needed.

One of the men was O'Brien, and Bruie cast the Irishman an inquiring glance.

"Picard?" he asked.

"A bit under the weather, sir," the Irishman said with a smile. "He's indisposed, in his cabin. Bertrand is in acting command of the

Princesse."

"Good. What are they doing on that damned ship, Drouin?"

The lieutenant shrugged. "But little. I put the spyglass to them. They seem to be getting a ship's boat ready for launch."

Bruie, who had set down his burdens except for the sword, now took one of them up again. Out of its small case he drew a heavy instrument that looked like two short telescopes braced together. It was a trophy of a long-ago battle with the Dutch, who had invented the instrument. They called them "binoculars." Bruie raised this instrument to eye-level, and looked.

There was indeed a lot of activity around the Rochester's launch. As he watched, it was lowered into the sea. There were six rowers and, it appeared, two officers in command. A few feet away from the mother ship, the rowers began pulling the oars, and one of the officers raised a piece of white cloth on the end of a long stick. Drouin, who could see the flash of white with unaided eye even at that distance, chuckled.

"A deputation! Compliments of the new governor of the Gambia, perhaps?"

Bruie snorted, lowering the binoculars.

"Perhaps. More likely a demand for the return of the ships they lost to us on the Little Coast. Well, they won't get them! The prize court awarded them to France."

"Orders, sir?"

"Stand easy for a moment. Remember, if we can see them, they can see us. One of the men in that boat has a spyglass, too. Appear smiling and unconcerned."

"I smile easily," the lieutenant replied. "My unconcern, however, would be a bit forced. But, very well."

There was silence on the platform for a while, as the ship's boat made its slow progress toward the harbor. In the interim, Bruie reviewed the situation and his options. There was really very little to discuss, but there were imponderables: it was unlikely the English would attack, but even the close balance of forces might not dissuade them if they misinterpreted something.

"I hope one of these English speaks decent French," Bruie

muttered. "O'Brien, you may have to translate."

"I hope to God not," the Irishman growled. "My English is like my French, only a second language to me. I wouldn't have learned even that, had it not been for that Breton here, those many years ago."

Bruie understood. The land of Brittany was part of France, but the Bretons spoke their own tongue, closely akin to the Celtic languages of Ireland, Scotland and Wales.

"Perhaps I may be of assistance," a quiet voice suggested.

Bruie turned, startled, to see Maurice de Gennes standing beside him, fully turned out in one of his formal attires, wearing a sword of his own and bearing no visible marks of the night's bout.

"You?"

"But of course. It so happens I speak English, and I can assure you of an accurate translation, down to the nuance. In both directions, of course."

Bruie stared at the young man. Then something clicked in his mind. Not just the bearing of de Gennes, or the calm confidence he seemed to exude in the situation, but something that had been described to him of de Gennes' last moments before passing out at the Stone House. A smile slowly crossed his face.

"So," he said. "How fortunate we are to have you with us, *Monsieur* de Gennes. I will welcome your... assistance." He gathered up his instrument case and his papers. "Let's go down to the quay. Our visitors are almost here."

Back at his desk later, writing a straightforward report of what had transpired with the English, Bruie found himself unable to suppress a laugh. The situation had developed almost comically. Not that it had seemed so at the time.

As Drouin had predicted, the English officer brought the compliments of Pinder, the new governor of Gambia, and of Captain Mayne, master of the *Rochester*. Also, as Bruie had predicted, he brought a polite demand for the return of the ships Bruie had captured over the last year or so.

However, the whole conference had turned on a point of honor. The English had demanded to know whether England and France were at war, and, if not, why Bruie had not fired a salute at the English flag's appearance in his waters.

Bruie had answered, quite properly he thought, that it was not for him to salute first. But, if the English would salute the French flag, he would certainly respond gun-for-gun. This message was relayed back by signals from the English officer to the English ship, who passed on a return message. The English captain declined to fire first. Instead, he, in turn, proposed to respond gun-for-gun if Bruie would initiate the exchange.

The upshot was that there was no shooting.

Since neither Bruie nor Captain Mayne would salute first, the English ultimately took their leave, retrieving their boat and sailing away. The only trophy they carried with them was Bruie's negative answer about those prize ships.

As he finished the report, Bruie was still chuckling to himself. His chuckles ceased, however, when he heard footsteps in the hall. He started to put his report away in the desk, then thought better of it, and left matters as they stood. There was a knock at the door, and, at Bruie's response, Maurice de Gennes entered. Bruie waved him to a chair.

"I was just finishing my report," he said. "I would have incorporated any comments of yours, if you had been here to make them. Where have you been?"

"Aboard the *Princesse*," de Gennes replied. "I was curious as to its state of readiness, given the circumstances."

"Ah! Remarkable initiative. What did you find?"

"Fairly good conditions, all considered. Bertrand, the first officer, seems to do rather well with the ship and crew, when left to his own initiative. He does work under constraints..."

"I take it you saw Picard."

"Something that was shown to me as Picard, yes." He paused. "A very sad case."

"Indeed. Well, we all work within our limits, is it not so?"

Suddenly, the Chief Factor of Senegal fixed the younger man
with a steady gaze.

"But I have reached mine, *m'sieu.*" From his desk he drew
out the packet of credentials de Gennes had given him on his arrival.
"There's something missing from this pack, I'm quite sure. When
am I to know the real story? And the real Maurice de Gennes, if that
truly is your name?"

The younger man stared back. Then a very slight smile
crossed his face, and he bowed his head in a quick nod.

"How did I slip? Was it my way with the English?"

"That, yes. That and something the *signarés* told me, about
how, when you were at the end of your drunk, you ran *toward* those
black giants, rather than away from them. Even a drunken young
puppy would know better than that, unless he was far more than a
drunken young puppy. Well?"

The young man seemed almost relieved.

"The name is real," he said at last. "My connections were not
exaggerated. Actually, they were minimized. I am the second son of
the Comte de Gennes, and a naval officer of His Majesty."

"Well, good. So you came here with a watching brief, to find
out how things stood and then to report. And you played a part in the
meantime. Am I to know the rest of it now?"

De Gennes reached inside his shirt and drew out a smaller
packet of papers, sealed in the same fashion as his original credentials. He started to hand them to Bruie, then held back for a moment.

"One moment, sir. Let me speak first. This... performance
was not exactly my idea. I would have preferred to be straight with
you from the beginning."

"Whatever. Orders are orders, as we both know. Were you
really that drunk?"

De Gennes grinned, rather sheepishly. "Very much so. I got
too caught up in my role. I'm not much of an actor, unless I'm able
to live the part." He gave the papers to Bruie. "I was constrained to
play that part, however, until I could analyze the situation from a
naval point of view. Then, I was to act. And, I act now. I'm not
your new assistant, sir. If it is proper in my judgment, and it seems

eminently so, and necessary as well, I am to relieve Captain Picard of command of the *Princesse*, and assume it myself. Consider him relieved."

"You? In command of that warship? You are very young."

"Twenty-seven, sir, and this will be my second command. During my first I sank three privateers and an English sloop. This was aboard the *Hermione*, four years ago."

"I've never heard of a ship's captain of twenty-three."

"I was first officer, sir, until the captain was killed. When I fought my way back to France, they left me in command."

Bruie opened the packet of papers, and read them long enough to confirm what de Gennes had stated; that, and perhaps more. He closed up the packet and put it in his desk, on top of the original credentials.

His mind was racing, and suddenly all the numbers added up. "There is to be war, then."

"It's expected," de Gennes responded. "And there's likely to be fighting in the homeland long before we get word of it here. In which case, the side that receives first knowledge of the fact will have the power to strike the first stroke. If that stroke is bold enough, it may be decisive." He smiled. "I will submit that I have the boldness, if nothing else."

Bruie snorted. "No doubt. But what are we to do in the meantime?"

"Appear to play a waiting game, and be polite to the English without giving anything away....just as you played it today, sir. Of course I speak for the Navy, not your company, and our respective superiors are still wrangling about priorities. The last word I received, however, is that the company wants to get a tighter grip on mainland trade and better relations with the mainland chiefs. They want to make sure the whole structure doesn't fall like a house of cards before the English, if it comes to war. I'm to back you in such an enterprise, which I can see you are already preparing to carry out."

Bruie nodded. "I suppose the company reiterated its opposition to my acknowledgment of the *signaré* system."

"I did hear a few complaints about it. But your directors are practical men. They won't interfere, if you get results. If you don't, on the other hand, they'll use this *signaré* business as an excuse to get rid of you. In that case, all the failures will land on your head."

Bruie nodded. "Well, we'd best get at it then. Welcome aboard, Captain de Gennes. I can't guarantee the days ahead will be uniformly pleasant, but I do believe I can guarantee they will be interesting."

Chapter Thirteen

Sunlight streaming in the window-flap of his tent wakened Captain Charles Tousaint in degrees. First, he was aware of the light, then of birdsong, and lastly the smell of earth. He had been a long way away in his dreams, so it was with some difficulty that he accepted the fact that he was on land, not at sea. Even so, his sleep-clouded mind mistook the locale. The birds, the breeze, and the unmistakable smell of grain being cut for harvest, convinced him that he must be home in France. That is, they convinced him until he stumbled outside the tent. Only then did he realize he was this morning exactly where he had been the day before... deep in the plains of West Africa.

He walked to the well, drew up a bucket, and poured it over his head. In a few moments, he had his bearings, and in some additional moments, having joined the rest of his party at the campfire, he had his breakfast. At that point, he was truly himself once again.

The rest of the party had waited for him, for he was the senior member of this expedition. He was the only ship's master present.

Three other ships were represented, but only by second or third officers. This was becoming customary. Not long before, a French expedition had been attacked and three captains had been lost in one day. Now, only one captain went to negotiate. The others, the seconds and thirds in command, accompanied him to learn the system and to guard their own captains' interests.

Whatever his rank, each white man was accompanied by a servant and a *signaré*; in the case of junior officers, of course, by junior *signarés*. Together, the women and the servants had prepared the breakfast. Exotic as it might be in appearance and flavorings, the meal, with all its extra touches, was basically composed of eggs and flour: a porridge. But such was usually the case during harvest time.

"Has anyone seen Sasha?" Tousaint asked the group as he finished his first bowl.

"Only in passing," came the answer from Desbien, third officer of the *Haut-Garonne* and the youngest man present. "I think she went into the village."

Tousaint nodded, saying nothing, grateful for once that the other captains were not around. Without a doubt, another captain would have mocked him for losing track of his *signaré*. It was almost as certain the mocker would have added some impudent explanations for her absence. But from his juniors, Tousaint didn't have to contend with that, at least to his face.

Sasha knew what she was doing, he was quite certain. Although this was less than a full-scale trading expedition, its mission was still very important. They were to coax traders from the interior to the coast. Sasha would smooth the way for them.

"Well then," Tousaint said as he finished his second bowl of porridge, "we shall wait and see what news she brings us."

Tousaint got up and walked away from the campfire, taking his morning exercise, a vigorous walk. His route was roughly in the form of a circle, clockwise heading westward from the camp, taking him close to a field that was being harvested.

Once again it was easy for him to think himself in France. He wasn't close enough to see the color of the farm workers' skins; their hats were broad like those of European peasants, and the lush grains waving on either side of the narrow river bisecting this broad valley were as high as those of Picardy in autumn.

There were differences, of course. The peasants served not the King of France but the King of Sine, a West African potentate, who was usually at war with the King of Bawol, ruler of the territory to the immediate west. The grain being harvested was also not the standard wheat of Europe. Instead it was a variety called "spelt," an ancient form as old as cultivation itself. At least to a European palate, this grain was much inferior in taste. The Africans probably felt the same way about it, Tousaint reflected, given that they enriched their porridge with egg.

As for the river itself, well, it was neither the Seine nor the Loire, but the east branch of the Senegal, rising out of the south.

Coming back toward the camp at last, Tousaint reminded himself that this was as deep into Africa as he had ever been, if his maps were right, and that was always open to question. Given that maps of the interior were even more inaccurate than the sea charts, he might walk fifty miles due west and touch the headwaters of the Gambia.

He might also go fifty miles to the southeast, and touch the headwaters of a river greater than either the Gambia or the Senegal, or even both put together: the mighty Niger, beginning its thousand-mile journey east and south to the Atlantic.

Abruptly, Tousaint spat on the ground. Both the Gambia and the Niger were British rivers now, and the Brits would probably come after the Senegal again someday. Perhaps he might yet make one or two more voyages in peace.

At the tent, Sasha was waiting for him.

"You were looking for me, *M'sieu?*"

Tousaint set down the long stick he'd picked up on the way as a staff to ease his aging legs. Somewhat stiffly, he sat down outside the tent. Much more easily and fluidly, Sasha sat down beside him.

"You have news, no doubt," he said after a while.

"Good news, I think."

"You think?"

"I'm not sure. There are good prospects, but there's an ele-

149

ment of danger, too."

"So be it," Tousaint scoffed. "Danger is necessary to good trade, but then, you know this as well as I. But I saw you shiver when you spoke of this. Sasha, there has only been one man we've met in our travels who ever made you shiver. So our old acquaintance, that Arab called the Ghoul, must be nearby."

"Yes," Sasha said. "And no."

Tousaint paused. He knew Sasha well enough to realize she would speak of the details only when she was ready. She was still digesting things she had learned in town. There must be a great deal.

Tousaint waited, and while he waited he let his thoughts range. It had been a very successful trip so far, and it had clearly justified his decision to come inland himself. He had come to Gorée on the *Beausoliel*, the Good Sun, which was the first fully-armed merchant-man he had ever commanded. He hoped it would also be the last. Guns took up space that should have been available for trade goods, and therefore the goods had to be selected for maximum value per pound. There was tobacco, and a little cloth, but for the most part his cargo consisted of small arms and ammunition. These sold very well in Africa.

At first, Tousaint had been somewhat concerned that he might arrive at a time when the tribal chiefs were at peace, not even think-ing about the possibility of future wars. Sheer folly, of course. There had never been such a time in Africa, and he doubted there ever would be. The King of Bawol and the King of Sine were at peace, for the moment, but that would change with the seasons.

Tousaint pondered the trading goods. Even if the two kings had no slaves to sell, they both had a plenty of other goods, including ivory and gum-arabic. More important, it was now possible, given the temporary peace, to entice representatives of both Sine and Bawol down to the coast at the same time. In all probability, they could be maneuvered into bidding against each other, handing Tousaint and his colleagues a buyer's market.

Not only that, Sine and Bawol might not be selling each other's people this week, but there were captives within range. The Dinka had once again tried arms against the Ashanti. This time, however, despite great personal bravery on the part of many, Ashanti numbers had prevailed. The Ashanti had sold their captives to an Arab trader, nicknamed the Ghoul. Tousaint, doubting whether many other men bore that moniker, was pleased.

He had dealt with this one before. A slimy, oily, depraved man indeed; probably a pervert as well, since he seemed to cast his sidelong glances at young men, and ignored the likes of Sasha as if she didn't exist. Normally, Tousaint would have been in a bit of a quandary in a situation with which Sasha could not deal. But he had been a ship's captain for better than half his life. Yes, he could deal with the Ghoul on his own.

Tousaint shook his head. Hopefully, this time *the batarde* wouldn't try to make an impression by destroying a captive prince.

Still, what mattered was how to persuade the Ghoul it would be worth his while to bring his caffle of captives down to the coast. That was the best place for hard bargains, at least from a French point of view. Tousaint had learned that lesson well. He hadn't brought his trade goods, only samples. When the Ghoul saw what the newest French muskets could do, Tousaint was sure he would set out for the *Petit-Cote* without a second thought.

Eventually, despite himself, he became aware once again of Sasha beside him; Sasha staring ahead of herself, features clear and calm, but absorbed. He was about to speak when she turned to him and preempted the conversation.

"This is not the same Ghoul."

Tousaint frowned. "Not the same? Then why does he go by that name, and what happened to the other?"

"Shortly after he sold us the Ashanti captives several years ago, the old Ghoul was killed in his tent. Disemboweled, in fact, and then chopped up like so much meat and thrown out to the carrion birds."

"So! A not unfitting end for such as he, *c'est pas*? I take it this new Ghoul did the honors?"

"That is true, sir. Or at least so I'm told. We must deal now with one called El Haji Khalil al-Ghul."

Frowning, Tousaint mulled over one of the words.

151

"Haji, eh? So he's made the pilgrimage to Mecca, has he now?"

"Yes. The son of an indulgent father, it seems. One rich enough to send him there."

"Ah. Well, no doubt we shall hear much praise of Allah in the next few hours." He paused. "But who was this father of his?"

"Abdullah al-Ghul."

Tousaint simply stared at her. Being a ship's captain, a trader and a Frenchman, he simply nodded.

"It is perhaps fitting, eh?"

Sasha's expression didn't change. Slowly, she nodded her own head.

"And this faithful son is nearby?" the captain persisted.

"Yes, from what I've heard. It's said in town that he has a camp six miles to the east. I've arranged for messengers to go to him, inviting him to meet us in the town."

"Ah. You don't suggest that we visit *him, in his camp?*"

"I don't think that would be prudent, captain."

Tousaint chuckled. "Indeed. Well, then we wait and see what this new Ghoul is like. In the meantime, we shall have to find some way to pass the time. Can you suggest any?"

Sasha finally looked at him. "I'm sure I don't know what the captain means."

Tousaint laughed, and, standing up, extended his hand to raise her. That done, he lifted the front flap of the tent, and drew her inside.

"You are truly a remarkable woman," he said. "Remind me to marry you again, if I should chance to make another voyage in this direction."

A spyglass, Andre Bruie decided, was indeed a wonderful instrument. But as he stood on the quarterdeck of the *Princesse*, surveying the palm-covered coastal ridges of the Little Coast, he wished he had brought along his binoculars. They would have given him a sense of depth, more valuable for his purpose than a flat image.

Nevertheless, there were some things he could spot, and he focused in on a wisp of smoke that rose over a headland to the south. He studied it carefully, then drew the instrument away from his eyes, handing it to the man who stood next to him.

"Have a look, Captain."

Maurice de Gennes, commander of the *Princesse*, took the telescope and stared through it. Moments later he handed it back to Bruie.

"Interesting, eh?" the Chief Factor asked.

"It is that," de Gennes agreed. "Certainly a fire of some kind. Ordinarily I would think it a mere community fire of some village."

"*If* we were near a village, which I don't believe we are."

De Gennes nodded. "There is a village further north. Perhaps a hunting party has come down from this northern village in search of its quarry, and has made a camp."

"Assuming there's anything to hunt along the coast. Do you get the feeling our visitors are of another stripe?"

De Gennes smiled. "It's a pleasure to have you with us, *Monsieur*."

Bruie snorted. "I don't mean to jostle your elbow, de Gennes, but I believe in being prepared."

"I wasn't being ironic, sir. It is indeed a pleasure to have you aboard. After all, we who have engaged the English can only profit by sharing our ideas and approaches. Yours is an eye that's capable of appreciating my acts. I gather that you, if you were in command today, would call to battle stations at this moment."

Bruie nodded, but said nothing.

"I only wait a little longer. Perhaps three minutes."

"Your thought?"

"With battle stations, we go to full sail. If anyone is watching from that camp, they're far less likely to spot our bare masts. Achievement of surprise is always worth striving for."

Bruie nodded, this time more emphatically. He was quite satisfied. After all, he hadn't really been all that concerned. The only reason he had come along on this particular voyage was to see how de Gennes operated. In the few short months that de Gennes had been in charge of French enforcement operations along the *Petit-Cote*, he had taken four prizes; as many as Bruie himself had been able to grab in the space of three years. Bruie simply wanted to see him in action.

In the back of his mind was a grudging appreciation of the company's directors. They hadn't sent him an assistant, in his own terms, but after this voyage, he was quite certain he could get back to his proper work in the offices of Saint-Louis and Gorée. He no longer had to pretend to be a sea-dog. Now there was an authentic one on the scene.

Watching and listening as the headland approached, Bruie heard de Gennes pass a few orders down from the quarterdeck. This was done quietly through messengers, rather than at the top of a bawling command voice. Bruie understood some of what was happening. Ordinarily they would round the headland just outside the shoals, but in this case they would stand out a ways to sea first. From that position, they would then sweep in with the port guns bearing full on the coast.

Just before they rounded the headland, Bruie smiled, casting the amused glance at de Gennes.

"Well, would you have me say it?"

De Gennes smiled in turn. "If the Chief Factor please."

"Well, then, guard the coast."

The two had joked about this formality, and in fact it was not only trivial, but unheard. Bruie's last words were drowned out by de Gennes' call to battle stations. Flags accompanied the sails to the tops of the masts, and men scurried amidships with loud shouts and the inevitable curses.

An instant later, the headland fell away and a ship appeared at anchor in the lee of the cape. De Gennes, gazing at it through the spyglass, suddenly exploded in laughter.

"Oh, spare us! Not *them* again!"

"English?" Bruie demanded

"*Au contraire*, sir. Dutch."

"What? The Dutch? They haven't tried to poach our coast for more than five years."

"Perhaps by now they've had time to forget the consequences, eh? Ah!"

This last exclamation of surprise came in response to the appearance of a flash from the anchored ship. There was a swish of air, and the splash of a cannonball in the sea beyond the *Princesse.*

"Good shooting," de Gennes observed. "And quick too. I fear, sir, this is one prize we will not be able to take back to the island."

Bruie shrugged. "Do what's prudent."

"Port guns," de Gennes called out, "Fire!"

As he spoke, there were more flashes from the side of the anchored ship, but they were erratic. Obviously, that ship's crew and their captain, if he was aboard, were acting in desperate panic, hoping to land a lucky hit before the French could strike effectively. Their attempts failed, and the *Princesse's* guns roared a response in the form of hot and cold shot.

The *Princesse* was close enough for its crew to hear the splintering wood and the agonized cries of the maimed sailors. They were close enough to see the flames sprout from the regions amidships, far down below.

There was a moment's hesitation between the two vessels. Then abruptly, the Dutch flag came down from the mizzenmast. The French crew cheered.

De Gennes, however, wore a sour look, and after a moment Bruie asked him why.

"After all," he noted, "you didn't sink it. It's still a prize."

"Yes, sir. If our prize crew can board it, patch it up enough, and steer it to Gorée without foundering. If I'd known they were going to give in that quickly I wouldn't have given them full blast. I'd have stuck to cold shot instead, and left the hot shot for another time. It only makes a prize crew's task tougher."

Bruie chuckled. He understood. Some men were never satisfied with less than one hundred percent of the possible.

The Pilgrim, Khalil al-Ghul, was a singularly unprepossess-ing-looking young man, at least to the eyes of anyone who had ever seen his late unlamented father. Unlike the elder Ghoul, this one had neither scars nor pockmarks on his face, and the perpetually cruel expression of the old man was reflected but palely in his son's cat-like smile. Only the manner was the same, Tousaint reflected; as oily and as offensive as ever.

"Why should I come to your coast?" the young man purred. "I can get as good a deal from the British along the Gambia, and the travel is easier."

"The travel may be easy or hard, I won't claim to know," Tousaint said casually. "I'm no expert on the Gambia. But as for the deal you can get, you are well aware that we bring more goods you can use than the English do."

"Perhaps."

"Little 'perhaps' about it, I would think. Or is it possible that someone has found something more valuable to African potentates than firearms?"

"No, that's not possible, as you suggest. But it is possible that by the time I arrive, the English, as you call them, will have destroyed you French. In which case I would wind up dealing with them, anyway. Besides, you hardly bring enough merchandise to make a convincing case."

Hearing this as an accusation, Tousaint controlled himself. They were seated, the two dissimilar men, across from each other at a table in what passed for the African village's tavern. They had quickly completed the opening ceremonies of their discussion.

"You mistake my purpose," Tousaint said at last. "I have not come here to sell, my young friend. I have come to inform you that you have the opportunity to buy, if you choose to pursue it. That opportunity doesn't exist here, and will not exist here. It exists only along the *Petit-Cote*."

Tousaint ignored the Arab's return stare, and his eyes fell for a moment on Sasha, sitting some ways away at another table. She was not part of this discussion. The Arab seemed to regard her mere presence as an insult. Perhaps this was affected, perhaps not. The elder Ghoul had been less insistent on such points. But perhaps the younger one, whatever his real feelings, had more to prove.

After a moment the discussions continued. Tousaint was not slow to realize that the Haji Khalil wanted to make his deal close to where he was, without a great deal of travel, not because of what the French did or didn't have, but because of what the Arab himself had. Inevitably, on the trip to the coast, a great many slaves would become ill or perish. The rest would be in varying states of exhaustion. This was something Tousaint had discovered on earlier visits, and it was exactly the reason why he, himself, would not finalize a deal in the interior.

Eventually, the impasse filled the room. Contrary to trader custom, to say nothing of Arab tradition, Khalil rose up and thumped the table with both hands.

"Enough talk! I waste my time on you infidels. If I go to the coast, I shall take my time getting there, for I go wherever and whenever I please. And I shall not be as easy to deal with as you seem to expect. You shall not cheat me as you cheated my father!"

He turned away as if to go, and then, catching sight of Sasha at the table nearby, spoke a few rapid words to her. Tousaint saw her body stiffen, but no expression crossed her face.

It was only after the Arab had gone, and the two of them were making their way back to the camp, that Tousaint got a chance to ask her what the Haji Khalil had said to her.

"It was nothing," she replied at first. "Typical of the man, I suppose. He likes to create an aura of menace."

"Sasha, if it was 'nothing', it would not menace you. Tell me, was it a threat of some kind? I must know. It may be significant for my purposes as well as your welfare."

"I doubt it, sir. It's personal to me."

"Sasha..."

She sighed. "Oh, all right. He said that he knew all about the whores of Gorée, and that one day he would seize our island and sell us all. He also said that he had heard my foster-mother and the storyteller, Hadithe Zakale, were on the Ivory Coast. He said one day he would take them, too, and send me their heads to prove the sincerity of his promises."

She cast Tousaint a wan smile. "It seems he doesn't like to have women interfering in his business."

They walked in silence for a while. After a time, however, Tousaint spoke.

"I think," he said, "that if this Ghoul does come down to the coast, I shall bring along my man Duvalier for the negotiations."

"Duvalier?" Sasha echoed. "I don't know the man. You say he's of your crew?"

"Yes, and you do know him, though not by that name. Everyone calls him the Claw, because his left arm is cut off below the elbow and a hook is in its place."

"Oh, him. What use would he be? He's but a sailor."

Tousaint smiled. "The young Ghoul, as you have no doubt observed, lacks his father's face. It might do him good to give that face a harder look. Of course, if the Claw ever had to do the job, there might not be much left of his face. Still, it would give our young friend there something to think about. Menace works both ways, Sasha."

Chapter Fourteen

Had the town of Lahtse not been on the coast, there would have been no reason for its existence. Hadithe Zakale was certain of this. In all his travels throughout Africa, he had only once run across a community so dependent upon its location.

What was puzzling to the storyteller was the fact that despite its dependence on the sea, the village of Lahtse had, in the remote past, resolutely turned its back on the Atlantic, and had grown into a town through activities having as little to do with salt water as possible.

Even the social system of the town reflected Lahtse's contempt for the ocean. Among the castes, of which there were several, the fisherman ranked only a little above the slave and considerably below the hired servant. The people of Lahtse hunted and herded on the broad parkland north of the coast. What trade they had was mostly inland, reaching up into the Great Deserts.

All this was on Hadithe Zakale's mind as his footsteps brought him closer to the spacious hut on the outskirts of the town that was his home during his stay in Lahtse. They might be somewhat strange, these townsmen, and they were certainly stubborn and opinionated, but they did respect the storyteller's profession, and they did know how to honor one.

He found a hearty lunch awaiting him. Helene-Marie had seen him in the distance and had prepared it. There was plenty of food for her to work with, for the gifts had been heavy to correspond with the success of the harvest. In fact, when it came time for them to leave Lahtse, they would have to give a great deal away in order to lighten their load.

Eating lunch, Hadithe Zakale glanced around the hut, summing up in his own mind exactly how much had been accumulated. These days it seemed that each move required more agonizing decisions over the discard of possessions. Dimly, he recalled the days when he had first taken up the wandering craft, when his only possessions had been his drum, his clothes, and the trinkets he wore. He wondered how much the changes were due to time, to his recent tendency to stay a little longer at each stop, and how much to his having a companion, who happened to be a woman.

"Have they asked you yet?" Helene-Marie asked suddenly.

Hadithe Zakale looked up from the meal he was finishing, and smiled.

"Yes. This morning Mutatu returned from Aro Chuku with a favorable omen, and told me the expedition would leave tomorrow. They want me to go along."

Helene-Marie said nothing, and Hadithe Zakale knew she was digesting the news. The storyteller's way with his woman was almost the exact reverse of his way of telling a tale. With a tale, he exploited every possible dramatic effect: repetition, embellishment, circumlocution. He was master of them all. With Helene-Marie, however, he spoke directly, cramming as much meaning as possible into a few words. She didn't need embellishment to understand him.

"I wonder," she said at last, "what the Tuareg really look like, behind those masks."

Hadithe Zakale laughed. "Is that what troubles you? They unveil in their tents. I've seen them. They look like ordinary men,

160

no different from any other Berber tribesmen." He paused. "Of course, if you wonder about their women, I've never seen them, veiled or not. They would be as likely to take their women on a caravan as the people of Lahtse would be to bring their women along to meet it."

He smiled. "I shall miss your attentions, Helene-Marie, but I shall be all right."

Helene-Marie sighed, accepting the situation, but hardly acting as if she were convinced it was a good idea. That was perhaps to be expected. It was only the second time Hadithe Zakale had accompanied Lahtse's annual expedition to the north. The expedition was designed to cross paths with the Tuareg. Each year the Tuareg brought a caravan down through the desert and the passes between the Niger and Volta valleys. Its ultimate destination was the southwestern coast of West Africa.

The storyteller didn't expect the routine to vary. First the deliberate meeting, played out by both parties as if it were a mere chance occurrence. Then the elaborate ceremonials, endless discussions, feasting, and finally the hardest of hard bargainings between experts skilled in trade. Hadithe Zakale was sure the people of Lahtse would hold their own. The Tuareg were famous dickerers, but Mutatu the son of N'Gazan, was a master-trader, the like of which even the Europeans seldom produced.

Besides, Mutatu had an automatic advantage, knowing how prized his trade goods were. The bulk of the cargo of the Lahtse expedition would consist of the elephant's tooth, as it was called. Traded up from the south by land, it came in a continual stream in return for products of Lahtse's fields and herds. This was not known among the whites as the Ivory Coast for nothing.

The storyteller was certain that Mutatu and his comrades would relieve the Tuareg of almost every item the caravan carried, except for slaves. The slaves would, of course, attract the Lahtse people's interest, but they were not interested in dealing with the whites. They never had been. Of all the places on the Ivory Coast, Lahtse was known as the most fiercely inhospitable place Europeans could possibly touch, and they gave it a wide berth. Lahtse had little use for the sea, or anyone who made use of the sea. A curious people.

161

"And what stories will you tell?"

Hadithe Zakale looked up from his reverie to see that Helene-Marie's face had brightened to match the lighter tone of her voice. He was glad to see she wasn't giving his pending absence any great brooding-space in her mind, so he answered in perhaps more detail, and with a little more self-mockery, than he might otherwise have done.

"Men's stories, of course," he replied. "Tales of daring and ferocity and prowess; tales highly complimentary to the Lahtse people and the Tuareg, and showing absolutely no consideration for their enemies."

"Won't that be a problem? After all, between them they hate almost everyone in this part of Africa."

"That's true, but I range rather widely in time and space." He smiled at her. "I'll tell them tales of Jenne-Jeno, and how the old city was stormed at last when the Songhai empire fell. I'll tell about Radama the Malagasy, how he came to the oracle at Aro Chuku, and how it sent him into the boiling forests of the south. I'll tell about Aladdin and Ali Baba to please the Tuaregs. Can't mention Sindbad of course, he was a seaman and that would displease our Lahtse friends. Perhaps Osei Tutu's victory over the Denkyra would go over well. Our audience isn't fond of the Ashanti, but the Denkyra were cordially hated by everyone whose lives they touched. And, of course, I'll tell the tale of Singlehand, who killed the lion all by himself."

"Yes, that should please them," Helene-Marie agreed. "But what will happen when you return here?"

"Hm? Why, we go, of course. It's time."

"A long journey?"

"Not that long. I should like to go among the Ashanti again. It's been almost three years. I wonder if old Anokye is still alive, and if Sokolo has yet become King Opuku Ware's chief messenger. He should have made it by now."

Helene-Marie smiled. "I've always enjoyed the Ashanti."

"I should think so, woman. They regard you more highly than they do me!"

Helene-Marie blushed, and protested that he was exaggerating, which was true, but just barely so. On their first visit to the Ashanti, they found that their fame had preceded them, a result of Sokolo's report to the Ashanti king. Much honor had been showered on Hadithe Zakale, and attentions unique for a woman on Helene-Marie. The Ashanti people praised her for aiding Hadithe Zakale and Sokolo in their efforts, despite the risk of banishment. Hadithe Zakale was reminded by both Sokolo and the village potentate, Kwame-Uhru, that the Ashanti did not forget their friends. Neither man had exaggerated.

"If it's to be a short trip to the Ashanti," Helene-Marie said thoughtfully, "perhaps I can pack more than we would otherwise be able to take."

Hadithe Zakale looked at her in mock terror. "Not the hut too, woman!"

"Only a few things we really need. Not all storytellers travel as lightly as you do. Look at Moshesh, the Fulani. He travels in a litter, and has nine servants."

Hadithe Zakale smiled. Moshesh was the only other storyteller who had crossed their path in the years he and Helene-Marie had traveled together. It had been a brief contact, but she had remembered.

"Moshesh," the storyteller replied, "was a Fulani before he was a teller of tales. He's also older than your Mama-Lise, older even than Anokye the Magician. When Moshesh tells a Creation Tale, you get the feeling it all happened in his youth. I can still walk."

"Well, as I said, just a few things."

"I leave it to your discretion, Helene-Marie."

"And will we stay long with the Ashanti?"

Hadithe Zakale gazed at her in surprise.

"You know there's no telling. Why do you ask? We can't know until we arrive there, and size up the situation." He paused, reflecting. "I'd like to stay the summer, though, if possible."

"That would be good."

At which point the teller of tales rose up.

"But before the Ashanti, the Tuareg. I shall take my drum

and cloak."

"Nothing more? You might need..."

"...Any number of things," he finished for her. Then he grinned. "But I will confide my needs to my hosts, as a good story-teller should."

"*M'sieu* Pochette!"

At the rough sound of Andre Bruie's voice the clerk, Denis Pochette, now dignified with the higher title of Assistant Chief Factor, scrambled to his feet as he had in the old days. He was, after all, still a clerk at heart.

"*Oui, M'sieu* Bruie?"

"Get down to the harbor and order somebody to fire off a round across the bow of that ship!"

"Ship, sir?"

Bruie, standing at the window of his office on the island-city of Saint-Louis, thrust his trusty binoculars into the assistant's hands.

"That one, man! Look! Yes, I know, all you can see is a mast or two, but nobody passes this close to my coast without identifying himself. Get the fastest and best-armed merchantman in the harbor ready, too. Just in case he wants to play games!"

Pochette took a quick glance through the binoculars and was off, almost before Bruie had time to seize the instrument back. The Chief Factor took another look himself, cursing matters. He never bothered with the small details, such as to whom such curses should be directed.

He wasn't altogether unhappy. He had spent more time in Saint-Louis these past few months than he had ever been able to spend there before. And, while he was grateful that matters elsewhere in the Senegal Colony allowed him to be away from Gorée, he found himself becoming bored and restless.

He was an administrator, and what he was doing in Saint-Louis was certainly administrator's work... but it lacked a sense of action. His work was now caught up, and he was aware that in his rare daydreams, rare reveries, he stalked the decks of the *Princesse* in pursuit of intruders along the Little Coast. Somewhere along the line, he had acquired the heart of a captain.

Binoculars raised again, he studied what little of the passing ship he could see from that distance. The curvature of the earth hid the hull, but from the mast configuration he could tell it had to be a large vessel. Something about it suggested that it might be French, but that made no sense. A French vessel, above all others, would be bound to put in at Saint-Louis. Whatever its nationality, the ship was clearly trying to bypass the post.

Then Bruie heard one of the seaward fort's cannon boom, and saw signal flags go up in the harbor. He couldn't read the naval signals himself from this angle, but he knew what they would say: Identify yourself and sail into the harbor, or be treated as an enemy. Loud voices reached him. The call for all hands to report sounded from the largest of the armed merchant vessels.

Bruie permitted himself a smile. Pochette had been efficient. He was glad, once again, that he had taken the fainthearted clerk off Gorée before the *signarés* had totally ruined him. At least he wrote in a fair hand, and could keep up with Bruie's demanding routine, for the most part anyway.

He saw a flicker at sea, and then realized it also came from flags shooting up masts, this time on the passing vessel. He raised the binoculars again, then snapped them down in exasperation. They were signal flags, all right, but they made no sense. Unless they were in code, and that made no sense, either.

The ship kept going. Down below, the crew of the merchant vessel prepared to sail. Bruie calculated it would be ready in perhaps ten minutes. That was time enough for him to prepare, if he was going along with it, and he most definitely was going.

He moved quickly. In fact, everything he needed was packed, except the binoculars, by the time he heard feet racing his way down the corridors.

"*M'sieu!*" Pochette gasped, trying to catch his breath. He had a small slip of paper in his hand. Bruie sized up the situation at once.

"So! French, is it... and in code? It must be a naval vessel. But what on earth is the man's excuse for not stopping?"

Pochette, finding he could not speak even a single word in response, just handed Bruie the slip of paper. Bruie read it:

I AM THE SIEUR DE LA ROQUE, IN COMMAND OF HIS MAJESTY'S WARSHIP *MUTINE* : THE *HERMIONE* FOLLOWS UNDER CAPTAIN DE ST-VAUDRILLE. WE ARE BOUND FOR THE GAMBIA TO TAKE THE ENGLISH FORT JAMES, HIS MAJESTY NOW BEING IN A STATE OF WAR WITH ENGLAND. I SHALL SIGNAL THE NEWS TO GORÉE AS I PASS.

Bruie stared at the paper, and then crumpled it. He stared out the window at the masts of the passing ship, now slowly disappearing in the distance. And then, in one abrupt move, he thrust the binoculars into the sea-case and closed it.

"Take charge here, Pochette, until I get back."

"But sir! If this is war, shouldn't you remain ..."

"... Here? What good will I do here? The enemy is to the south. Or at least," the Chief Factor reflected, "he was."

He strode out of the room, satchel in hand, without another word.

It was nearly dusk on the day Hadithe Zakale returned to the hut on the outskirts of Lahtse. Even so, he found a hot meal waiting for him. Helene-Marie sat silent while he ate, and only when he began sipping the wine she'd poured as a special treat did she begin to ask her questions. There were a lot of them, and it took a while for the storyteller to describe his visit to the Tuareg caravan, even without embellishments.

"But there were no women?" she asked at last.

Hadithe Zakale laughed. "No. Well, only one, but we saw little of her."

"Really? What sort of woman?"

Hadithe Zakale waved a dismissing hand. He hadn't meant to mention that aspect of his journey at all, and for a reason, so he passed it off.

"The Tuareg chief had one of his wives with him. Not by design, however. It seems he acquired her en route."

"Acquired a wife en route? You mean a concubine, I think."

"No, a wife. She seems to have made quite an impression. She rose rapidly in his esteem, no matter how she may have started out."

"Obviously. The Tuareg usually don't marry slaves, do they?"

"Not that I know of. But perhaps she's a special case. Anyway, as I said, we saw little of her."

Helene-Marie nodded, and then abruptly changed the subject, for which Hadithe Zakale was glad.

"Then we shall go to the Ashanti?"

"Yes," he replied. "Three, perhaps four days from now. One or two last entertainments and it will be time."

"And we shall stay the summer?"

Hadithe Zakale put down his winecup.

"Helene-Marie, never before have I seen you so concerned about how long we will remain in one particular place. Why this sudden interest? Or do the Ashanti please you as much as that?"

"Not that, no," she said quickly. "But it would be a good thing, if we did stay the summer. It might be a hardship otherwise."

"You're giving me a riddle. What hardship?"

Helene-Marie stared out the window of the hut. After a while she spoke.

"Do you remember our first night together, after I agreed to come with you, to share your travels?"

"I remember many good nights, Helene-Marie."

"That first night, I told you that I could and would give you myself gladly, but that I was too old for that gift to have any consequences. I remember how you laughed. You said that you yourself were too old to engender any consequences, so you wouldn't be disappointed in me."

"I seem to remember. What's the point?"

"It seems we were both wrong."

For once in his adult life, Hadithe Zakale, the teller of tales, was totally without words. After a moment, Helene-Marie continued.

"It will be born in the summer."

The storyteller, staring at her, found his voice at last.

"You knew this, then, before I left for the Tuareg."

"I thought it might be so. Now I am sure."

Hadithe Zakale shook his head.

"Incredible. But yes, I should have known. My father was an old man when I was born and when I left home as a grown man, I had a younger brother not two years old." He gestured at his hair, now fully white, hair that had been silvery since his youth. "With my family, it seems, the gods aged our hair and preserved other parts." He fixed her with his eyes. "Boy or girl, of course, does not matter to me, but I hope whatever the sex of the child, it takes to a wandering life."

Helene-Marie exhaled a breath. She had been worried, deep down, that the storyteller might think of abandoning her and the child. It was, after, all something that neither of them had expected. Yet her relief was mixed. For once that fear was disposed of, a natural desire took its place and came into voice.

"If you want to wander until you're as old as Mosesh, I shall go with you, and I'm sure the child will take to our way of life. Yet, if you wish at some point to return to your homeland and settle down, we'll follow you there, too."

Hadithe Zakale smiled. He could see through the screen.

"I might settle one day, if circumstances made it advisable...or necessary."

They fell silent then, not needing speech. Hadithe Zakale was glad for this silence. It gave him time to think about the baby, and time to think about the bride he had seen.

Hadithe Zakale had, in fact, seen that new bride much more closely than he had let on. He had recognized her, and she had recognized him.. There had been a cruel, cunning look on that briefly unveiled face. The teller of tales had no desire to see that look again. The face belonged to the former *signaré* of the island of Gorée. The face belonged to Desiree.

Tousaint could smell the sea, and that was a relief.

The bush was thick on the coast opposite Gorée island. Although the palms lining the shore were not in sight yet, the Captain knew he was close. Behind him straggled the tired and staggering bearers. Even further back were the junior Europeans. Although they carried nothing, they were the most tired of all. The leaders went ahead with two bearers. They were given wicked-looking blades of Spanish manufacture to cut through the bush to the sea.

"The machetes will make us a path," he told Sasha as they walked behind the slashing bearers. "It's much easier than trying to find the path we used on our inland journey."

"That's true," she replied. "The path is probably bushed over by now anyway, even if we could find it."

All of a sudden the Captain came to a halt, sniffed the air, and frowned.

"What is it, sir?"

"Smoke," he said after a moment's hesitation. Then he swore, and called out to the slashing bearers to redouble their efforts.

"Is there something wrong? Smoke could be anything."

"Not with tar-pitch in it!" he shot back. "That's the smell of a burning ship, Sasha. Follow me. We're going through!"

Through the dense undergrowth they went, right behind the slashers, bending brush out of the way that had not been swept or cut aside. Finally, as one of the slashing bearers seemed a trifle slow, Tousaint took the machete from him and began wielding it himself. He had picked up several of these blades in the Americas, and knowing their value, had kept them sharpened and oiled. But the African bush dulled them very quickly, as the bearers had discovered.

Then at last they were among the palms, and it was from there that they first noticed, in the falling dusk, the red glow of flames.

With a cry, Tousaint rushed the last few yards and broke through to the beach. Sasha was only a few steps behind her captain. Then, at the shore, they both halted and stared.

Before them lay the island, an island in flames.

Smoke rose from Fort St. Francois above the harbor. Smoke came from a ship burning in the harbor itself. Flames seemed to be engulfing even the humble huts of the islanders, and there was a red glow off the Stone House. Figures darted in and out, but it was impossible to tell from that distance who they were, or what they were shouting.

"My ship!" Tousaint roared. "Where in hell is my ship?"

Hesitatingly, Sasha pointed to the far side of the harbor, where a ship lay aground, its masts shot away.

"That's not mine," the Captain growled. "That's a warship. Must be what's left of the *Princesse*."

Over his shoulder, in a loud voice, he called for the trailing party to come up on the double. There was silence in the thickets. The bearers had either run or they were being uncommonly slow. No matter. Either way they would confront the tired Europeans who were trailing them, and those tired men would have muskets to persuade them to turn their course or speed up on it.

For a moment he couldn't find Sasha. Then, looking up the beach, he saw her, scurrying for some destination he couldn't see. He followed, quickly, and a few moments later came upon her pushing at a small boat that had been drawn up on the shore. He was puzzled by its existence. It wasn't the waterboat and there was no evidence of ownership.

"Hold off," he called. "We can signal the island, and they can send us a boat. That looks like it might have been abandoned for a reason."

Sasha, panting, shook her head violently.

"I will get us there, *M'sieu*, if I have to row the boat myself. If it leaks I shall plug the leaks. That's my home, burning over there. Will you help me?"

Tousaint looked from her to the island, then back to her. Finally he nodded his head slowly.

"I haven't pulled an oar in some years, Sasha," he said as he joined her in pushing the boat to sea. "But I haven't forgotten how."

Chapter Fifteen

Maurice de Gennes, propped up on cushions in one of the alcoves of the Stone House, waited patiently while the *signaré* Arsene finished cutting his meat for him. When the pieces were bite-sized, he thanked her and fell to his breakfast. The assistance Arsene rendered hadn't been a courtesy but a necessity, for while de Gennes' right hand was still reliable, his left was not. There was, in fact, no longer a hand at all. The wide swaths of bandage around his left arm, or what remained of it, did nothing to conceal this fact.

Sitting around the curve of the table, Captain Tousaint restrained himself. Normally he ate with great dispatch even when he wasn't hungry, and he was hungry now. But he was determined not to outpace his companion.

"What do you think, Tousaint?" de Gennes asked after a lengthy silence. "Would you advise a hook, or a ball?"

Tousaint smiled. "You're young, Captain. I'd advise... flexibility. A steel cap, with a threaded indentation, perhaps. Then you could screw in a hook, or a ball, or anything else, as needed."

"Ah! I hadn't thought of that. But then, I really haven't given much thought to the matter. After all, I'm right-handed, so this is more of an inconvenience than a catastrophe."

Tousaint smiled again. "If you say so."

"Oh, I do. My ship's in worse shape than I am. And it will be hard to replace the men I lost... good ones. Why is it always the good ones who get hit? But we took care of the matter at hand. The island still lives."

"*Oui,*" Tousaint said softly. Although one might debate the status of the *Princesse* or its captain, de Gennes was right about the island; it did still live.

Gorée was indeed in good shape, much better shape than it had appeared to Tousaint and Sasha from the mainland shore. Most of the fire they had sighted had produced a lot of smoke and some spectacular flames, but little structural damage. The islanders' huts were, for the most part, intact; three of them on fire had made it seem as though all of them were engulfed. Sasha's Stone House was largely undamaged, also, and the two forts, creations of earth and stone, had taken little more than superficial damage. The island looked bad, scorched, but structurally was very sound.

By contrast, the *Princesse,* with its masts restored and hull repaired, seemed quite fit and ready for any new expedition. However, the truth of the matter was that without major repairs, it might never sail the again. The warship had taken the brunt of the English surprise attack, engaging both the *Rochester* and two armed merchant vessels, while the French merchant vessels made their escape to the north. Hot and cold shot had gone through the timbers, and while little of this damage was visible from the outside, the inside resembled a slaughterhouse.

Fifteen men had died below the *Princesse's* decks, and another score had been injured. The sudden arrival of the *Sieur de la Roque* and coincident damage to one of the English merchantmen, however, had saved *the Princesse* from further damage. The English Captain Mayne had called for a retreat.

One French merchant vessel had remained to assist de Gennes, and that had been Tousaint's. By contrast, those captains who had remained aboard their vessels and sent subordinates to accompany Tousaint proved quite willing to abandon their junior officers. Not even the sight of the ships of the *Sieur de la Roque* had persuaded them to turn around. When a furious Andre Bruie, trailing the warships, had signalled them to reverse course and return to the island, they had ignored him.

In all of this, as usual, the ruling principle for a captain was supposed to be the safety of his ship. Tousaint didn't pretend to judge his fellow captains. Quite possibly it would be an Admiralty court that did this, at some later date.

But this course of thought did remind him of a question he had meant to ask.

"Has Bruie been to see you this morning?"

"Briefly," de Gennes replied. A sudden movement made him wince, but he covered it with a smile. "Bruie is a bit preoccupied, as you may imagine."

"Truly. How's his temper?"

"Not as vile as when he arrived, or so I'm told. I wasn't there to greet him. They tell me I passed out."

Tousaint let a chuckle escape him. He shook his head in mild wonder. De Gennes had passed out all right, on his quarterdeck from loss of blood, moments after beaching his ship in order to save it. The crew of the *Princesse* had carried him to the Stone House, while the other wounded were brought only as far as the fort. Islanders were making them as comfortable as possible under the circumstances. Old Mama-Lise, shuffling her great bulk from bed to bed, had been dispensing some vile-smelling and vile-tasting African remedies. If they were half as potent as they smelled, they would certainly help.

"No doubt," de Gennes said, "You're wondering if he asked me about La Roque and his intentions."

Tousaint nodded. "La Roque didn't give him any clue, from what I understand. All he said was that he was headed for the Gambia. I don't imagine having warships fleeing in front of him would have made a material difference in his plans at that point. But we still don't know whether it's to be raid or conquest."

"That was what Bruie wondered about. Well, La Roque did

174

sail with my father, against Fort James, so he does know the weak points of the place. But I don't know his orders."

"And if he were left to his own discretion, you think?"

De Gennes laughed. "He would storm it and this time burn it to the ground. We should never have let them have it back intact, after the last peace."

"No doubt they thought there were good reasons at the time."

"Oh, no doubt. But you are to see Bruie today?"

"Yes, when he's through with his morning appointment."

"Morning appointment?" de Gennes repeated with a frown. "Not even Lieutenant Drouin takes up half a day on our Chief Factor, Tousaint. Who's seeing him?"

"Sasha, of course."

"Oh, yes, of course. Well, no doubt important island affairs must be addressed. He may spare you a few minutes, eh?"

"Perhaps. Many adjustments must be made. I fear many of us have grown soft, de Gennes. We're not used to war."

The young warship captain smiled. "I am."

Andre Bruie closed his calipers, put them away in his desk, and carefully rolled up the large map that had been spread across his desktop. He put it back beneath the side table that held the other map rolls, poured himself a glass of wine, and refilled the one that sat before Sasha.

"So," he said, "You see the situation. We're in for very rough times."

"I see that," Sasha replied quietly. "Much seems to depend on how long this war with the English lasts.

Bruie allowed himself a thin smile. "You are perceptive, as usual. But the difficulty is that we don't know how long the war will last. It may even be over in the homelands before the last few battles are fought along this coast." His face wore a sour expression. "Not that it would matter to *them*. They know little of our situation, and care even less. One has to be on the spot to realize how important this island is to France."

He paused to fix Sasha with his searching gaze. It developed into a stare. She continued to look back at him.

"Your people were most helpful during the attack," he said at last. "Drouin and de Gennes both remarked on their assistance in their reports. I gather your people helped us for a number of reasons, not the least of which that they thought you would have expected them to do so."

"Truly?" she replied. "If so, they were correct."

"That is, of course, commendable. But I'm a curious man. I must know the reason why."

"Reason? Isn't it reason enough for people to defend their homes?"

"Ordinarily, more than sufficient. However, I can't overlook the fact that some islanders, yourself excluded, of course, believe a deal might be made with the English. A deal to secure a more favorable situation, perhaps. After all, though the English may act like it sometimes, they're not pirates. They might like to come here and stay."

Sasha smiled. "And who would speak to them?"

"Perhaps you."

"Me? *M'sieu* Bruie, it's taken me most of my life to learn how to speak French properly. Only now am I beginning to be able to read it well. I would hardly be able to deal with the English until I knew the tongue. All I know now is its curses."

Bruie smiled, a trifle more fully than before.

"You prefer the devil you know?"

"I always prefer what I know to what I don't. This seems pointless, sir. We are all with you in this war."

Bruie nodded. "I accept that, and I'm gratified. But I'm not so much concerned with the goodwill at present, but with its maintenance in the face of some very pressing necessities."

"We're used to hardship."

"That's not what I mean. I doubt that Gorée will be attacked again, at least directly. It's the indirect that concerns me."

"Indirect?"

"This island's importance is based on trade. The war might interrupt that trade. Especially if word gets round the mainland tribes that the English can, and may, attack us at any time. Africans who were once eager to deal with us, on our terms, may suddenly take it into their heads to drive harder bargains. To play us off, in fact, against the English."

Sasha considered the matter. After a while she spoke.

"The kings and the Arab traders respect power," she said. "They despise its absence. As long as they see us strong, they will not try to change the rules in their favor."

Bruie smiled. "And we are strong?"

"We still have that appearance. The English didn't land, truly. French warships, in fact, drove them off, and pursued them. If we continue to carry out trade as in the past, if we meet the traders at the coast points, and show no fear...we will prevail."

Bruie frowned. "You're suggesting that we meet the caravans on the Little Coast as before? We risk a sudden English raid."

"Yes, but isn't the risk worth it? As opposed to the risks of losing? If we try to redirect the trade to a place the French can control more easily, we lose respect."

Bruie, silent for a moment, considered a number of things. He had been Chief Factor for many years now, and as far as trading went, there was little left for him to learn. He knew Saint-Louis, he knew Gorée, he knew the Petit-Cote and the kings and traders of the inland. He could even claim, in almost any company, to know Africa better than any European of his time. But he knew it from the outside. He was not of it.

He brought his hand down on the desk.

"So be it. We will play the strong hand, Sasha, and not worry about the possible arrival of rude visitors. Now tell me, what of this young Ghoul, who runs his late father's slave-trading enterprise? Truly, he does seem to be his father's son!"

He was an unremarkable man, with an unremarkable face, scarred only lightly despite his years, which had to be more than fifty. He sat on an unremarkable-looking piece of furniture, a three-legged stool, and around him were unremarkable people who seemed to fade into the background whenever an observer's eye came to rest upon them. Yet, when Hadithe Zakale finished his tale and patted his drum one last time, he inclined his head in as respectful a bow as a storyteller ever made, for the man who sat on the stool was the Asantahene, Opuku Ware, Chief of the Kumasi, King of Ashanti. Opuku Ware nodded his head, and smiled.

"Well done, Sir Storyteller. Once again you have spoken so as to touch the higher truth, and have made our hearts glad."

"I am pleased that this is so."

"Now enough of the formalities," the king said. "You and the brave woman who accompanies you are always welcome guests in this house. Be good enough to enter, and take your ease, until I can get away from my duties and come to you."

Hadithe Zakale bowed his head again, and without another word walked away from the King Stool and the man who sat on it. He walked, with Helene-Marie beside him, into the large thatched-roof building off to the king's right side. There was no trace of tension in Hadithe Zakale, and though Helene-Marie was nervous, as always she was determined not to let that nervousness show.

Behind them a dance began, and the sounds of many drums marked the pace of their steps.

Inside, as they had expected, was a reception committee: A man and a woman, designated to split up the two for the moment; to take Helene-Marie to the Women's Parlor and to hold Hadithe Zakale in the front part, the Men's Parlor. The storyteller did not recognize the woman who greeted them, but it seemed Helene-Marie did, for the two went off laughing. He did, however, recognize the male greeter, for it was his old companion.

"It's good to see you," he said to Sokolo. "I see by your badges that you've made your way to the right place. You are senior messenger."

"Senior messenger?" Sokolo grunted. "Precious little do I

carry these days in the way of messages, teller of tales. They hold me to court, now, and have me training others." He paused, then waved his hand around the room. "You know most of us, I imagine, if your eyes have pulled far enough away from daylight."

Hadithe Zakale squinted. His eyes were indeed growing accustomed to the changed light, although perhaps not as quickly as they would have once. He recognized one figure almost immediately, for he was a mere wisp of a man, aged, bent, thin, almost a caricature of Death. But he was still very much alive, and wore a young man's amused grin.

"Greetings, Anokye," Hadithe Zakale said. "It's good that you still live."

"And good that you do likewise," the old magician replied sharply. "Despite the careless neglect of health that is so typical of storytellers." He broadened his grin. "I have only gums left, but I would guess they're harder than the teeth in *your* head."

"My teeth still bite, Old One, but they are more careful than they used to be."

Anokye the magician chuckled, and fell silent, as Hadithe Zakale sat down in the men's circle. Others gave their greetings, some that the storyteller remembered from previous visits, some that he didn't remember and had to place in the court hierarchy from their badges and decorations. It seemed odd to him that they were all, in one way or another, trainers of the young. It was understandable in the cases of Sokolo and Anokye, of course, for one had proclaimed himself a trainer and the other had been so for a long time. But there was also the Asantahene's master of arms, and masters of the various weapons.

Still, Hadithe Zakale found himself concentrating on the oldest of them, Anokye. He was the ruling presence, which was natural enough, for it had been Anokye who had established the Kumasi as leaders of Ashanti. It was he who had made the Stool of Royalty descend as if from heaven for the King to sit on. That king had been Osei Tutu, and now he served his nephew and successor, Opuku Ware, just as faithfully.

"You stare at me, young storyteller."

Hadithe Zakale shook his head. "I watch you, old sir. There are many stories in you."

"No doubt. But the story of the Captive Prince is perhaps the one we are all thinking of today."

Hadithe Zakale was surprised to hear this, for it was a tale he had deliberately not told on this visit. It was the story of Opuku Ware's son, the one who'd been captured and later murdered by the slave-trader called the Ghoul. The teller of tales had told it once on de-mand, some years ago, and it had left Opuku Ware in tears. Hadithe Zakale would not tell that story among the Ashanti again, unless by specific command.

"We are all trainers," Anokye said. "We are right now all training one man, a young man, for a special mission." The old man coughed. "I tell you this, storyteller, because if I did not do so, you would guess it for yourself eventually. It's best, however, that we speak no more of it at this time."

Hadithe Zakale looked long and searchingly into the old man's eyes. Then it came upon him, a thought that made him shiver. Yes, he understood.

On the shores of the Little Coast, halfway between the mouths of the Senegal and the Gambia, a large Persian rug was spread on the sand. It served as the seating-place for two men who sat cross-legged facing each other. Their retainers stood back, at a respectful but useful distance. On the one side, stood two bearded Arabs with curved swords. On the other side, two giant Africans with crippled feet called Samson and Hercule.

"This is good," said the Arab who sat. "At last I meet the famous Andre Bruie. It's about time I was given to deal with some-thing other than stupid ship captains."

He said this last with a malevolent glance, not at Bruie but at Captain Tousaint. Tousaint was some yards back behind the rug, standing with Sasha, and though he heard what was said, he didn't betray any feelings by word or gesture. Bruie, though, smiled at the Arab, pleasantly enough.

"You have five hundred and some slaves to sell," Bruie noted.

"*Monsieur!*" Khalil the Pilgrim cried in mock astonishment. "I thought you were aware of the proprieties. We are not ready to discuss business yet."

"Yes, yes, one must exchange questions. But you see, Pilgrim, I have no desire to waste valuable time asking after the health of one who would be better dead."

The face with the oily expression darkened perceptibly. "You insult me, dog? I will have your heart's blood."

"Not while my men are close enough to spill yours, Pilgrim. You will deal with me, and you will do so now, sparing insults and false compliments both. Or we will go away, and you can do what you like with your slaves. Feed them, water them, or impale them on stakes."

A sneer crossed Khalil's face. "The English will buy."

"Then let them. I will show you the English, soon enough." Bruie stood up, kicked the edge of the carpet, and wiped his feet on it before stepping off onto the sand. "I came to do business, Pilgrim. You are indeed a young man, if you want to play games like this instead. I offer an ounce of gold for each of your captives. Get a better bargain if you can."

"Two ounces," Khalil snapped.

"I didn't come to bargain, Pilgrim. Take it or leave it."

Khalil the Pilgrim stood up suddenly, sweeping his flowing robe around him.

"Then I leave it! No Christian dog plays with me."

Bruie chuckled, looking the man in the eye, for they were about the same height.

"Deal with the English, Pilgrim."

"I shall," the Arab said, spitting on the ground. "They will come by here soon enough. I have already sent messengers. When your Sieur de la Roque came against him at the Gambia, they killed him. Oh, yes, I am well aware of that!"

Bruie smiled. "That's true enough. It was a stray cannon shot, but the sort of thing one must expect in war. However, the second in command, St. Vaudrille, beat the English and took a hundred thousand crowns in booty, not to mention two hundred fifty slaves."

"You lie, French dog!"

"He also took another token of his conquest," Bruie added.

"Token? You speak riddles."

Bruie waved a hand backward, which was understood by those behind him. A young man of the crew of the *Princesse* brought forward a large sack, as big as a wine keg. He had to drag it most of the way. On Bruie's signal, he opened the sack and dumped its contents at the Pilgrim's feet. The Pilgrim roared a mighty oath that certainly would have offended Allah. The sack's contents consisted of forty-seven whitened skulls.

"You dog! Filthy swine! May your mother rot in the shithouse where she bore you!"

"No doubt," Bruie remarked pleasantly, "the same place where you learned to eat pork."

Khalil al-Ghul, the Pilgrim, burning in face and in stomach, tried to stare Andre Bruie down. He was a hard man, this Ghoul, but his was a hollow, brittle kind of hardness. It was breaking up against a hardness that was both real and substantial. One scratches the bully to find the coward, Bruie mused.

"One ounce," the Ghoul snarled.

"I should now make it half an ounce," Bruie said with as oily a smile as he could manage. "But in the interest of good trade relations, one ounce it is."

Chapter Sixteen

Silently, Mama-Lise set a large bowl of porridge and a small bowl of nuts before old Gilbert, the water skiff captain. Despite her size, and the narrow passages she had to navigate, she moved with apparent ease, for this was her own hut, and the small table where the old man sat was the place where she herself usually ate alone. The light in the room was strong and heavy with contrasts, for there was but one window for the sunlight to pour through.

As she sat down to join him over the bowls she had prepared for herself, Gilbert reached down into the small satchel he had brought along. From it, he produced a bottle. Mama-Lise's eyes widened, and a shocked exclamation escaped her lips.

"Wine! Where did you get this, Gilbert?"

The old man smiled. "A present from the Lieutenant, some time ago. It has been sitting around for too long. We shouldn't let it take the chance of spoiling, truly?"

A trifle reluctantly, the old woman shook her head.

"This is good of you, Gilbert, but it's been a long time since

183

I had wine, and I've always had a weak head for it."

"Well, I too can get by with very little. But a taste, Elise."

She nodded. "A taste, then."

For a while they ate and drank in silence, somewhat more than a taste flowing from the wine bottle. At last, when the food was gone and only the wine remained, Mama-Lise spoke again.

"This is an occasion, then, Gilbert? You don't often visit me. And now you come bringing wine, perhaps to addle my wits? I must satisfy myself as to your intentions, sir."

The old man chuckled. "Perhaps somewhat different from what I might have intended, some years ago, in bringing wine to a woman's hut. But we have each seen a lot of life, Elise. What happens to us, or between us, would concern no one but ourselves. I'm concerned about others, who haven't lived quite as long."

The old woman nodded. They had been speaking in French, as was their habit, although both were at home in the island dialect and each had spoken Portuguese in youth. Speaking in French, naturally, they required gestures to accompany the words. Mama-Lise's were perhaps heavier and somewhat more expressive than Gilbert's.

"What troubles you, Gilbert? Certainly things seem to be going well. The French have drubbed the English, carrying away gold as well as slaves from the wreckage of Fort James. They don't have the strength to retaliate. And Bruie has acquired all the slaves the Ghoul brought down to the coast, at the cheapest of prices. One would almost think he had frightened the Arab, no?"

Gilbert nodded gravely.

"I, too, might be wary at the sight of so many skulls. I wonder where Sasha got them?"

The old woman shook her head. "I have no idea. Of course, you and I both know the French took no English captives, and wouldn't have slaughtered them like that if they had. The skulls probably came from one of the kings along the coast. Little matter, of course. Hard to tell an Englishman from a Dinka, when the skin's off."

"I would think it would be difficult. But then, I'm only a simple carpenter and water-runner, who keeps posted on the comings and goings of ships."

"Ah!" Mama-Lise said at once. "So that's it. What's coming, then, Gilbert? Another English warship? I suppose it would find good plunder here, if it were interested in slaves. We have so many on this island now...but warships are not equipped to handle slaves."

"That's not my concern."

"Pirates, then? I look at you now, and I am sure of it."

"On the contrary, Elise. I'm concerned because there are *no* ships coming."

Mama-Lise frowned. "No ships? But that's impossible. The French have cargo waiting for them, and we can't keep so many slaves here for very long. Surely Bruie has sent word for company packets to come, if not independent traders."

"I'm sure he has. In fact, I know he has. But it seems those ships that fled when the English attacked brought tales of horror to the French. No doubt they exaggerated to cover their own cowardice. But whatever the case, the independent traders have been frightened off. And even the company, it seems, is waiting for things to settle down."

"Gilbert," she said reprovingly, "these things don't come from your usual sources. You've been eavesdropping."

"I would have done so if there was such an opportunity," he said. "But in fact, I trade information with the Lieutenant and sometimes with Bruie. It's from my usual sources, as you call them, that I know no ships are now coming. It's from the French that I know why. It may be two or three months before any summon the courage to come, Elise."

"But that is...I see. Meanwhile we must feed and water these slaves. I don't know their number, but they pack the lower fort and some are now held in the warehouse. There have never been as many, in my time. You'll be making many water-runs."

"Runs for water, runs for food. Even so, we won't be able to keep up with the demand. As you say, we can't keep that many here for very long."

The old woman fixed her eyes on the old man.

"There will be trouble."

"I'm sure of it."

"You've heard what, mutterings?"

"Nothing definite, no. I know a little of the Dinka speech, and our largest group of slaves is the Dinka captives. They're restless. Bruie and Drouin will keep them busy, of course. There will be more stone buildings around here shortly. But meanwhile, Elise, I believe you should think about moving the creche to the upper fort. If there is trouble, it would grieve me to see the children caught in the middle of it."

Mama-Lise grunted. "If anyone attacks the children, they will have to deal with me first. But you're right. I, too, have seen a lot of life, and am not all I used to be. Is Sasha aware of this?"

"I believe so. Perhaps she's not aware of the implications." He smiled. "She has many things on her mind these days, and perhaps one day she may regret that she took on her large burden so suddenly."

The old woman laughed. "Shall I say it would serve her right? She was young, and eager for control, and now she has it. It was different in our time, Gilbert."

"To a degree. I recall that you, Elise, once had all the answers... as did I."

The old woman frowned. "You're comparing me to Sasha? We might yet quarrel, Gilbert, which would be a pity. I was never like her."

Gilbert held up his hands, still smiling.

"I seek no quarrel, Elise, but there was a time when you dealt with the Portuguese as strongly as she now deals with the French."

"That may be so, but for different objectives."

"Yes, that's true. Sasha simply has more imagination, then."

"And little conscience."

Gilbert shook his head.

"It's there, Elise, never doubt it. It may be sleeping, as she deals with all the affairs of this wider world she lives in now. But, it will come forward one day... perhaps in a way she doesn't like. At any rate," he added, reaching for the bottle, "you might want to think about putting in an order for a stone house, while the opportunity is there."

At which they both laughed, and finished the wine.

Andre Bruie, shoving stacks of paper from one side of his desk to the other, cast a measuring glance at his visitors. His eye fell first on Drouin, then on Sasha, and finally came to rest on Captain de Gennes.

"What do you think, Captain?" Bruie asked. "Am I too old to get a commission in the naval service?"

De Gennes smiled. "I'm sure you could have it for the asking, sir. But you've made a great career with the company. Why would you throw it away to eat salt water with the likes of us?"

"Because I might grow to like the taste of salt water, de Gennes, sooner than put up with dealing with cowards. Damn them! I would have thought at least LeClerc would have had the guts to show his face and ship in our harbors by now!" He frowned. "You are sure there's no possibility of an English attack?"

De Gennes shook his head. "There's always the possibility. But given the commitments the English have already made in this war, it would be extremely foolish of them to come down here and waste ships on what must be, to them, essentially a sideshow. Even revenge or restitution aren't sufficient motives. And I never assume the enemy to be foolish."

Bruie smiled. "Of course not. But you must allow for the possibility."

"True. I also allow for the possibility of lightning striking one of us dead within the quarter-hour."

Bruie wore a sour face.

"There are a lot of people around here who seem to assume that if something is possible, then it will happen."

"That's their problem."

187

"And mine too, as long as I must depend upon them." His eyes fell on Sasha, and held.

"Is there something you would ask?" she inquired.

"Need I do so?"

"Perhaps not," she said after a moment. "Am I to guarantee that the people of the island will stand fast, even if there's trouble? I can do that, sir, but you could make life easier for all of us, *Monsieur*."

"And how is that?"

"We must keep the slaves occupied," she said. Bruie stared at her. "Sasha...we're doing that. In point of fact, we're keeping them occupied for a great part on tasks you yourself have thought up. Quarrying and building, pulling and hauling. Are you thinking even now of adding to your own list?"

Sasha shook her head quickly.

"No, *M'sieu*. The situation is satisfactory at the moment. We of the island are doing extra work to feed and water these people, but since they are, in their turn, making things better for us, it works out well. However, the rainy season will be coming shortly, and that will be the end of the quarrying and building for a time."

Bruie saw her point. It had occurred to him in passing, but it was different to have it driven home.

"Ah. Then at that time, the islanders will still have to feed and water the slaves, and we'll see that they're getting nothing for it."

"That's minor, sir. It is the slaves I worry about. They'll have to be kept confined. There will then be nothing to occupy their time but their own thoughts. These thoughts may not be useful."

"No doubt. Well, Drouin? You have the same problem with soldiers, during the rainy season. You still manage to keep them busy."

"That's true," Drouin said. "It is always necessary to keep troops occupied. But troops can be put to tasks that prisoners cannot. I see what Sasha is getting at, sir. There's really little that we're equipped to use these slaves for, except what they're doing now. When the rain ends that occupation, they'll be idle, unless someone has ideas."

"Well, damn it," Bruie exploded in the silence that followed, "somebody better have some ideas!"

"Ease the crowding," Sasha said promptly. "Get some of them off the island. At least enough to make it so none of them has to be confined to the warehouse."

"That's impossible," Bruie replied. "We've thought of shipping some to Saint-Louis, but we have no ships. And even though one or two of the local kings might buy a few for their own purposes, we couldn't afford to sell them at the bargain prices those kings would insist on getting. No!" he said finally, his hand falling to slap the table decisively. "We'll keep them working until the ships come. Even if the rains come first, we'll keep them working."

His measuring glance ran across the room again. The faces were blank. But Bruie didn't care. He was determined, and his determination had made up for others' lack of enthusiasm in stranger circumstances than these.

The midwife was a tall, thin, old woman, and lecture was more her way than discussion. Helene-Marie heard her out, indicating her understanding and agreement at the appropriate points. She waited a long time after the old woman left the Ashanti King's guest house to rise from her cushioned couch. Slowly, she crossed over the room and took a seat across from Hadithe Zakale at the table.

The storyteller smiled at her.

"You don't seem impressed," he said.

"She's very good," Helene-Marie said quickly. "She knows things about preparing for childbirth that I, for one, wish I'd known when I was dealing with pregnant women back on the island. But perhaps I'm just not used to all this attention."

"It was inevitable," he replied. "She's the senior of the three midwives at Court. Once Opuku Ware found out what was in the winds, he insisted on putting her on your case."

"I understand that. But women are always having children. Do Ashanti princesses really follow such a strict regimen as she suggests I observe?"

The teller of tales laughed. "I imagine they do, when they can't avoid it. It is hard to separate what is really necessary from what's just tradition and superstition. But I'd be pleased if, as far as possible, you would do what she asks."

Helene-Marie nodded. "I shall." Then she hesitated. "Has she told you anything she hasn't told me?"

Hadithe Zakale's eyebrows went up a bit.

"Told *me* ? Midwives don't speak to mere men, Helene-Marie. Except to tell them to get out of the way."

"I wonder," she said, "if that applies to the King as well?"

"Hardly. But then, the Ashanti don't regard their King as a mere man. He, like his throne-stool, is supposed to have descended from the gods. As is thought of most kings, I imagine."

Abruptly she changed the subject.

"What will you do today?"

"I have to spend some time with the young man called Tasso," he replied. "There's also an entertainment tonight, for which I must prepare an appropriate tale."

Helene-Marie nodded. Before Hadithe Zakale left, she was back on her couch, trying to make herself at ease on the cushions. He had a feeling that she wouldn't remain there quite as long as the midwife had demanded.

On his way to the King's training ground, Hadithe Zakale stopped a moment by a well to refresh himself with a drink. As he lifted the cup to his lips, he felt a slight vibration in the air; felt it or heard it, he wasn't sure. Cautiously, he sniffed the air. Yes, there was a certain tang to it, and although there were no clouds visible in the west, they had to be somewhere not far over the horizon. In a short while, and for a short while, the Ashanti would not have to depend on wells for water.

At the training ground, he found the master-at-arms called Shakar working with the young man Tasso. Sokolo, the messenger, looked on. Hadithe Zakale took a seat by his old companion, and together they watched the warriors go through their paces.

Shakar was master of the short knife, and of its use in close combat. Normally he trained his pupils with dummy knives, but today, Hadithe Zakale saw, it was a full-dress drill with real weapons. Both Shakar and Tasso were armed with thin blades about seven inches long. Even from where he and Sokolo sat, Hadithe Zakale could tell that the knives being used were not European trade articles, the kind which armed most of the Ashanti. They were of African manufacture, with distinctive hilts, forged, probably, by an ironworker in Dahomey.

Both Tasso and his trainer wore wide padded belts about their bellies, for this was the target area. Already the padding on each was ripped in a few places, with threads dangling. It was, of course, very dangerous training, and a slip could be fatal. The trainer would not, however, permit a full-dress drill until he was as sure of his pupil as he was of himself.

The lesson ended abruptly. The master-at-arms broke off, saluted Sokolo, and departed without saying anything to Tasso, who came over and sat down beside the older men. He was in his late teens, with all of the youthful energy characteristic of that age. He was sweating a bit, but he wasn't even breathing hard.

"It seems you have almost mastered the knife," the storyteller observed.

"I believe I'm doing well, sir," was the young man's response. He smiled up at the storyteller. "Do I hear a tale today, or a geography lesson?"

Hadithe Zakale laughed. "The latter, Tasso, I fear. But I'll dress it up a bit, so the medicine will go down more easily."

It was an unusual role for Hadithe Zakale, but it was a command performance. And for once he had a colleague, for it was Sokolo's task to take over when Hadithe Zakale's description of the Western territory touched on matters of more concern to a warrior than to a teller of tales.

Later, returning the way he had come and stopping by the same well for another drink, Hadithe Zakale noticed that a thin line

191

of purple had emerged at the western horizon. He felt himself shudder. Of course, the rainy season was coming. In fact it was long overdue, and it was nothing more than a natural phenomenon. Hadithe Zakale had been too long in the world, and seen too much, to have any real superstitions. But he was of Africa, and he was not one to totally disregard omens

He had to admit his worries. There were some grounds for them. He hadn't lied to Helene-Marie about the midwife, for indeed she hadn't spoken a word to him. It was the Ashanti King's doctor who had spoken to him, after reviewing Helene-Marie's history: the complications of her last child-bearing, and the long interval since. This pregnancy might be dangerous, for her and for the child.

And even if all went well, what would be the child's fate? He had to wonder about that. How did a wandering storyteller provide, for instance, for a girl's future? Or steer a boy's? The storyteller's thoughts shifted to Tasso.

Perhaps, Hadithe Zakale thought, that was what was really bothering him. The young man called Tasso was being trained as few men ever were, and could put that training to good use in the field. But he was not destined for that. He was to go on a special mission, which would probably be his death.

In a way, Hadithe Zakale felt himself responsible for this. It was he who had told Sokolo the details of what had happened to Opuku Ware's son. It was he who had told him of the Arab trader known as the Ghoul. Sokolo also had a part in the story-telling, of course, but it was Hadithe Zakale who supplied the details. Now the King had declared, as he was bound to do, that he would have blood for blood.

It made no difference that the original Ghoul was dead, and none whatsoever that the Ghoul's son had been the hand that murdered him. Some day soon, Khalil the Pilgrim would find Tasso beside him, and feel Tasso's short knife probe his guts.

Hadithe Zakale sighed, and left the well for home. It was, of course, justice. But it was also a waste.

The rains had already come to the island. There had been thunder at first, but it was brief. It was more like a hurricane in some respects than a thunderstorm. The winds were high and the rain fell in sheets, attacking the thin soil, turning it to light mud, and washing a great deal of it away in rivulets and puddles. Huts were shut up. The lower fort was shuttered. Dawn had not brought much light.

But in the Stone House there was plenty of light, and even laughter pealing in the heavily curtained alcoves. The party of the night before was breaking up with breakfast, and all attention was focused on one visitor, the object of the festivities and the guest of honor.

He was a short, dumpy fellow, by name Gustave Colbert, in his middle fifties; hardly the sort of man to cut a dashing figure among the *signarés* . But whatever else he might or might not be, he was a ship's captain, and that was what counted. His ship, the *Largesse*, had come into port unexpectedly just as the rains began. And its cargo holds were fitted to carry slaves— large numbers of them.

Colbert, now somewhat heavy with wine, had taken it all as his due. It amused Maurice de Gennes to see the contrast between Colbert and the company man who had come with him from Saint-Louis. Andre Bruie had been detained on another matter, and the Company representative on this day was the exalted clerk, Denis Pochette, returning to the island for the first time in many months.

"No Wolof, no Fulani," the ship captain was saying solemnly to Sasha in her alcove. "Only Dinka make good slaves in the Americas."

"You've said that before, sir," Sasha replied easily, moving somewhat closer to him as if to hear his words more clearly. "But why should that be?"

"Better workers," Colbert mumbled. "Know more. Complain less. Always the same, wherever I go... Louisiana, the Dominicas. All want Dinka. If they can't have more, why, they'll wait and breed them on their own, rather than take your Wolof. Your Wolof makes a sorry slave. Yes indeed, a sorry, sorry slave."

"I don't think I understand you," Sasha said. "About breeding. How do you mean?"

Colbert laughed, a big, roaring laugh for a small man, the only thing in fact that was sailor-like about him.

"Why, my dear, you take a male slave, and put him to a female slave, and in about nine months you usually get another slave. Just like with cattle, no?"

Sasha frowned. "I hadn't thought of it that way. Here in Africa, the children of slaves are not automatically and forever slaves themselves."

The booming laugh came again.

"How you talk, my dear girl! What else could they be?" He belched. "But enough of such talk. Let's have more wine instead. I leave the arrangements to my crew and to *Monsieur* Pochette here. You hear me, Pochette? Don't try to slip any Wolof in on me."

Pochette, who had deliberately not been drinking wine, stifled a sigh.

"Captain, I assure you the cargo you selected yesterday will be exactly what's loaded aboard your ship this morning. As a matter of fact, the loading will begin shortly, if you would care to see it."

Colbert shook his head as if to clear it. "It can't be dawn already!"

"The rains darken the skies, sir. But yes, it's dawn."

De Gennes tugged unobtrusively at Pochette's sleeve, and the latter turned to him.

"You're sure all is ready? No need to call Drouin back from the upper fort?" The lieutenant was customarily on hand, with his soldiers, at loadings.

Pochette shook his head. "I've taken care of things. No need to worry."

De Gennes was satisfied. Once again it had been a case of nothing happening and then everything happening at once. On the very day the *Largesse* had come in, the first rains had revealed a hidden weakness in the walls of the upper fort; revealed it by washing out the foundations of a wall, causing it to collapse. Drouin had quickly assembled a crew to repair the walls, rains or no, for after all it was wartime. He had also left word that he was to be called back for the actual loading of captives. De Gennes and Pochette, however, thought Drouin's return unnecessary, and took on the responsibility themselves.

Most of what was coming would be routine, anyway. The slaves selected by Colbert on the previous day were now housed in the most secure part of the fort. They had survived a thorough inspection, being forced to run, jump, do various other exercises and to show their teeth. Now there was another ordeal ahead of them before the agony of the trip: They would have to be branded. This was done just before they boarded ship.

De Gennes didn't need to sigh to show his relief. The *Largesse*, as its name implied, was a generous ship, and generously provided. It could hold a larger cargo of slaves than any vessel the island had yet seen. It was a most welcome and unexpected relief from the overcrowding. It also opened up the route for trade again. Now that one ship had called, word would go back, and they would probably have more ships than they could handle by the time the rainy season ended.

The relief was palpable. The *signarés* arranged for an unusual rainy-season party at the Stone House as a celebration. Sasha played her part by showering attentions on the dumpy old sailor who had brought the *Largesse* into harbor. De Gennes smiled to himself. Her attentions were not as commendable as they seemed; earlier in the evening, she had given the duties to a junior *signaré* named Amy. Either Colbert didn't have a reputation for being as generous as his ship, or else the senior *signaré* was getting picky.

Pochette, at this point, disentangled himself from the crowd in Sasha's alcove, and rose as if to go. De Gennes approached him.

"Time to go, eh? I'll join you shortly. Then again... hell. Wait a second. I'll go with you."

De Gennes reached for his cloak with his good hand, and then draped the cloth casually over his left arm. The limb now ended in an iron stump which, for this occasion, was decorated with a ball rather than a hook.

Together with Pochette, de Gennes walked the last few steps through the Stone House and braced himself for the rain that would hit them as soon as they raised the curtain.

"What remains to be done?" the captain asked.

Pochette smiled. "Nothing but to check the branding irons, to make sure they're hot. I set up that operation yesterday."

"So you did," de Gennes replied, remembering something. "By the way, I did change one thing on you."

"Oh? What's that?"

"You set up the branding operation inside the fort," de Gennes said. "It's awfully close in there, what with the rains...and I remember the last loading with rain falling, the operation was moved outside. So I had that done."

"Ah. Under awnings, then, right outside the seaward door?"

"Under awnings, of course. But not by the door. I had them move the whole thing down to the docks, where there is more room."

"The docks!" Pochette burst out. "But that's in sight of the upper dungeons of the fort, and the warehouse!"

"True...what of it?"

"The slaves who are waiting can see what's happening. For all they know, it could be that we are planning to boil the men and eat them. At least the fire could be misinterpreted as that."

"You're joking."

"Not at all. It happened like that once, or so Bruie told me. That's why they moved the branding inside in the first place, and why the setup goes just outside the door if the rain isn't too heavy."

"So no one sees what awaits him until he's there on the scene, eh?" de Gennes mused. "Well, that makes sense. But I wouldn't worry about it. After all, the slaves in the upper dungeons aren't going themselves... not yet, and they're not even of the same tribe as the ones who've been chosen. Certainly they must know that by now."

"Certainly, sir, but the Wolof and Fulani hate the Dinka. They'll lose no time in passing the word down to them. Besides, the Dinka will be able to smell the fires burning. They won't know it's just for branding. We'd better get down there and move that operation back beneath the walls, before it's too late!"

De Gennes laughed. "Too late for what? Even if they got the idea we were going to cook them, what could they do about it?"

"It would make them very desperate, sir. And God only knows what desperate men are capable of doing."

De Gennes laughed again, and opened the curtain. The rain hit them both, and they moved quickly down the stairs toward the dockyards.

"Our real problem is this damn rain," de Gennes called out. "About the other, Pochette, I still say you worry too much."

Pochette didn't answer. He came to a halt instead, as if he had heard or seen something. Then de Gennes halted too, for he himself had heard something that time. The battering noise of the rain obscured it at first, but then another sound carried through it, unmistakable in its nature. It was a man's scream, the scream of a dying one, and it was followed quickly by two shots. Then came another shot, and another.

"The devil!"

"No," Pochette yelled over the rain. "The Dinka!"

De Gennes whirled on him and stared. Then, as other sounds came from the docks and the fort, he gave a quick nod.

"I beg your pardon, *M'sieu* Pochette," he said formally. Then he turned on his heel and raced down the pathway, heedless of the rain. Pochette stumbled along behind him.

Already in the distance the dockside was beginning to glow red.

Chapter Seventeen

The old man in the alcove waited patiently while Sasha changed the bandage on his hip. There were other wounded in the Stone House, and several of them were seriously hurt. Old Gilbert had merely been cut by a knife. But the old man had been very brave, and there were others to care for the rest of the invalids. Sasha had marked Gilbert out as her special case.

"I think that should do it," she said at last. "For today at least, as long as the wound doesn't get wet. You will stay here, of course."

The old man shook his head. "I must get back down to the docks."

Sasha smiled down at him. "What for, old sir? The cisterns are full by now, full to overflowing. You and your water skiff crew can take a long holiday."

Gilbert grunted. "There's work to be done on the skiff, if it has survived."

"It survives," Sasha reassured him. "Thanks to you and the three men who stood with you. It seems others among your crew were less brave."

"Not true!" Gilbert responded quickly. "They were merely away from the shore and caught unawares, unable to get back through the fighting. I don't blame them, and you shouldn't blame them either, Sasha."

Sasha, smiling again, said nothing more and moved away among the other wounded. There were enough alcoves to provide one for each. Although it had been a fierce and confused battle, there were few wounded. More lay dead: several soldiers, three crewmen from the ships, five male islanders and one *signaré*. The young Antoinette had been caught in the sudden eruption of the revolt.

As Sasha moved around the great hall, a scattering of small firearms drew her attention back to the lower fort complex. It was barely visible in the distance through the rain and smoky haze.

Sasha wasn't sure how the battle was going, perhaps less sure about what had really happened during the brief, savage encounter on the shore. Each of the wounded, her only sources of information, had seen but a portion of the conflict. Some things, however, were fairly certain.

It had all started when some of the first Dinka being led to the Door of No Return had overpowered a guard, stabbed him repeatedly, and taken his keys. While others flailed about, surprisingly agile despite their long linked chains, the first line had managed to unmanacle itself. Then it performed this service for others, interrupted by the soldiers who rushed in, stabbing and clubbing with their weapons.

That fight had been sharp, but brief. Only a few of the slaves had managed to break out into the open, and they had gone off in all different directions. One group had overturned the branding iron setup, spilling the coals and instruments. Another group had made for the nearest available boat, the water skiff, where they were fended off by Gilbert and his companions. Still, a third group had rushed upland, away from the shore, through the town, grabbing any instrument on the way that might serve as a weapon. Many islanders had had their heads crushed by these frenzied slaves.

The chaotic escape, however, was certainly without a plan.

199

Instead of seizing the Stone House, in the hope of fortifying it, they had not come near with any force. Three who made the attempt had been immediately destroyed by Sasha's attendants, Samson and Hercule.

It had all been confusion, and it might have ended quickly. But, the disturbance at the fort had drawn away some soldiers from the warehouse, where the overflow crowd of slaves had been confined. And the slaves in the warehouse had seized the opportunity, overpowering and killing their remaining guards and taking over the warehouse itself. They remained in control of it even now, though they were surrounded and cut off.

So now, everyone waited, while three white men met to consider what to do next: Drouin, de Gennes and Pochette. This fact bothered Sasha, for she was used to seeing decisions made quickly. But of course, Bruie was not around at the moment, and there appeared to be conflicting ideas on what to do next.

Meanwhile, no ships were being loaded, no slaves were being sent away, and the slaves who were not now under heavy restraints in the lower fort could be heard chanting and singing. They were under careful guard of course, but the fever of freedom was contagious.

Sasha's rounds finally brought her back to old Gilbert, propped up on pillows and looking distinctly unhappy about it all. Sasha was unsure whether he was upset because he wasn't able to get back to inspect his water skiff, or because he wasn't used to pillows.

"I had almost forgotten to thank you," she said to him, "for suggesting that Mama-Lise take the creche to the upper fort. The slaves who got away ran right through the places the children would have been. You no doubt saved many young lives, *m'zee*."

This brought a smile to the old man's face. He had second-guessed his suggestion when the first rains fell. The collapse of the upper fort wall had almost taken the temporary creche with it. Gilbert had feared he'd endangered the children to no purpose, but it was a different matter now.

"I'm glad that is so," he said. "The men in the fort went crazy. They might have done anything."

"That's true," Sasha replied. "In such cases, men seem to want to shed blood above and before all else. They didn't even attempt to rape poor Antoinette when they found her. They just cut her down like a wild animal, then hacked her to pieces."

"It's different now, though, with the ones remaining," the old man said.

"How is that, sir?"

"They are led. Yes, those in the warehouse are led. They are organized. It won't be so easy to defeat them."

Sasha stared at the old man, then quietly sat down beside him on the alcove couch.

"How do you know this, sir?"

Gilbert snorted. "My eyes may have dimmed a bit, Sasha, but my ears are still as good as a young man's. Better than most, is it not so? I know several tongues, especially Wolof, and I have heard the Wolof slaves speaking guardedly of one upon whom they would rely."

"Wolofs?" Sasha echoed doubtfully. "The whites are not fond of the Wolofs as slaves, any more than the Arabs are fond of them as captives. They make a practice of rooting out and killing any leaders who survive among Wolof captives."

"It would seem they missed one, this time," Gilbert replied. "I did warn the Lieutenant that such appeared to be the case, but the French are not frightened of any Wolofs, leaders or not."

"No, they hold them all in contempt. But perhaps for once the Arabs were wiser...or would have been. You say you didn't hear a name?"

Gilbert shook his head. "I'm sure they would not speak it, even among themselves, for fear of betrayal. But the warehouse was full of Wolofs. The Dinka, whom the French thought more dangerous, were the ones locked up in the fort."

Sasha sat for a few moments longer, mulling over what she had heard. After a while, she got up.

"Thank you, Gilbert. Please try to make yourself comfortable. I shall look at your wound again when I return."

Gilbert frowned. "Sasha, I see you are thinking of something. If I know you, it's something dangerous. This time, please, leave it to the French."

She smiled. "I might, if Bruie were here. But he is not, eh? And there are things that must be done."

Without further word, she left, taking up a cloak to fend off the rain.

"I must say that I'm not impressed," Denis Pochette said with suitable gravity in his well-chosen words. "Neither of you has an acceptable solution. Until I hear one, we shall wait. Now if you'll excuse me, I have work to do. We'll meet again this evening in the Chief Factor's office."

Drouin and de Gennes rose and bowed as the Assistant Chief Factor left the room. After Pochette left, they both sat back down, and Drouin drew out a bottle of wine with two glasses. De Gennes accepted one with a smile.

"Well! I'm glad to see that, despite our difference, I rate higher with you than the substitute Factor."

"*Merde!*" Drouin muttered as he poured. "This is too good to waste on clerks." He paused, bottle still held in hand. "He is that, you know. Whatever his title, he's still a clerk at heart."

De Gennes smiled, ruefully.

"Yes, I know. Afraid of risking damage to company property, whether it be slaves or the warehouse that contains them. Although I grant he was wiser than I, when it came to moving that damned branding setup."

"Don't berate yourself," Drouin replied with a dismissing wave of his hand. "Pochette picked that up from Bruie. It's true, I would have known to hide the thing from the slaves' view, myself, but that's in the past. We must deal with the present. And I don't think *Monsieur* Pochette has the answer."

"I agree," de Gennes replied. "At least we agree on that. But it didn't help that you and I each advocated a different approach. Perhaps if we agreed on what to do, we two together could prevail over the clerk."

Drouin shook his head.

"Little chance of that. Only Bruie could do it, I fear. Pochette, you see, is quite conscious of his authority, if not his responsibility. And he is in charge, which is rare."

"So?"

Drouin sighed. "So let's discuss it again anyway. If we do have to wait for Bruie to get here, and with the rains, that will be several days at least, we might well be wise to present a plan we both agree is valid."

De Gennes smiled. "Days, you say? You are optimistic, Marcel, and not a sailor. It might be weeks."

"I think not. I sent my message to Saint-Louis overland. If I know Bruie, he will come here at once, even if he has to travel overland himself, most of the way." The Lieutenant allowed some satisfaction to show in his smile. "He will not be slow to realize the implications of having Pochette in charge of this fiasco."

"Well, it's a rough journey...but perhaps you're right. Where shall we begin?"

Once again the men resumed their discussion of strategy and tactics. Both were professionals and each respected the other, but there was little common ground between the two.

It was Drouin's idea that the warehouse should be stormed in a sudden rush by his soldiers, after a brief cannonade to distract the slaves from the troop movements. De Gennes, on the other hand, wanted to blast the warehouse with the *Princesse's* cannon, until either that building came down on the slaves' heads or they marched out in surrender.

Of course, either plan involved a risk to company property a considerable risk. The alternative, however, was to wait and starve the slaves out, and neither Drouin nor de Gennes liked the implications of that.

So intent were they on their discussion that neither heard the approach of footsteps down the hall. But then again, the footsteps were light.

"I still say a sudden rush would do it," Drouin summed up at last.

De Gennes shook his head. "I'm sorry, old man. A cannonade would be more effective, and perhaps more impressive."

Drouin spread his hands, exasperated. "We would make an impression, true, but who would be impressed? Islanders, who don't need the impression, and slaves bound for Hell or America, not likely to come here again, in any case."

"Perhaps there's a way out of your impasse," said a quiet voice from the doorway.

Drouin needed only to look up and stare in order to recognize their visitor, but de Gennes had to turn his head. He did so with a catlike abruptness. Disliking being taken by surprise, he merely glowered at the woman in the white dress. It was Drouin who spoke.

"Sasha, it's good of you to try to help us, but it's not your place to interfere. Now let us be."

De Gennes recovered quickly from his surprise. "Oh, let her have a say," he sighed. "Everyone else has had one. So tell us, Sasha, who is right? The Lieutenant or myself? Which plan would you choose?"

Sasha, a cloak draped over her arm, and her eyes bright with determination, met de Gennes' gaze straight on without a smile.

"Neither," she said quietly. "Here is what we must do..."

The small stream ran quickly down the sloping hillside, splashing white water in some places, overflowing its narrow banks in others, and looking for all the world as if it would keep on doing so for the rest of time.

In fact, its life would be brief. It would last only as long as the heavy rains did, which in the central part of West Africa didn't promise to be a long life. It was a seasonal stream, the kind the Arabs called a *wadi* , and for most of the year it was merely a dry, caked and barren track meandering down the hillside. For this brief time, however, it was a full-fledged spillway, emptying its swollen waters at last into the larger river that ran through the village of Kumasi, the Ashanti capital.

From that stream, Sokolo the King's Senior Messenger emerged, refreshed and suddenly surprised. Approaching the lean-to shelter near the stream's edge was Hadithe Zakale, the teller of tales. Hastily, Sokolo wrapped himself in a towel, not out of modesty but out of protocol. People did not, after all, receive storytellers naked.

Then he called out, and the old man trudging through the rain came over to join him. He was clad in a cloak and little else, and that cloak was barren. He wasn't even wearing the badges of his trade this morning.

"You take a wet walk, old sir," Sokolo said after his old companion had seated himself under the lean-to. "And anyone would think you were a farmer or a herder. Incognito does not suit you."

Hadithe Zakale smiled. "Those who have a need to recognize me do so, Sokolo, badges or no. I often take a long walk the morning after a great ceremony. But what brings you here to the hills? I'm sure you could get as good a bath in the village, with people to attend you."

"Perhaps I'm the same as you," Sokolo replied. "After a great ceremony, I get tired of looking at people, especially at people who want to fuss over me. I go off by myself. I spend much time, as it is, in the company with those who know nothing of my life or my ways. It does get to be tedious." He shot a quick glance at the storyteller. "Not you, *m'zee*, of course. You know more about my life, I think, than I know myself."

Sokolo, dressed now in his own less-than-formal outfit, came over to sit beside the storyteller, drawing out a mixture of fruits and nuts from a small sack at the back of the lean-to. The small outbuilding was old, and ill-kept, even for such a structure. But it was seldom used, used only by travelers, for the most part, and then only during the rainy season.

For a while, the two men sat gazing at the stream, the waters splashing and tumbling over the rocks. Beneath the waters the thirsty earth was now sated, the cracked bed now a uniform sea of mud.

Sokolo chuckled at last. "No doubt this place reminds you of a story?"

Hadithe Zakale, as if breaking out of a reverie, glanced over at him, but answered only after thinking a while.

"Quite a current, at least today," he said at last. "Has this stream a name, Sokolo?"

"No," the messenger replied. "Other than the Dry Run. I've heard it called that." He smiled. "Not suitable now, of course, but it will be again before long."

"Still, today it is something other than *dry*," the storyteller commented. "With that current, we cannot call it by its right name, lest we be thought ridiculous and improper. A curious phenomenon. There should be a name for it while it is bright and vibrant, rather than when it's dead and dry."

Sokolo grunted, uncertainly. He was often uncertain when the storyteller winged his way through his thoughts aloud like this. But he understood that it was part of Hadithe Zakale's method of meditation. Sokolo, who had heard him do so before in their travels, didn't put too much stock in this kind of rambling. He preferred stories that had a beginning and had an end. But one couldn't be telling stories all the time. One must spend some time thinking and shaping them, just as one must learn a message before bearing it, or a weapon before wielding it.

Briefly his thoughts flashed back to the night before, to the great ceremony they had both mentioned. It had been the Mission Ceremony, carried out in observance of the sending of someone on a special mission on behalf of the King. Tasso, the young man, had finally been sent on his way at the appointed time, the first rains.

Both men had been deeply involved in the formalities. Sokolo's duty was to present the young man to the King. Hadithe Zakale had told a tale, this time the story of Singlehand.

Afterwards, Anokye, the old Magician, had given Tasso his "marching orders," his mission statement. He was to go to the South, into the heart of the rain forest, to find out whether or not the tales of certain travelers might possibly be true.

Like everyone else who knew the real mission, Sokolo had kept a straight face. The mask was, after all, essential to the success of the real mission, and was based on character.

The young man, Sokolo held himself back from even thinking the name, for a second time... The young man's name was not supposed to be mentioned among the Ashanti until he returned from his exploit, or until reliable word came concerning his fate.

Abruptly Sokolo stared at Hadithe Zakale, remembering what he had said about the Dry Run. Suddenly he realized that the apparent rambling had carried a point.

"Perhaps we shall have to change the name of the Dry Run," Sokolo said slowly. "Perhaps some day we shall call this stream by someone's name, as would be fitting, when it is bright and running with fresh water."

Hadithe Zakale smiled, knowing his point had been made. He had long known that whatever thoughts Sokolo might have on the matter, no word in criticism of the Ashanti king or an Ashanti mission would ever drop from his lips. But the message had been passed, and Hadithe Zakale was content.

Sokolo, too, thought it was a waste.

It was a strange scene, but there was something compelling about it. A young woman in white, two gold bracelets her only adornment, faced a half-dozen men in loincloths; men seething with rage and fear, carrying makeshift weapons and iron tools, looking ready to devour her as they had expected to be devoured on the shore of the island.

They surrounded Sasha in the front room of the warehouse, a room that had been an office. Through the door in the back, she could hear a mixture of chants, yells and screams, all words spoken in anger. Through it also came the smell of a charnel-house, mixed with that of a latrine.

Only one man there appeared in control of himself and the situation. He was a tall, heavily scarred warrior with a gold medallion around his neck. He stood staring at her with the unsmiling, implacable look of a chief. He was totally bald, not shaven, but bald, and around the top of his head was a line of lighter skin; undoubtedly some kind of circlet was habitually worn there. They should have spotted him, Sasha thought to herself. If not by that, then by the way he carried himself.

"Who are you, woman?" he asked in a surprisingly soft voice; soft, but clear and deep. "Who sent you?"

"I am called Sasha," she replied. "No one sent me. They merely allowed me to come, when I asked permission to do so."

"For what purpose?"

"To spare my people further suffering."

The stony face measured her.

"We are not your people, woman. You are not all of Africa. There is the white in you."

"I do not speak of you," she said quietly. "I speak of my people who live on this island. Already you have killed five of them. If they're forced to attack you, these Frenchmen... well, more may die in the fight."

Men behind the leader muttered, and some laughed about a woman's aversion to fighting. One sneered openly at her, but Sasha ignored this.

"And you, sir? Am I to know *your* name?"

The face remained impassive.

"I am..." the man said at last. "I am Fara Oburu, general of Bawol. I lead my men. We shall be free, or we shall die in battle. No white pigs will make dinner of us."

Sasha shrugged. "They didn't plan to eat you, but to put their mark on each of you, and take you west to be sold as slaves."

The dark eyes of the leader glittered. "Well, they shall not have even that! We will not accept it. And we shall fight, fight with any weapon that comes to hand. We shall fight and we shall win, because no one has ever defeated us in battle."

Sasha stared at the leader, saying nothing, until finally a grim smile crossed the scarred face.

"You do not ask the question, but it's written in your eyes, woman. How came we to be captives, if undefeated? Easily enough. We were taken by the treachery of the King of Sine, whom we all but destroyed on the field. He sued for peace and gave hostages. I sent a messenger back to my own King, and camped awaiting instructions. One morning I awoke with a Sine spear at my throat. The dogs had planned their action well."

"I see," Sasha said. "Dishonorable, of course. But nonetheless, effective. The end result was the same as if you had been defeated."

"Not to me, or to my men. We don't deserve the shame of defeat, nor are we about to bear its consequences without a struggle. We will fight to the finish for the things we cherish."

"And what are those, Fara Oburu? Freedom?"

"Freedom of course. Home. Family."

"Home and family, I fear, you have already lost. Will it really matter to the King of Bawol, or the people of Bawol, that you were captured by treachery rather than defeated on the field? You have still lost. They will write you off. If you did manage to get home, they would not welcome you. But you know this."

The scarred man shrugged. "Then we will go somewhere else, and make a new life for ourselves. A new land. New families. It's happened before."

Sasha nodded. "I see that you are a bold and determined man, sir, and a leader of men. But tell me, what is the first duty of a leader?"

The scarred man's lip curled.

"Do you seek instruction, woman, or seek to instruct *me*?"

"Neither," Sasha replied promptly. "I want to see if we agree. It seems to me that the first duty of a leader is to put all thought of himself aside, and to do what will save his people in the end."

An eyebrow went up on the face of the Bawol.

"I would not quarrel with that. And I see where you're leading, woman. But no matter how great the odds, while there's still a chance for freedom it's a chance worth taking." He gestured at the assortment of weapons in the room, none of them really designed as weapons, but hardly less effective. "Even death is preferable to slavery, if in dying we can still strike a blow... and we *can* do this."

"A slave can live," Sasha replied. "He will go somewhere else, and make a new life, and perhaps he can prevail in the end. It's not the same with a dead man."

The Bawol general waved a hand. "Enough. You are about to suggest that I surrender, since the whites have overwhelming force. Well, I've heard that they do, but I've seen no evidence of it. Their big guns didn't fire at us, and even if they did, I still don't believe they would do as much damage as your islanders insist they would do. Besides, I would still prefer death without striking a blow, to life in slavery."

"And your people feel the same?"

There was no answer. Sasha glanced around the room, tuning her ear for muttered comments. But there was no indication of how the men really felt.

"If I could demonstrate their powers," she said, "would that change your mind?"

The leader laughed. "You? And how would you do that?"

"Clear the sea-ward room of this warehouse on the top floor. I shall advise the whites to fire at it. When the firing ceases, just go up and look. You can judge for yourself, when you see the damage."

After a while Fara Oburu nodded his head. "We are not afraid of demonstrations," he said. Then he turned about and gave orders. One by one, and rapidly, the other men left the room and he was alone with Sasha.

"And I suppose," he said quietly, "You will now promise, for my ear alone, that the whites will spare me if I surrender."

Sasha shook her head. "We both know they will kill you. But they will spare your people. As many of them as possible, so they can be sold as slaves. The choice is yours."

The scarred general nodded. "Go make your demonstration, then, woman. But don't come back here when it's over. You will have your answer soon enough."

The *Princesse*, out in the harbor, signalled that all was ready. Confirming the signal from the shore, Lieutenant Drouin gave orders of his own. Beside him, Pochette stood with a sour look on his face, the only expression he could muster that would ever remind anyone of Andre Bruie.

He still didn't like the idea of firing on the warehouse. But he hadn't been able to prevail against the combined, supposedly professional, opinions of Drouin and de Gennes.

"Well?" he asked.

"We're all set," Drouin replied.

"How many of your guns will be involved?"

"Only six," the Lieutenant said. "All we could get turned around on such short notice. After all, the fort's guns were sited to be fired at sea, not at land."

"A contingency for which I'm sure you will be prepared in the future."

Drouin bit his lip, wishing with a sudden raging fervency that one day this *clerk* would come under his command. Just five minutes would be enough! But he said nothing.

The silent warehouse waited. Finally Pochette shrugged.

"Proceed."

Drouin shouted an order. In response, a soldier down by the dock relayed the order up to the merchant ship tied there. Slowly at first, then briskly, a flag rose toward the peak of the mainmast. Many eyes were on it, for when it reached the top, that would be the signal for both Drouin's and de Gennes' guns to fire.

Upon reaching the top, a huge explosion was heard. Steel balls and scatter-shot were hurled in the direction of the warehouse. In reply there came a sound of shattering wood. Dust billowed up from the seaward upper room of the warehouse. It seemed as if the whole building vibrated.

211

"Cease!" Pochette yelled. "You were not to *destroy* the place!"

Drouin shrugged. "One salvo only, as agreed. As designed, it merely smashed the one room."

"But the noise... "

"Was impressive, no? That seaward room is where your people store empty crates, remember?" He grinned suddenly. "Or, as of now, toothpicks." He turned to Sasha, standing beside him on the quay. "I imagine that was part of your plan?"

Sasha smiled. "It should give them something to think about."

"Well, good. At least you didn't suggest carrying powder under the warehouse."

Sasha's smile faded only a little. "That would have been repetitive, sir, and not much to the point."

"Well?" Pochette broke in. "How long are we to wait? And for what?"

"I imagine we won't have to wait long," Drouin replied, and they all fell silent, watching the warehouse.

At first there was no discernible noise from the building, but after a while, shouts started to come down from the upper story. They were followed and accompanied by other noises, sure signs of a violent quarrel. Then at last there was a clear, single voice, stilling argument and saying a few words that Sasha couldn't quite make out. She recognized the voice, however, as that of Fara Oburu, the Bawol general.

Then there was complete silence.

Moments later, the door to the warehouse opened. Two men came out; the general, and a Bawol warrior carrying a white cloth on the end of a stick. They marched in purposeful silence toward the quay.

For a moment, everyone watched in silence, as if stunned. Then a cheer erupted from the gunners on the fort, a cheer that was carried across the harbor by the merchant sailors and the navy men aboard the *Princesse.*

Drouin didn't cheer, but allowed himself a smile of satisfaction. Out of curiosity, he stole a glance at Pochette, wondering how the Assistant Chief Factor would react. It wasn't anything he would have expected. There was no look of astonishment, or of relief, or even of triumph. Across the face of Denis Pochette there flowed nothing but the unmistakable ferocity of revenge in the making; a cruel and savage look, focused on the Bawol general.

Chapter Eighteen

Lieutenant Drouin glanced at the scrawled note the *signaré* Paulette had given him. The writing wasn't smooth. In fact, in some ways it was childish. But the language was clear enough and it was in French. Drouin frowned, then nodded.

"Tell Sasha I shall come as soon as I can," he answered. "I hope it will be soon enough."

The island woman left without a word, closing the door of Andre Bruie's office behind her. Drouin bent back to his paperwork. It was an unfamiliar place for him to be, and he was working at unfamiliar tasks. But as Andre Bruie had predicted, Drouin had seen enough of what a Chief Factor did to produce a passable imitation. Nevertheless, he would be more than happy to relinquish a certain amount of power and responsibility as soon as the Chief Factor returned.

Bruie's departure with de Gennes on the *Princesse* had left Drouin the senior officer on the island. Hence, he had temporary authority over company operations as well as command of the forts.

Normally a company man would have been given the task, even a very junior clerk if necessary, but for reasons of his own, Bruie had not taken that course. Drouin knew the reasons well enough, though they hadn't spoken about them. It was obvious that Bruie was deeply dissatisfied with current company personnel, particularly Pochette.

Drouin smiled to himself, but the smile didn't last long. It was pleasant to think of how Pochette's face must have looked when Bruie, arriving two days after the slave revolt had ended, had received the Assistant Chief Factor's report. It was less pleasant to think of the major reason for Bruie's dissatisfaction and anger. Drouin, although he wouldn't have told Bruie this to his face, had deep doubts about the effectiveness of Bruie's corrective actions.

Instead of sending Pochette back to Saint-Louis, or perhaps even back to France in disgrace, Bruie had saved face for him. He had removed him from the island by dispatching him on an expedition to the interior with two visiting captains. The errand was legitimate and twofold; they were to visit the gold fields, and if possible, make contact with a Tuareg trading expedition that was reported westbound with slaves, ivory and some of the other typical trade goods. Past experience had shown that the captains themselves could have handled the affair, with the aid of their *signarés* . Pochette was excess baggage.

Drouin broke off his reverie and went back to work. He had other things to think about. The rainy season was nearly at an end, and it would soon become necessary to start up the water skiff schedule again. When that happened someone would have to be chosen to run it; old Gilbert was no longer fit for duty. The wound in his hip hadn't healed properly. He was still convalescing at the Stone House, and if the note Sasha had sent was correct, his condition had taken a turn for the worse.

Whatever happened, Gilbert's days on the water were over. To succeed him, Drouin saw a choice between two former *laptots*, Marcel and Desmond. Between them, they had all the qualifications Gilbert possessed. The problem was that the qualities were divided, neither one having the full complement.

Marcel was a bluff, hearty man, heavy set and sinewy. The

men respected him and would follow without question. Marcel, however, was lacking the special kind of knowledge that Gilbert brought to the task. Desmond, on the other hand, had this knowledge, but he was a frail and somewhat nervous young man; the men didn't respect him to any great degree.

Drouin reviewed his notes on the matter, and finally made his decision. With that, he glanced at the sky and decided it was time to take a break. He closed up Bruie's desk, locked the hidden drawer where the most sensitive documents rested, and pocketed the key. He found himself staring at the locked drawer for a moment. There was something that needed doing here... but was it for him to do? Surely Bruie must know, and must have the matter in hand.

Drouin shrugged his shoulders and put such thoughts out of his mind for the moment. He left the office, locking it as he did so, and walked out of the fort into the driving rain. It was a short trip to the Stone House, but nevertheless, he was a dripping apparition when he arrived.

"It was good of you to come, sir," Sasha said on meeting him at the door.

"How bad is he?" the Lieutenant asked.

"Very bad, I'm afraid. Tonight, or tomorrow morning." Drouin sighed and walked through the main room of the Stone House to the alcove where Gilbert rested. Bagatelle the parrot bellowed a chatter of calls and screeches as he passed, but said no words.

Sitting down beside the old man, Drouin saw at once that Sasha's judgment was correct. The dark face was tinged with a yellow pallor, and the hands picked at the blankets; blankets that covered him, but didn't seem to warm him. He shivered as if with a chill. Drouin had seen more men die in battle than in bed, but he had seen enough of the latter to know the signs.

Gilbert seemed fairly alert and pleased to see him. At once he began questioning the Lieutenant about the water skiff, urging him to pick a new man. Drouin told him of the decision he had just made, to put Marcel in charge. Marcel might not possess any special wisdom, or even any great intelligence, but the power to command was the first requirement of anyone in charge of an operation.

216

"He will do well," Gilbert said quietly. "The men trust him, and what he doesn't know, Desmond can supply. They are good friends. I think the friendship will survive Marcel's promotion."

Drouin smiled. "Now quit worrying about it, and get better, so you can enjoy your retirement."

Gilbert slowly shook his head. Drouin's heart sank a bit, for that signal completed the fatal picture. Nevertheless, he tried one more time.

"I wouldn't think that you'd give up," he said.

Gilbert smiled. "It's not a matter of giving up, sir. It's simply time. I've lived a good long life, is it not so?"

"It is so. You have lived it well. You did your tasks with more than competence, and I haven't seen you bear any grudges, even against those who harmed you. Even against those, for instance, who gave you that wound in the hip."

Gilbert seemed surprised. "Why should I bear a grudge? They were brave men, willing to risk their lives to be free. Of course, they had to be stopped, and I helped to do that. But one can't hate such men. Or at least one shouldn't, truly?"

Drouin nodded, studying the old man's changing expressions.

"It was a bad thing, Gilbert, what was done after the surrender. Had it been up to me..." He let the sentence go unfinished.

Gilbert smiled. "I know you would have had no part in it, sir, but I've also never seen you refuse a legitimate order. It was good of you to try to evade it."

Drouin hid his astonishment as best he could, but he couldn't hide a wry smile. It was quite true that once he'd learned of Pochette's intentions for the disposal of the Bawol general, Drouin had tried to circumvent the plan. Surprisingly enough, de Gennes had, too; a fact Drouin had not realized until too late. If they'd been able to work together.... but, what was done was done.

Gilbert was right, though. It wasn't all that surprising that even at death's door, he would have both excellent information and the ability to analyze it.

"Not all men are brave," Gilbert said, resuming the conversation. "Those who are not are often vicious instead. I've tried to

217

explain this to Sasha, but I find I can't get the words right. Perhaps you can do it for me, sir?"

Drouin was surprised again, though only mildly this time. "Sasha? She is puzzled by this?"

Gilbert nodded. "She has asked me several times why a man would do a thing like Pochette did to the Bawol. But then again, being a brave person herself, she is perhaps incapable of understanding what goes on in the minds of others. Still, it bothers her."

"And you?"

"No, I am not bothered. It won't matter that much in a short while. But you, Lieutenant...you and *M'sieu* Bruie have been good to me, and good for this island. Do be careful. Men like Pochette are dangerous, no?"

Drouin didn't reply at once. When he did, he spoke carefully.

"I shall watch my step," he said with an air of light unconcern. "But have you seen something, Gilbert? Something you want to tell me?"

Gilbert shook his head. "Clouds and smoke, sir. Nothing definite. Nonetheless, from time to time I smell things. Perhaps that's the best way to put it."

Drouin chuckled. "Very well put indeed. And you have an excellent nose, Gilbert, as I've learned over the years. What do you smell this time?"

"Treachery."

Drouin kept his face a mask. "Well, as I said, I shall be careful." This time he didn't try to appear unconcerned. "And," he added, "Bruie can protect himself, too. He has the best protection of all, an instinct for doing the right thing."

Gilbert shook his head. "That isn't always protection enough. Sometimes even when a man does right, it gives his enemies an opening."

"For example?"

"It would be sensible to make a separate peace between the French and English companies. I realize this might be dangerous while the homelands are still at war."

This time Drouin did not try to hide his astonishment.

"Gilbert, I must know your sources this time."

"I have no sources, really, sir. Just a guess. It seems to have been a good one, no? Bruie talks long with you and de Gennes after Pochette leaves. Then he and de Gennes take the *Princesse* and head south. We all know the captains and the company people have been complaining that the mainland tribes are more demanding now, with a war going on. They play the French off against the English, and both sides suffer. Add to that the fact that Sasha has been told to prepare the Stone House for many important guests. No more French captains can be expected until the rains cease...well, those are my sources, sir."

Drouin studied him. "You have told no one of this?"

Gilbert shook his head. "Not even Sasha, though she may also guess it on her own. But she wouldn't speak of it, either."

Drouin didn't pursue the matter, and the conversation ended a while later with trivialities and a last exhortation from the Lieutenant to the old man to get better.

At the door of the Stone House, Drouin drew Sasha aside, and took something from his tunic. He hesitated momentarily.

"You're sure there's no chance?"

Sasha shook her head. Drouin couldn't read her face, but then again, he seldom could. He thrust a small bottle into her hand.

"Then before he drifts away, give him a taste of this. It's brandy. Some of the best. But a brave man deserves a last tribute, no?"

Sasha smiled at him. "*Oui, m'sieu.* I shall see that he gets it."

On his way to the Stone House, Drouin had taken a roundabout course, even though it meant spending more time in the rain. He had done this to avoid passing through the small cemetery adjacent to the island's chapel. Returning to the fort, however, he walked resolutely through the burial ground. He walked slowly, reading the writing that remained on some of the white crosses.

Some of that writing he couldn't read at all; either it was too faded, or in a foreign language, or both. The cemetery had been set aside in the time of the Portuguese, and there were Dutch and even

English inscriptions, as well as French. The newest cross, however, still carried fresh writing: FARA OBURU/LOYAL TO HIS PEOPLE.

Drouin stood by the grave a moment, thinking about how the Bawol general had met his doom. There could have been no mercy for him, of course, no pardon. Hanging or a firing squad would have been the proper alternatives. Drouin had suggested the latter. But Pochette had been in charge, and Pochette had ordered the Bawol cannonaded.

The vision would stay with Drouin for a long time: men tying the Bawol to the mouth of a cannon, with the cannon mouth against his lower back; the subdued slaves, all in heavy chains, lined up to watch; the reading of a fulsome execution order; and finally, the order to fire.

Then the eruption of flame, the explosion of blood spattering forward, and a ribbon of guts spiked with shattered bones spiraling out for several yards from two halves of a severed corpse. One final touch: hanging the two split halves of the Bawol on either side of the Door of No Return, so the slaves could take a last look as they marched out to the ships. The parts had hung on the door for two days until Bruie arrived, and ordered the burial. He had chosen the inscription himself, after, it seems, talking to Sasha.

Drouin remembered how the Bawol had acted those last moments. He had met his fate in stony silence, brave even in the face of what, for him, must have been an unknown terror. He had been a man, Drouin found himself thinking, a man, just as Gilbert was. And Gilbert, Drouin could not help thinking, was more than a man. He was more than an African. He was.... a true Frenchman.

The Lieutenant smiled to himself and allowed the thought to slip from his mind. It was certainly not a common thought for people of his generation. Even when such a thought did surface, it was often consciously weeded out, like the seed of a dangerous plant. It would be nearly a hundred years before such thoughts took root in the minds of men; and even longer before they took root and began transforming the landscape of the world.

For Drouin, however, trudging back to the fort in the rain,

there was another pressing matter to think about. It might not be his place to do anything, but old Gilbert had given him a parting piece of intelligence. Somehow it wouldn't be right for him ignore it. There were many papers in the secret drawer that suggested reexamination, and Drouin, after all, had the key.

For a man of business who had just been resoundingly beaten in a three-way trading session, the Pilgrim Khalil wore a singularly satisfied expression on his face as he rose from his evening prayers and approached his tent.

Observers who were of the Faithful, but not retainers of the Pilgrim, would no doubt have regarded his demeanor as obvious piety, a ready acknowledgment that things had gone, as always, according to the way God willed them: *Inshallah.* Even some of his retainers might have attributed it so. Others, however, the keener observers, would have realized that something more was required to explain the smug look. Deep inside, the Pilgrim Khalil was no more a faithful son of Islam than he was a faithful son of his father. Even his youthful pilgrimage had been for show, and his one enduring memory of Mecca was of the astonishing extent to which some people actually appeared to believe in Allah, his Prophet, and the Koran.

But he maintained the show. He had learned that the appearance of piety had lulled many sheep to the shearing-ground. It didn't always work, but it was worth keeping up appearances, in the long run.

Over the last three days, however, he had been reminded of the instances when piety didn't work. As planned, he had crossed paths with a Tuareg trading caravan just as the rains ended to the south of them, on the edge of the great desert. He was on the verge of making what might have been the first of a very profitable series of deals with the Tuareg, when, to the surprise of all sides, a third party had intervened, the Europeans. Not just the normal run of Eu-

221

ropeans, either; not the kind of people who could be swindled past comprehension with great ease. No, these had been those damnable, hard-nosed Frenchmen from that cursed island of Gorée.

The man in nominal charge of the group had been a glorified clerk by the name of Pochette. He, however, had little say in the bargaining. The other two men with him, veteran seacaptains and traders, had done most of the talking. They had sized up the situation with astonishing speed, analyzing strengths and weaknesses. Then, before Khalil could convince the Tuaregs to combine with *him*, the French had convinced the Tuaregs to combine with *them*, against Khalil.

It had all been done to the accompaniment of the usual trader's dance, endless discussions replete with flowery compliments, recurring assurances of everyone's good health, and invocations of one's own honesty. But at the end of it, when the three expeditions went their separate ways, it was Khalil who had been left holding the proverbial bag, a very empty one at that.

He hadn't even been able to secure from the Tuareg one small object, a woman, very attractive if no doubt troublesome, who would have fetched a high price from a certain king Khalil knew. She was just the type he liked. The Tuareg had been eager to get rid of her, too. She was a disgraced wife of one of their leaders, one who had apparently plotted against her husband and master. She was lucky to be suffering sale as a slave rather than the normal fate reserved for such wives. Somehow, she had eluded Khalil. Somehow, she had contacted the French clerk, Pochette, and had convinced him to buy her.

But all of these setbacks paled before the prize that Khalil now felt was within his grasp.

News of this prospect had arrived just as the caravans were breaking up. Khalil's men had secured a certain captive, as directed, and if that captive could be persuaded to talk, the Pilgrim could well reap a fortune that would offset a hundred trading losses such as the one he had just suffered.

Inside his tent, seating himself to await the arrival of that captive, Khalil permitted a catlike smile to cross his unscarred face.

It had been a bold stroke, but remarkably easy to accomplish.

A short while back, rumors had begun to reach Khalil from reliable sources that the King of Ashanti had dispatched a messenger to the southern forests. His mission, it was hinted, was to find out if a fable of a fabulous treasure of ivory, an elephant's graveyard, had any basis in fact.

This had amused Khalil at the time, but later he had learned from similar reliable sources that the messenger was now returning posthaste, having indeed verified the existence of such a place. What was more, he had located it.

Khalil had, at this point, changed his mind about the situation, and had dispatched half a dozen of his most trusted men to intercept the messenger and bring him to the Pilgrim's tent. They'd had little trouble, for the messenger had been traveling in the open. He'd walked right into their clutches. As it turned out, the messenger was even able to speak Arabic, although naturally he hadn't spoken of his King's business.

As the footsteps approached, the Pilgrim arose smiling. There were many ways of persuasion, and he was master of them all.

Four men brought the young African in, two maintaining a firm grip on his arms and two behind him for insurance. He was indeed young for his office, Khalil decided, and very much overconfident if he had been traveling openly as reported. But he was certainly strong-looking, and to all appearances he was unafraid.

Khalil had rehearsed his men well. He took a long, measuring look at the Ashanti, fixing his eyes on the tokens that spoke of his office. Then he flew into a carefully calculated rage.

"Dogs! Fools! *This* is the young slave you claimed to have taken? Can't you see from the badges? He's just what he claimed to be! Oh, you fools! You have disgraced me, taking a King's Messenger! How shall... never mind, never mind! Release him! At once! And get out of here while your heads are still on your shoulders!"

The Arabs, appearing shaken, quickly did as they were bid, leaving the young African standing alone in front of the Pilgrim. He said nothing, only began to rub his arms where he'd been held. He stared at the son of the Ghoul.

"A thousand pardons, my young friend, a thousand pardons," Khalil effused. "I shall have these ignorant wretches whipped, you may rest assured of that."

"Whipping," observed the young man in slightly accented Arabic, "does not seem to cure fools."

Khalil cocked a sidelong glance at him, and smiled.

"Ah, that's true, young sir, true indeed. You are very wise for one so young. Nevertheless, it's necessary in this instance, even if it doesn't work. Please sit down, sit down over there. Make yourself comfortable while I prepare some refreshment. Stay the night, if you please, and in the morning I will see you on your way with the fastest means available."

The young man, appearing to consider the matter for the moment, nodded abruptly and went to sit on the cushion Khalil had indicated. The Pilgrim fussed over a table in the corner, and came forward at last with a full cup of dark red liquid, which he pressed on the young African.

Warily the young man tasted it. He seemed surprised.

"Wine, sir? I thought it was forbidden."

Khalil grinned with a show of unconcern. "But not to you, young man. And I will even drink with you... a bit, just to show that I am truly hospitable. Things may be forbidden, yet, as it's written, let the name of Allah be mentioned over them, and much is forgiven."

So saying, he took a cup of his own and drank from it sparingly. Normally, he was not that sparing of the bottle. In fact, it was no occasional thing with him, either, but rather a habit. But this night, he was resolved to stay sober. It was the young man who would get drunk. Wine was a powerful persuader, or if nothing more, a powerful loosener of the tongue.

The young man took a healthy gulp, then glanced about him as if seeing the tent for the first time.

"You are truly a trader, then?" he asked at last.

"Very much so," the Pilgrim said affably. "I do fairly well, as Allah wills. But you, young sir? I am called Khalil ibn-Abdullah, the Hajji. Please, call me Khalil. Am I to know your name?"

"I am called Tasso, sir," the young man said. "If you will

pardon me, I cannot bring myself to call an elder man by a given name."

Khalil nodded approvingly. "You were well raised, young man. Very good breeding indeed. Well, permit me at least to call you Tasso, or does that make conflict with your high calling?"

"No, sir. May I ask what it is that you trade? I've never seen a place like this."

"Ah, I see, I see. Well, I trade in the usual things, Tasso... ivory, and gum, and gold, and slaves. I trade for western goods in the west, and eastern goods in the east, and whatever comes my way in the great desert. I might say that you've seen goods that I've traded, for much of what the Ashanti import comes through my hands, at one stage or another."

"We don't import much," Tasso replied. "The King doesn't trust the white man or his ways, so he doesn't trust their goods, either. Some of their knives and axes are useful."

Khalil nodded. Taking thought as he refilled Tasso's cup, he crossed the room to a small box he kept near the head of his bed. He drew out a long, simply fashioned knife with a wooden handle.

"Knives like these?" he asked.

"Yes. They are European?"

"Indeed. This one is English. Very cheap, and plentiful. But the steel doesn't compare to that of Damascus, my young friend. Real knives are made like this." He held up an Arab dagger.

Tasso seemed impressed. "May I see it?"

At the request, Khalil hesitated a brief second. The young man was obviously neither a hothead nor a fool, and the Pilgrim couldn't believe himself in any danger at the moment. Besides, it would not do to show suspicion. So he brought the knife over to Tasso and handed it to him, seating himself once again on his own cushion and taking up the cup.

"A very strange design," Tasso said, inspecting it.

"On the handle? That's writing... Arabic script. It says *inshallah*, as God wills it."

"And the material of the hilt? It seems familiar, but I cannot place it."

"Ivory."

"Ah," Tasso said with a smile, "ivory." He seemed about to add something, but instead raised the cup to his lips and drained it. Khalil took it from him instantly, rose up, got a refill, and came back. As he did so, Tasso took the cup, and then held out the knife, hilt toward the Pilgrim.

"Ivory, and as God wills it," the young man said quietly as Khalil reached for the knife. Then, in a sudden, blinding flurry of motion, he flipped the knife, grasped it by the hilt, and drove it into Khalil ibn-Abdullah's belly with a ferocious twist.

"For Opuku Dara!" Tasso cried as he ripped the knife out.

Khalil's scream of agony arose behind Tasso as the Ashanti made for the tent's exit. The Pilgrim sank back on his cushions, holding his guts with both hands, for if he hadn't done so, they would have tumbled out in front of him. He heard, through the red haze that was beginning to take the place of both sight and hearing, the sounds of a scuffle outside. Then one of his retainers poked a head into the tent, saw what had happened, and rushed in calling an order over his shoulder.

"No!" Khalil gasped. "Bring him in here! I must know who did this and why...why.!"

But it was too late for that. As he finished speaking, a second retainer entered, bearing the news that Tasso had escaped. The fact that the young man had been seriously wounded in the process did not impress Khalil in the least. His face bloated with anger and pain.

"Damn it all!" Khalil moaned. "He said a name, but I didn't catch it. Help me up."

"But sir..."

Khalil, unheeding, struggled to his feet himself. He stared down at the ivory-handled knife on the ground.

"Why?" he growled. Then he repeated the question several times, his voice rising with each repetition. At last he brought back a foot, and with a vicious oath, kicked the knife across the floor of the tent. It hit the box with the knives in it, and scattered them.

Khalil the Pilgrim stood for the moment, staring at the distance. Then, his eyes glazed, his hands relaxed their grip, and his intestines fell to the floor. A second later, the rest of his mortal remains followed.

"A toast," the Englishman said in passable French, "to your health, *M'sieu Bruie*, and to the success of our respective companies."

"To the same," Bruie responded. He took a quick drink of the unfamiliar rum, hiding his dissatisfaction with the taste. Then he held up the glass again.

"A well-spoken toast, Mr. Pinder, and perhaps the best we can do for the moment. It is a great pity we can't pledge the health of our respective sovereigns, no? But while they remain at war, it would perhaps be excessive. Nevertheless, peace always comes, and I suggest we reserve such toasts for that time."

Interrupted briefly for the formalities, the hubbub of conversation now resumed. The Stone House was packed with more people that night than it had ever contained at one time; all the alcoves were taken, and the tables were set heaping high with food. There were but two French captains present, and a limited number of other ship and Company officers, but all of the *signarés* had companions. Andre Bruie was determined that his entertainment of the English East India Company's Governor of the Gambia, and his minions, was going to be a success.

Lieutenant Drouin, watching from one of the alcoves close to where Bruie and Governor Pinder sat, took in the scenery with the wine. He was thankful that he wasn't at the head table this time, and honor-bound to drink the English rum. It was indeed a remarkable occasion.

Once again Bruie had done the impossible, and with a flourish. Meeting the Englishman at Albreda in the Gambia's mouth, he had proposed that the two companies agree to assist each other against both the competition of other Europeans and the conspiracies of the

Africans themselves. The latter showed signs of getting out of hand. The agreement would be passed on to the respective capitals, which could, of course, veto the arrangements. But in the meantime, they would be fully respected by both sides.

Governor Pinder, Drouin knew by now, had been most willing to agree. It had been hard enough on the English, with men like de Gennes prowling the Little Coast in relentless search of trespassers on the French domain. But now interlopers were getting into the act; privateers with royal licenses to plunder the enemy. One such captain, Henri Baton, commanding a little brigantine called *Fanfaron*, had just recently caught the English by surprise and plundered their fort at the Gambia mouth.

It also appeared that the English had been more than willing to come to Gorée for the formalities. Lieutenant Drouin thought he knew why. There were few women in the English establishment, and fewer who could compare to the women of Gorée. Drouin was sure of this fact as he studied the English and the ways they were reacting to the *signarés*. Even the land agents acted like sailors who hadn't seen a woman in two or three years.

"Another toast," came an English voice from across the room. "To the women of Gorée island!" There was a pause. "And to our charming hostess, Miss Sasha Fara!"

There were cheers at this, and glasses raised and drained. Sasha, bowed and smiled in acknowledgment. Now, as she returned to her place on the dais in the central alcove, Drouin caught her eye with a wave of his glass, and she came over to where he sat.

"Yes, *M'sieu*?"

"An endorsement to that toast," Drouin said. "You have outdone yourself today. But tell me, where on earth did that Englishman get the idea that you were called Sasha *Fara*?"

Sasha waved, and called out something to someone up on the dais. Then she nodded toward the *signaré* Arsene, who had been sitting next to Drouin. Arsene immediately found something else to do, and Sasha herself sat down by the Lieutenant.

"He called me that, Lieutenant, because that is my name. I decided to take a second one, as the Europeans do."

"But why Fara?"

"Because he was a brave man. I thought it would be good for me to do."

"Well, yes, I can understand that. After all, I'm a soldier. But...."

Sasha laughed and tapped her arm. "Although my father was white, my mother was still a slave, *M'sieu*. I find it fitting that I should also have an African name."

Drouin nodded gravely, then changed the subject . "This is a great success, Sasha, and I think the deal is now done in earnest."

Sasha nodded more slowly. "They are in complete agreement, except in one minor detail."

A wry smile crossed Drouin's face. "Minor details have a way of causing trouble. What is it that you see?"

"I suppose it's a matter of protocol. Both *M'sieu* Bruie and Governor Pinder agree that neither of them can be spared from here at the moment, so each will send his number-two man home with a copy of the agreement, to help put it across. The English will be sending that one over there. He's called Mr. Snelling. Bruie intends to send *M'sieu* Delacroix, who is now in charge in Saint-Louis. But Pinder has discovered that Delacroix is number three, and wants Bruie to wait for his number two to get back from the interior."

Drouin paused, then sighed.

"That would be a mistake, Sasha. Pochette is not the man for such an assignment."

"I agree. I thought it most convenient that Pochette was away from the island at this time. But he'll be back soon."

Drouin shot a glance at her. "You know this? I haven't had that kind of information...reliable information...since old Gilbert died."

"It's true," Sasha said quietly. "I, too, have my sources. Since Gilbert has gone, I'll try to help you, sir...but, I must ask for your help in this. Help for us all, in fact. Bruie must not wait to send this mission back to France."

Drouin studied her. "If you can't convince him, Sasha, how am I to do it?"

"I believe you might be able."

"And what leads you to this conclusion?"

Sasha spread her hands. "Guesses. But I believe my guesses are good, and you might have what's called a compelling argument."

Drouin, emitting a grunt, stared in front of him. Then he rose without another word, and went over to where Bruie sat, at the head table up on the dais.

"A word with you in your office, sir?" he asked quietly.

Bruie, already flushed from the unexpected ravages of the rum, looked up sourly.

"Now? Surely a more appropriate time..."

"The importance is grave, sir. I so believe."

Bruie took a long look at the Lieutenant and measured the words he had chosen. Then he excused himself with a shrug, and went with Drouin out of the Stone House and down the path to the fort.

Bruie eased himself behind his desk, tapping his fingers briefly on its surface. Drouin reached behind some old records to bring out a packet of papers. Then the Lieutenant seated himself before the Chief Factor, packet in his lap.

"All right, Marcel. Out with it. What's so damned important that it was necessary to drag me away from a crucial dinner?" He raised a hand and then dropped it. "Not that I didn't need a break. The rum was getting to me. How can those English ... but never mind. I must get back there shortly."

Briefly, Drouin told him that it was necessary to have Delacroix sail, and not wait for Pochette. Bruie heard him out without interrupting.

"So," he said at last. "Sasha told you about that. Well, Pochette wouldn't be my first choice for such a mission, but if it's going to be an issue with the English, hell, I will send him. This is too important

230

a matter to get lost in detail."

"It is indeed," Drouin said quietly. "But that makes it even more important that Pochette not go." Hesitating a moment, he handed Bruie the packet. "I believe this will explain it all."

Bruie frowned, opening a letter that was on top of the package.

"What's this? Marcel, this is a letter of resignation! I didn't ask for this!"

"When you have read the rest," Drouin said, "you might feel it necessary to do so. I've spared you the trouble, having perhaps caused enough already. You didn't tell me to do this, sir, when you put me in charge here...and I feel that I have very much exceeded my authority...but..."

Bruie cut him off, becoming irritated by the incoherent babble. "All right. I'll read."

At first a puzzled look came over his face, then a frown, and finally a glare of rage. At last he finished the final document and shoved the pile aside.

"So! You've been investigating Pochette, which has led you through some of the most sensitive documents in this file...all unauthorized. And all you've come up with is a theory...a possibility, with no real evidence. The things you have noted could have happened by chance."

"One or two of them perhaps," Drouin responded. "The laws of chance cannot really be pressed to cover nine or ten."

"And you think Pochette has been getting me to sign reports, and then has been rewriting them before submitting them to France? Forging my signature on the false report?"

"He's capable of it, physically," Drouin commented. "As you have often said, his hand is his fortune, and he can follow any pattern in drawing up a document."

"Could, could, could. Even so, Marcel, you are a soldier. You know the military saying that capability does not imply intention."

"Pochette is no soldier."

"True. But even if it were so, how would I prove such a deception?"

"Copies of the documents must exist as submitted, sir. A false file to back up the originals. They must be somewhere in or near your office in Saint-Louis... somewhere hidden out of view, where you wouldn't find them. They wouldn't be in the main files, but they could be inserted quickly as a cover."

Bruie snorted. "And I can only find out in Saint-Louis... if indeed this second set of documents exists!"

"Perhaps you can find out sooner," Drouin said. From his tunic he drew a smaller packet, just several papers thick. He handed the packet to Bruie. "Did you write these, sir?"

Bruie studied the documents, the color draining from his face as he did so.

"Where did you get these?"

"I took the liberty of searching Pochette's quarters. They were inside his mattress." A ghost of a smile appeared. "I dare say you didn't write *that* report!"

Bruie was sputtering. "This... this has me saying that I gave the order to have the Bawol general cannonaded, over Pochette's objections! He presents himself as a sane man, dealing with a maniac!"

"Obviously those were prepared as copies for the Saint-Louis files. I wonder where the originals are?"

"Spare me, Marcel." Bruie stood up. "You and de Gennes argued over who should hold the Bawol until his execution..."

Drouin gave him a puzzled glance. "Yes?"

"Both planning secretly...to let him go rather than have Pochette's plan carried out?"

"Sir..."

Bruie held up a hand. "Peace. I know you both, Marcel. I wish you had done so, at least one of you. I would have been glad to pardon an excess of authority, in that instance." He waved at the papers. "In this instance, well, I suppose you are forgetting that *I* ordered the investigation of Pochette?"

Drouin let out a long sigh of relief, then grinned.

"Thank you, Andre."

"Forget it. But what in hell does the snot-nose want?"

" That's obvious, I would think. Your job."

"My job? Who'd want that? My colleagues at the company were astounded that I took this position in the first place. It was considered a hellhole, the least of the Cap-Verde establishments we acquired."

"So it was, until you got here, Andre. You've changed it into one of the plums of His Majesty's colonial empire. You won't lack for eager would-be successors, even if Pochette fails to get the job for himself."

"I suppose you're right," Bruie muttered. "But as for Pochette, damn it! I do want a letter of resignation, Marcel, from him. And when I get back to Saint-Louis, I will find this other file. And dispatch Delacroix to France. At once, and without worrying about details."

Drouin nodded. "And the English?"

Bruie waved a hand. "A few more bottles of wine and they will be agreeing to it. They've run out of rum, you know."

Drouin was surprised. "How so? I saw them bring several kegs ashore."

Bruie yawned, then smiled. "Yes, yes, they had them brought ashore. But it seems our islanders took over from there, and they were clumsy in transporting them. Broke a couple. A real pity. I suppose we'll just have to make do with some of our better wine...and our *signarés*."

There was a moment of silence. Then both men burst out laughing.

Chapter Nineteen

"Wake up, mistress. Mistress, wake up! There's something that must be done."

Sasha roused from a sound sleep in the middle of the night and mumbled the equivalent of "all right, all right," as submissive to the command as anyone in the process of clearing dreams. Then, she sat bolt upright, an angry look on her face.

"Samson! What... you too, Hercule? What do you think you're doing? Get out of here!"

But as neither of the giant black men moved, and as her stares were met by unmoving faces as well, she paused for a moment.

Neither of the giants was a complete stranger to this place, her bedroom in the back of the Stone House. There were nights when she called on one of them or the other, when there was no captain in port. But they came only by invitation, command really, and never together.

Quite casually, the sheets were thrown back, and the men had a brief glimpse of the bronzed body before Sasha put on a large green robe that lay beside her bed. She shook the folds, almost as if shivering, and then faced them standing up.

"You must have a message."

"We do," Hercule responded. "Arsene wants to see you. She has found a man on the shore, and wants to help him. But she feels she cannot, unless you approve."

Sasha frowned. This was not a usual thing, but it wasn't unique. After all, shipwrecked sailors and failed raiders did wash ashore on the island from time to time. There was a procedure, however, for most cases. The senior Frenchman available on the island was notified, and he took charge of the interloper. Clearly this was something different.

"Very well," she said. "Why did you come, instead of Arsene herself?"

Samson tossed his head. "She didn't come here herself, mistress. She sent Calinda instead. We haven't been told to admit Calinda, even if she bears a message from Arsene."

Sasha would have smiled, if she hadn't caught herself. They were slaves, Hercule and Samson, and they knew their place; they also accepted it. But Sasha had noticed long ago that those who have accepted a place are the most determined to make sure all others stay in their places, as well.

"Well then, I will go out and see Calinda myself. Samson! Why did you both come?"

Samson bowed his head. "We judged you might be angry with whoever woke you. We didn't want you to be angrier with one than with the other."

Sasha did let herself smile this time. This much she understood. The lame giants were loyal to her, but they had been loyal to each other first; she would find it disturbing if that ever changed.

Calinda was waiting for her in the empty Main Room, seated in one of the back alcoves. It was a bare place, for whenever there was no event going on, the alcoves were swept clean and left alone. She could get, however, very little out of Calinda. The young *signaré*, who had only recently swept up the last footprint of her first captain, had been no more than a passerby enlisted to bear a message. Sasha would have to go see for herself.

She had already gathered that Arsene thought it best not to draw attention to her discovery. So Sasha went in darkness, accompanied by Samson and Hercule, but not by the torches they could easily have carried. Their route took them past the silent church, and in the darkness Sasha crossed herself dutifully, but a little more carefully than had been her habit.

Things were not going well. People were uneasy on the island. Most saw the still-unratified peace with the English as a kind of calm before the storm. There was a restlessness on the mainland as well, a host of minute changes in the attitudes and actions of customary contacts. Sasha was used to grappling with problems, but it was impossible to grapple with smoke in the darkness; this left her frustrated and, to some extent, worried. Not knowing exactly what was happening, she had to walk carefully, and be watchful.

The circumstance that made her most uneasy was the circumstance that was completely out of her control; the power struggle going on among the whites. She was aware that Pochette was somehow in the middle of it, but she was unclear about the details. One thing was clear, though; when Pochette returned from a surprisingly successful foray into the mainland, Bruie was anything but pleased. Also clear was the identity of the young female slave who accompanied him. The woman called herself Assha, but Sasha knew her as Desiree.

Sasha went to Bruie directly with her warnings. Bruie, however, had been powerless to act. A free island woman he could banish, but he couldn't interfere with another white man's possession of his property. For once, Bruie didn't have the upper hand. He could only reassign Pochette to Saint-Louis, and, of course, Desiree had departed with Pochette.

Sasha hoped Bruie would be keeping an eye on the both of them. She hadn't needed to meet Desiree's eyes to know what this woman had in mind. She needed no warning to tell her that this was a mortal enemy.

The situation with Pochette was far less clear. Knowing of Drouin's investigation, and of Gilbert's last warning, she was aware that he was involved in some kind of treachery. To make matters worse, tensions on the island were growing. Subtly, but not so subtly that she couldn't sense it, the white men on Gorée were dividing into distinct groups. They sat apart, ate apart, and even drank apart , even at events held at the Stone House. The cliquishness was even spilling over into the ranks of the *signarés* who were associated with some of the leading figures.

Drouin was certainly aware of this, though they had never discussed the matter. Fortunately, his *signaré* was Arsene, Sasha's closest friend and follower, and as long as Drouin stayed out of the factions, Arsene would do so as well. Sasha thought it odd that Arsene wouldn't involve Drouin in whatever problem was down on the shore. It was disturbing.

The western shore of the island was rocky, and the footing was often treacherous, but Sasha knew the island as well as anyone. Fortunately, the moon was full, also. It wasn't long before she and her companions came upon Arsene, sitting watchfully beside a man stretched out on a patch of sand, covered from his neck down by a blanket. Sasha gazed at his face, drawing her own conclusions. African, yes, a young man with a gaunt look and a child's face. He was breathing heavily, a rasping in his throat.

Hercule carried a small satchel Sasha had filled before leaving the Stone House, and now, at her signal, he set it down beside the heaving figure. Samson stood a few feet away, watching for anyone who might come that way.

"Is he ill?" Sasha asked.

"He's wounded," Arsene said quietly. "and exhausted. Looks as if he's been traveling for days. I found him moaning and speaking in some language I could not understand."

Sasha frowned at her. "Why didn't you just have him brought to the fort? That's the usual procedure."

"This man is different," Arsene said. "I don't know why.... "

"*Merde!*" Sasha exploded, and then quickly drew in a breath to calm herself. "He's a slave, Arsene! You know what's to be done with an escaped slave..!" Sasha's face was a mixture of anger and worry. She knew what had to be done. Drouin must be notified immediately. Still, Arsene had been correct in her assessment; there was something different about this man, something in his face...

Sasha thought hard for a moment. The situation itself was puzzling. There were no slaves on the island at the moment, and haven't been for a while.

Arsene seemed to read her thoughts. "Sasha, what if he isn't an escaped slave? There are no slaves on the island now and..."

Sasha interrupted her harshly. "He might have been brought over by Pochette, Arsene! Think! If that is the case, we must inform Drouin immediately!"

"But, we haven't heard anything," Arsene retorted. "There has been no news of an escape! What if..."

Sasha was becoming impatient now. She shot Arsene a severe look, to inform her that the discussion was over. Then, sensing her friend's disappointment, she softened her glare. "Maybe no one noticed an escaped slave from that small caffle yet, Arsene. But I'm sure they will discover it very soon."

"Maybe," Arsene said quietly, lowering her head to stare at the ground. "Still, he's wounded very badly. We must dress these wounds as soon as possible." Arsene drew back the blanket, exposing the wounds. "Look."

Sasha glanced down and caught her breath. His wounds were very bad, indeed. To make matters worse, it looked as if he had been traveling for days. Infection had already begun to set in. Sasha was surprised the man had survived this long. Still, there was something about him...

Abruptly, Sasha whirled around to face the water. Confusion and worry crossed her face. She found herself staring at the restless tides , searching them for answers. Who was this man? And why was he here? What was it about him that made her feel so unsure? Sasha scoured her brain for the answers.

Just then, the man stirred, moaned, and after that muttered something. He kept on muttering for a while, until finally Sasha understood what he was speaking. It was not, as Arsene had indicated, an unknown tongue; it was Ashanti. Sasha had learned a bit when Hadithe Zakale had come with Sokolo, the Ashanti King's messenger.

As they walked out into the sunlight, Samson and Hercule scrambled to their feet to accompany them. The group made slow progress through the village, in the direction of the hill at the far end of the island that was the site of the upper fort. Having once transferred the creche to the higher ground, Mama-Lise had found many excellent reasons for keeping it there. Despite the fact that there was a truce, she insisted on remaining in the upper fort and in the comfortable quarters that had come her way. It was a chore coming back to the village, but it made the old woman's presence an event, and there was a little vanity left in Mama-Lise.

There was also, however, native caution. As they walked, Mama-Lise considered the events of the last few hours and made adjustments. Sasha had been remarkably open, remarkably human in this encounter. There was nothing overt to suggest that there was anything beneath the surface. Yet Mama-Lise knew, better than most, how much the younger woman kept her own counsel. The possibility that there was a deeper game afoot couldn't help but cross the old woman's mind.

Suddenly, the small procession came to a halt. A call came from a rough French soldier at the garrison. He came running at them. Instantly Mama-Lise stiffened, although Sasha, still holding her arm, remained unperturbed.

"Glad I found you," the soldier said hastily. "Sasha, the Major wants to see you." He looked at the older woman. "You, too, Mama-Lise."

It took a moment for the matter to register in the mind of Mama-Lise; for the fact to sink in that it was Drouin who wanted to see them. Part of this delay was due to the fresh title. Drouin had been a Lieutenant for nearly a generation, passed over for promotion several times due to the remote and minuscule nature of his post. But Bruie had arranged a sudden promotion, a boost of two levels of rank, commensurate with his new duties as de facto Assistant Chief Factor in command of the island. The French might still be debating the truce, but word of this promotion had arrived promptly.

They found the newly minted Major in his office, Bruie's office. Drouin was using it more and more often; it was the place where he conducted company business. Seeing the sour look on his face, Mama-Lise almost let her apprehensions run loose. But she relaxed when he showed himself preoccupied with other matters. Had he discovered what was going on with the Ashanti visitor, he would have come to the point at once.

"Thank you for coming," he said absently, studying a document. "Please sit down."

Mama-Lise and Sasha sat, and for a while Drouin continued to look over the document. He seemed to hesitate. Then, abruptly, he tore the document up and threw the shreds into a small basket beside the desk. Mama-Lise was puzzled. It was rare for a white man, let alone a Frenchman, to treat documents with such disdain.

"Well, here it is," Drouin said. "First the good news. We have a ship coming, Sasha, fortunately...they're a little scarce, as you may have noticed, despite the peace. This ship has been to India, and will go to France after it leaves here. It's the *Marseilles*, with your old friend Tousaint in command."

Sasha smiled pleasantly. "It will be good to see him again."

"And," Drouin added, "it seems he's picked up a special passenger on the Gold Coast, rather irregular if I didn't know them both... your storyteller, the one called Hadithe Zakale."

Sasha caught her breath. "Truly? How would you know this?"

"Drums," Drouin said in an offhand way. "Without Gilbert, I've had to make my own connections...but like you, they are reliable. Although it seems unusual. Storytellers don't often take to ship, do they?"

Sasha shook her head, smiling. "I wouldn't know, sir. I only know the one, and that one might do anything."

"Well, now, more good news. There's word from Saint-Louis. The peace between the French and English companies has been approved by the respective directors, and with some reservations, by each king. War remains at home, however."

"Ah!" both women said at once.

"Not only that, but our friend Pochette's deception has been fully exposed. He's in chains at Saint-Louis, waiting his return to

France to face charges."

At this news, welcome though it was, the women held back. It wouldn't do to rejoice over the fall of a Frenchman, even such a one as Pochette.

"Well, I approve, anyway," Drouin said. "Now for some sad news. One of the peace terms calls for the replacement of the two warships, English and French, that have been in the habit of fighting hereabouts. It seems both companies agree that two ships are needed, one each; but not the ones that have been adversaries for so long. Captain de Gennes will be taking the *Princesse* back to France, and the *Rochester* will leave as well." He paused to let this information sink in. "Captain de Gennes will pay a last visit to Gorée in a few days. I'd like a suitable entertainment for him, and for one other."

"We shall arrange it," Sasha said promptly. "He's a good man, and a brave one. Who is the other?"

"Andre Bruie," Drouin said.

"Ah. He will bid farewell to the Captain, of course."

"No," Drouin said, with surprising bitterness. "He will sail with de Gennes. This will be his last visit to Gorée."

Sasha shook her head. "I don't understand. He is... preoccupied in Saint-Louis?"

"No, Sasha. *M'sieu* Bruie has been recalled. To France. His successor will arrive on the next ship from the north."

Sasha fixed him with a strong, angry gaze. Then it gave way to astonishment, and in turn to a bitterness to match Drouin's own.

"*Mon Dieu*, sir, how could they *do* such a thing?"

Seated in the main alcove at the Stone House, Andre Bruie raised the small wine glass to his lips and drained it, pausing to savor the deep and subtle flavor. It was an old wine, properly aged, from the grapes of Bordeaux...in short, of the best.

"How could they do such a thing?" he repeated when Sasha

asked him the identical question she'd posed to Drouin. "It's the way of companies, Sasha. They follow their own rules."

"It seems an odd way to reward a man whose actions have saved them from disaster."

Bruie just laughed. He found the laughter unechoed. All around the main room of the Stone House, people were trying to keep up the pretence of a party. But, as he realized, this was more in the nature of a wake. This disappointed him, even though he understood the reasons for it. He had wanted to keep a memory of the island at its best, and this wasn't exactly what he had in mind.

As always, Sasha was the key figure here, and he could sense her bitter disappointment. She made no attempt to hide it from him or from anyone else, and people, of course, picked up on it. Well, he would see if he could change that. If he was able to do so, there might be a party after all. He held out his glass and let her refill it.

"Not to worry," he said. "On two scores, Sasha."

"Oh, really?" she responded, not looking at him. "And what are they?"

"One, if you worry that I'm headed for the headsman, forget it. They'll make me cool my heels in Paris while affairs have a chance to settle, then they'll reassign me. Possibly to Quebec...or Louisiana."

He felt rather than saw her sudden shudder, and laughed.

"Heard too many tales about America? Don't believe them, Sasha. One day that land will be the making of France ... if we can keep it." He paused, drank, then continued. "And on another score, don't be afraid of Leon Lablanc. I've never met the man, but he has a good reputation in the service."

"I've never heard of him myself," she replied.

"Little reason for you to hear of him at all, until now. He's been in India, and in the Seychelles, and briefly in America. A very well traveled fellow. Very adaptable, they say. He's also bringing with him something... someone you requested me to get for Gorée, long ago."

"Oh? What? Or who?"

"A priest."

"Oh. Is the priest a Jesuit?

"I understand he is, as a matter of fact. But tell me, Sasha. Why is it so important that the priest be a Jesuit? You've never even met one."

"No, I haven't," Sasha replied. "But I've heard of their reputation. They're not fools, like some of the... what do you call the heretics?"

"Protestants?"

"Yes, those. The Jesuits are said to adapt to native customs. I would think that would be important here."

Bruie nodded. "Yes, it would be. But some customs even they might not tolerate, Sasha."

"I think they would blend in with us, in time. Well, I suppose we shall see, shall we not?"

"*You* shall see," Bruie said, laughing again. "I may hear of it, later."

Silence fell again, leaving Bruie unhappy. Luckily, he had a profound sense of irony. All his official career he had been as straight and as tough as any situation could possibly demand, and had, he was sure, ruined many a party mood. Now, his official duties being at an end, he was ready to relax; and now all the fun had gone out of the people of the island. He sighed, and took another drink.

A little later, he excused himself, saying he was tired. On impulse, in taking his leave, he kissed Sasha's hand and thanked her for the evening. There was an indescribable combination of emotions written on the young woman's face, but he made no attempt to decipher it. Instead, he walked out into the open air. Instead of walking back to his headquarters at the fort, however, he walked through the village and took the path in the direction of the hill and the upper fort.

It was a clear night, lit by a moon waning toward half, and he had no trouble finding his way. The silence of the place struck him, as it had on a few occasions in the past, but not with the same intensity.

There was much for him to think about if he chose to do so. Not that he was worried; he hadn't lied to Sasha about his prospects.

But he was bothered, and irritated, and frustrated. There was much left for him to do here, and while he knew the company's reasons for recalling him, his was no blind loyalty.

The English were really to blame, of course. They had insisted on trading the *Rochester* for the *Princesse*, and Bruie for Pinder, taking all out of the action. Well, the French company had been stupid enough to buy it, not realizing that the combination of de Gennes, Bruie and the *Princesse* versus their English counterparts was no contest at all. They had sacrificed a great advantage needlessly, and that, more than anything else, galled Andre Bruie.

Up on the high hill, the Chief Factor had time to reflect on the fact that he had spent the greater part of his adult life off the coast of Africa, either on Saint-Louis or Gorée, or on some assignment connected with them. He wasn't sure he had accomplished all that much. But deep in his heart, he knew he had done more than most. Searching for other thoughts, he finally came to the conclusion that these thoughts would have to do.

He went back through the lower fort, not pausing as he passed through the cemetery.

As he came down the hall toward his office, through which he had to pass in order to get to his quarters, he stopped for a moment. There was the light of a lamp coming from beneath the door.

"Who's there?" he called sharply.

"Only me," came the voice of Marcel Drouin.

Bruie marched up to the door, opened it, and assumed a pose with arms folded, facing the Major, who was at Bruie's old desk.

"May I ask, Marcel, what in hell you think you're doing?"

Drouin looked up and grinned.

"Paperwork," he said. "Whoever the new Assistant Chief Factor may be, I'd hate to have him criticize me for not leaving things in order."

"That fails as an explanation, let alone as an excuse."

Drouin sighed. "I feared it would. But the party wasn't exactly going well, eh? You went out into the island. I came here."

Bruie nodded, then sat down casually in one of the guest chairs. It was extremely uncomfortable, which both irritated and pleased him. For its purpose, it had been a good choice, more so than he had previously imagined.

There was talk, then, for a while; talk of very little consequence, almost no consequence at all, really. There wasn't much that could be said, of any significance, that hadn't already been said. Over the years, these two very dissimilar men had become very close. The most important fact looming over the conversation was the great likelihood that after Bruie sailed in the morning, neither would see the other again. The last thing either would have done at this point would have been to admit it.

In the end, Major Drouin excused himself, bade Andre Bruie good night, and, being a Frenchman, parted from him with an embrace.

"*Bon voyage*, Andre," Drouin muttered.

Bruie held him away for a moment. "A good voyage to you, too, Marcel. You may have rougher sailing than I will. But enough of this. Morning will be time enough to say our farewells."

Drouin left, and Bruie turned down the lamp. He didn't turn it off, expecting to have to carry it to his quarters in the back. But as the lamp went low, he saw to his surprise that there was still another light, coming through the base of the door to his quarters. For a moment, he considered the possibility that Drouin might have left another lamp in the back burning as a guide. Then he dismissed the thought, and thrust open the door.

Sasha, seated in a chair beside the bed, rose to greet him.

"Sasha," he said as severely as he could, "This isn't necessary. Or proper."

Sasha shrugged. "You don't understand me."

Bruie laughed, surprised at how easily laughter came to him now.

"I would never claim to understand you. Nor will I make light of your offer. I know you mean it, and mean well. But I repeat, it isn't necessary."

"You mistake me," she said quietly, reaching up to undo the top of her dress. "It's not an offer."

"Not an offer? Then what is it?"

"A request."

Bruie simply stared at her, and repeated her words as a question.

"Yes," she said, as the dress fell to the floor. "I want you."

It seemed to Andre Bruie that he hesitated, but that was, perhaps, only the effect of the wine.

Chapter Twenty

The *signaré* Arsene, one of the most placid and unemotional of the ladies of Gorée, found herself uncommonly disturbed. But then, she was in an uncommon position. Here was a ship coming into port, and Sasha was not there to greet it. Moreover, she had forbidden the rest of the *signarés* from showing their faces at the docks.

"Let them come to us, Arsene," she had said. "Two of them have never seen the Stone House, and I'd like to be the first to see their faces when they do. Now just relax. Samson and Hercule will give them our invitation. They've not seen them, either, and they will come. The house is ready, isn't it?"

Arsene had to agree. There had been great commotion at the Stone House for several days. It had been a welcome relief for the women to be active, for in the several months since the departure of Andre Bruie, things had been decidedly glum around the main building of the island.

Just lately, however, on notice that the ship *Marseilles* was nearing Gorée, things had been a bit frantic. Sasha had roused herself from an inexplicable listlessness, and had started giving orders. Most of those, to Arsene's puzzlement, had wound up going through her. She was not aware that there was such a thing as an executive officer, but if she had been acquainted with the concept, she would have recognized her place in things.

Now, hearing the dockside commotion in the distance, Arsene found herself fussing over details, checking out things that had been checked and rechecked long ago. After a few minutes of this she tired, and paused to take a long drink of water from one of the many large crockery bowls that had been carefully sited in the main room.

About the place were the *signarés* of Gorée, all of them, and in their finest attire. They wore dresses of many colors, headdresses of several turns of cloth, and an abundance of gold hung from their necks and arms. The alcoves were all occupied and their tables were full of food. And the *signarés* were all standing, now, as the procession from the ship approached. They knew it was approaching, for in front of that procession was a drummer, one who knew not only the African uses of that instrument, but the white men's marches as well.

Glancing around the Stone House, Arsene shook her head in wonder. Leave it to Sasha to have everything so perfect. She was taking no chances with this new Chief Factor.

The drumming drew closer, became louder, and suddenly ceased. Up to the front of the Stone House came a half-dozen people, the two men among them bearing a large jar. The jar itself was a kind of crockery, not dissimilar to the waterbowls in the room. Arsene recognized only two of the men, Captain Tousaint and the storyteller, Hadithe Zakale. Momentarily she was shocked. Both the Captain and the storyteller looked older than she had remembered, the storyteller by a large margin.

Sasha rose at this point to greet them.

"Welcome," she said, "to Gorée. I should say welcome back, to both of you. You, Captain Tousaint...and you, honored teller of tales. It's been a long time." She frowned slightly, then craned her neck as if looking behind them.

"But where is Helene-*M·ä·re*? Is she still aboard ship?"

"No, Sasha," the storyteller said quietly, his voice sounding

252

old and tired. "She is here...as she asked to be."

Sasha shook her head, frowning, puzzled. Arsene, whose eyes had been on the storyteller the entire time, noted his deep sadness, and quickly followed Sasha's gaze to the large jar the two strange men had borne into the room. Suddenly Arsene recognized its style and type. It was not a jar but an urn.

Sasha recognized it, too. Her scream rose through the air, and fell only when she did.

The silence in the Stone House belied the elaborate decorations and the heaping tables of food that had been set up for the welcoming celebration. So, too, did the crowd, for it was a crowd no longer. In fact, there were only half a dozen people left in the main room: Tousaint, Arsene, Samson, Hercule, Hadithe Zakale, and lying on the couch in the main alcove, Sasha. Everyone else had discreetly retreated.

Sasha's fainting spell, if it was that, didn't last long. Her first stirrings were followed rapidly by eyelids flickering. Suddenly she sat up, her hands pushing against the couch. Her head tossed once for good measure. There were tears in her eyes, but her voice was calm.

"How did she die?" she asked.

"Childbirth," Hadithe Zakale answered. "It was unexpected. We both thought we were too old. But she was in good hands the last months, among the Ashanti who have always honored her. They would have given her the funeral of an Ashanti princess, but it was her wish... her last wish, that she be returned here to the island for burial."

Sasha stared at the urn, as if not hearing him. Then the tears welled up and she spoke in anger.

"Ashes," she moaned. "You bring me ashes! You said she need fear only what you fear. You said she would be safe, Hadithe

253

Zakale. Is this your safety?"

Hadithe Zakale said nothing, only bowed his head slightly. He accepted this; he had been prepared for worse. The silence grew oppressive, interrupted only by a few sobs Sasha couldn't stifle.

At last the chief *signaré* wiped her eyes, let a long sigh out, and fixed the storyteller with her gaze. The anger seemed to die. She even made an attempt at a smile.

"Forgive me, Hadithe Zakale. That was unworthy of me, and I'm sure Helene-Marie would reprove me for it. I can almost hear the words she would have used. I can see that you grieve for her as I do, and this is something that happens. I've lived long enough to know that." Then she glanced around sharply. "Arsene, have Hercule and Samson bring him a chair."

There was a scurry in the room, and Sasha sat back on the couch. "You must tell me all of it, however, including how you came to sail with Captain Tousaint."

Hadithe Zakale nodded, sitting down gravely in the chair Samson and Hercule brought. As he did so, one of the giants said something to him in a tongue Sasha could not understand. The storyteller looked up in surprise and said something back, then fell silent as the two lame men stepped away.

He had no drum this time, for it was still aboard ship, and he wasn't dressed in his usual elaborate costume with its array of testimonial trinkets. Nor was the tale he told now an easy one for him to get through. But he was, after all, a master storyteller, and even in artlessness, he couldn't help but put art into it.

It was a long tale, for it covered not merely the last few months, but in reality all of his travels with Helene-Marie... the things they had seen and done. In passing, he told a great deal about the life of the tribes they had visited. As he spoke, the people were told of the bravery and the grandeur of the continent on whose edge they perched. They began drifting back into the Stone House, silently taking places in the alcoves. Each stole a glance at Sasha to make sure there was, if not a welcome, at least not a hint of anger. But Sasha didn't seem to notice their presence at all. She was listening.

Finally the storyteller came to their last stay among the

Ashanti, editing this part somewhat. Helene-Marie had suffered a great deal at the last, but there was no point in making Sasha suffer for the hearing of it. He told of her final days without embellishment; the birth of a child who never drew breath, followed by the bleeding that would not stop, and the inevitable end.

"The child," Sasha interrupted. "What was it? What became of it?"

"A boy," Hadithe Zakale replied. "As he drew no breath, there could be no name for him. But he isn't forgotten. Their ashes are together in the urn."

"How came you to sail with my captain?"

Hadithe Zakale spread his hands. "Good fortune, Sasha. The King of Ashanti gave me two men as bearers and helpers, assuming I would journey overland in my usual fashion until I came to your Little Coast. But I really didn't have the heart to go story-telling on the way, this time. So, I headed due south from Kumasi, hoping to find a ship at Accra. I had gold enough for my passage. But as it turns out, the ship in harbor at the time was Captain Tousaint's, and when he found out the nature of my errand, he refused my gold. This he said he would do for you and he refused to discuss it."

Sasha smiled over at Tousaint. "*Merci*, my captain."

There was little left to finish the tale, and it ended shortly. Hadithe Zakale found himself relieved to have it over, as he seldom did. He was thankful that he had carried it through properly, and that he hadn't slipped out with any of the details he had not wanted to include. There might be a time to mention them, but it wasn't now.

Sasha took her eyes off the urn for a while, staring into far space. Then abruptly she got up.

"We shall do as she asked," she said quietly. "We shall bury her ashes in the old cemetery. But not right away. Let's keep the urn here until the new Governor arrives, for he is bringing a priest, and I know she would have preferred a Christian burial. It's been a long time since anyone here had such a burial. I know it would please me to have her be the first, after so many years."

That said, she strode from the dais, and as the storyteller stood, she embraced him, gripping his arms hard and then holding him away.

255

"Stay with us, Hadithe Zakale, as long as it pleases you. I know it is not your habit to remain in one place long, but it would make us happy if you would extend the time in this instance."

The storyteller smiled. "I usually leave a place before I wear out my welcome. But I think I'll risk that, this time. It's good to be back."

The Ashanti bearers had been among the first to return to the Stone House after Sasha's return to consciousness. Now Hadithe Zakale motioned them to carry the urn back into the heart of the building, Arsene showing them the way. Then, at Sasha's insistence, he sat down in the main alcove for an overdue meal, while she went off to talk to Tousaint and some others. In a while there was a semblance of life as usual, though very much subdued.

Hadithe Zakale watched, sorting out his thoughts. He was pleased with Sasha's invitation, for he very much wanted to stay on the island for a while. There were many things to digest; many changes, many and diverse. And there was something ominous in the air, a feeling he disliked. He was not going to go until the clouds had cleared, or the special kind of rain that such clouds contained made itself felt.

After all, the return of her ashes to the island had been almost Helene-Marie's last wish. There was her final wish to consider as well.

Leon Lablanc was a pleasant surprise to the *signarés* . Like Sasha, they had no idea what to expect from the new leader of the Senegal establishments, who was now called Governor, instead of Chief Factor.

Only a few clues had filtered down from Saint-Louis, where he had arrived six weeks earlier to relieve Andre Bruie. Lablanc had seen Bruie off aboard the *Princesse*, bound directly for France. Those clues suggested that he was a first-rate administrator; at least they suggested that much to Sasha, who could appreciate such things. No one really knew, however, how he was going to react to his first visit to the island. But, to everyone's relief, he seemed to appreciate the exotic mixture of French and African ambience that characterized the small community.

He was a stocky man of medium height, a dark Frenchman from the south of that country, yet his manners were as polished as any courtier's. He ate with appreciation, unlike Andre Bruie, who, though he did appreciate a good meal, usually treated eating as a necessary inconvenience, time stolen from the business at hand. Lablanc watched appreciatively when the *signarés* danced, and he listened appreciatively when Hadithe Zakale favored the company with one of his European-flavored tales. He admired the storyteller's skill as he spoke in almost unaccented French. At the conclusion, the new Governor raised his glass.

"Well done, teller of tales. And well done also, Sasha Fara. I can see that the stories I've heard of your island, are no exaggeration. Even in India, you are known."

Sasha laughed lightly. "So far away? I wonder what they think of us there."

"Oh, the Indian people themselves have heard a little of you. They have storytellers too, perhaps not as accomplished as Hadithe Zakale, but storytellers, nonetheless. But of course, the stories are most popular among the colonists in Pondicherry, who deal with the sea and the sailors who ride it." He glanced around him. "They say this place, this palace, I should say, was your idea."

Sasha laughed again; this time her laughter was dismissing. "It's true I suggested something like it to *M'sieu* Bruie. But it was he who saw it carried through."

"I fear you are too modest. Well! I see Father Etienne was unable to join us, which is a pity."

"What could have delayed him?"

Lablanc laughed. "He's the first priest on this island in perhaps twenty years, no? There are many things for him to attend to. But we are to meet at my office in a while. Much to discuss...by the way, Sasha, if you can tear yourself away, you might want to stop

257

by. I told him of your request for a Christian burial for your foster-mother. He indicated that he was ready to make arrangements."

Sasha was pleased, and quickly agreed to come. "I would like that very much. I've set eyes on him, sir, but I haven't met him since you and he landed."

"As I say, he's been busy. But continue, continue. What's next? Another dance?"

"Yes. Perhaps a little more exotic than the last." She smiled confidentially. "Of such a nature, in fact, as might be uncomfortable for Father Etienne. But since he's not here, it shouldn't offend him."

Lablanc's laughter boomed again. "He's no prude, Sasha. Perhaps more of what we in France call the Renaissance Man. I can only say it's his loss. Proceed, proceed."

Much later, Lablanc, after once more expressing his appreciation, rose with an apology on his lips.

"I fear I must be going."

"So soon, sir?"

"Sadly, I must. But do come down, say in about half an hour. Father Etienne and I should be through with our inconsequentials by then."

He left, but the party continued. There were other distinguished guests: many seacaptains this time, at least four in addition to Tousaint, who was scheduled to depart in the morning. Sasha glanced around for him, and noticed him talking to Major Drouin and one other whom she didn't recognize. She went up to them, and as she approached, the stranger glided away into an alcove.

"Enjoying, sirs?" she asked.

"Of course, Sasha, very much indeed," the captain replied. "This will be a good night to remember as I chew salt water on the way home." He seemed to study her. "But I seem to be leaving with no news. Usually when people arrive here after a stay at Saint-Louis, they're full of news, to call it by no better name. *Monsieur* Lablanc, however, has a tight-lipped following."

Sasha laughed. "Perhaps I shall be able to supply some."

"What have you heard?"

"About as much as you have, so far. But I should learn some

shortly, I think."

He looked at her with an odd glance. "Yes," he said gravely, "the night is not over yet. But are you going somewhere?"

"Yes, down to the fort office. I must make arrangements with Father Etienne about the burial."

Tousaint's face stiffened and his eyes became very dark. "Can't that wait, Sasha? It seems an odd time for such a talk."

Sasha laughed. "Don't worry, Captain. I shall be back in time to see you off properly."

With that, she started away. Suddenly she felt a hand on her arm.

"Sasha."

She turned to see Tousaint with a hard expression on his face.

"Don't go down there," the captain said quickly. "At least, not alone. Let me come with you."

She stared at him. "Sir, I'm perfectly able to take care of myself. Don't worry, I won't be long. You are too eager... and you are hurting my arm."

Tousaint sighed, and let her go. She paid no more attention to him, but focused on the matter at hand. Pausing by the entrance to give some instructions to Arsene, she hurried out into the night.

It was a clear, calm night, and once again the moon was full. She had no difficulty making her way. At the fort entrance she was stopped briefly, but allowed to pass once she had explained her errand. One of Drouin's men conducted her to the door of the office that had once belonged to Andre Bruie, and there he left her.

Inside that office, little seemed to have changed. Of course, Lablanc had only been on the island for a couple of days. Still, it was strange to see comfortable chairs in front of the desk as well as behind it. Obviously the new man didn't put as much stock in discomfiting visitors. What was even more strange to her was that neither chair was occupied.

"Ah, Sasha, come in," Lablanc called out. "Please sit down."

"But where is Father Etienne?" she asked as she sat.

"Delayed again, I'm afraid," the Governor replied. "He'll be here in a while...but I'm glad we have this chance to talk. You have a strange little society here, my dear girl."

Sasha laughed. "It's not France, but then, it isn't all Africa, either."

"Truly. And a fine house indeed. I would treasure one like it."

"I do, myself. But, of course, the house is yours, any time you wish to use it. After all, it belongs to the company, as all the buildings do...even the huts."

"Ah, yes, so I've noticed. But it's always a problem for factors or governors, for that matter, when they confuse private and company property. It's been the downfall of many men."

"I trust," she said slowly, "you don't mean *M'sieu* Bruie. He kept those things apart, quite strictly."

"Oh, of course not. He was a good man. I was thinking rather of the likes of Pochette, who seems to have been a bit of a thief as well as a forger. Did you know?"

Sasha shook her head. "I'm not surprised. I did hear that they managed to separate his property from the company's, and that they were going to auction it off."

"You are well informed. Pochette was a stupid thief. Basically he stole petty stuff. One must go into such matters in a big way or not at all. But what he had, you're right, was auctioned off in Saint-Louis some days ago. I bought most of his property, including an interesting young slave girl by the name of Assha."

It wouldn't be accurate to say that Sasha was instantly on her guard, for she had been so for a few minutes; little things like the priest's absence and Tousaint's warning had been enough to trigger an instinct. She spoke slowly.

"I knew her as Desiree... when she lived here."

Lablanc grinned. "So she said. She mentioned your previous association. A pity you two didn't get along. You see, while I respect you free Africans, and I really do... I can't really trust one who doesn't know her place in the scheme of things. In other words, I prefer people who are bound to servitude and know it. I've decided to bring Assha back here, to take charge of the Stone House in my absence."

Some color drained from Sasha's face, but she remained resilient.

"I shall do my best to work with her, *Monsieur*, if that is truly your intention. Perhaps I misjudged her."

Lablanc chuckled. "Daresay you did. It would be nice to think you could, as you say, work together. But there is that matter of trust, no? Especially, " he suddenly clapped his hands, "of one who is so treacherous as to hide an escaped slave."

Before Sasha could rise, or even speak, the door opened and the two men who had waited there in silence were on her. She started to struggle, but quickly abandoned the idea. They were not soldiers, not Drouin's men, but strangers, obviously part of Lablanc's personal following.

"Take her below the fort," the Governor ordered. "The back cell. Drouin's men will show you where it is." He smiled at her, as if nothing unusual had happened. "You will realize the necessity, I'm sure. But we simply cannot afford people like you, Sasha Fara. This is my island now, and I shall run it as I see fit."

"You will do nothing of the kind, Arsene," Sasha said sharply.

"But ... they will kill you," the latter replied, a hint of fear in her voice.

"And if they do? What good will it do to kill Desiree? It would only mean more grief for the people. You've said yourself that several of the *signarés* are already with her...that they have made their terms. Perhaps, in a way, they did so some time ago. But think, Arsene! Think how many people you would have to kill, to really

261

change things. Most of all, you would have to wind up killing French-men, and that would mean death for every man, woman and child on this island. That, or at least a long trip to America as slaves. No. I will not have it."

"But what then?" Arsene asked quietly. "I must know. They will not let me come down here again, I think. I'm only here now because I went to Drouin in secret."

Sasha smiled at her. Arsene couldn't see the smile, for she hadn't grown accustomed to the dim light in the cell over the past two days, as Sasha had. The feeble light came only from a torch ensconced some distance down the hall.

"How did he know?" Arsene whispered. "How could he have known...?"

Sasha rose and embraced her, slipping a small item onto a finger of her right hand.

"Don't worry about that... or about me. Do your best to keep them safe for me. You are the leader now."

"I can't do this," she muttered.

"Well then, if you can't, give the ring back to Mama-Lise, until such time as the *signarés* can choose a new leader without con-straint. If they follow Desiree now, it's merely for necessity. There will come another time."

Arsene sighed.

"I shall hold on to the ring, then. But if Desiree should harm the people, Sasha... "

"Then you will do what's prudent. Now I hear that guard coming back, so... go. Please."

With that, Sasha went back to the mattress on the floor and sat down on it. It was the only piece of furniture in the cell. This, indeed, was the deepest of the depths. As Arsene left, Sasha caught a brief glimpse of her surroundings in the intruding light. It was a fa-mous place, last occupied by the pirate Torrington, and before that by such people as Sokolo, the Ashanti, and Hadithe Zakale, the teller of tales. Thinking of the storyteller, Sasha drew in her courage with a deep breath. She could stand this dungeon for a brief while. After all, the teller of tales had endured these depths for days. She would take her stength from the storyteller's courage.

Stretching her arms out above her, Sahsa's thoughts wandered back to the visit she had received the night before. With the help of Lieutenant Drouin, Hadithe Zakale and Captain Tousaint had secretly come to her cell. Sasha recalled the conversation with great joy.

They had talked of Helene-Marie and the loyalty she had possessed. Sasha recalled the warmth and love she had seen in the storyteller's eyes when he had talked of her. His words had been so passionate, so caring.

They also discussed the wounded Ashanti warrior who had washed up on the beach. With tears in her eyes, Sasha had related the young man's proud victory and his sorrowful death. She described his burial site, a tiny mound, covered by a flowering bush, near the perimeter of the cemetery. Sitting silently in her cell, Sasha remembered now how intently Hadithe Zakale had listened to her words, and how understanding his eyes had been toward her. At that moment, she had felt very proud and very strong.

With a slight smile, her thoughts now shifted to Tousaint. How brave he had been to visit her. And his plan! With Drouin's help, he had devised a plan for her to escape. Intently, he had informed her of an escape route: in one corner of the cell was the entrance to a tunnel, that let out into an isolated corner of the island.

"It's a very great secret," Tousaint had said. "Drouin takes a great risk for you in this. Use it, Sasha, to escape. I will meet you. We'll go to France... together. If you are with me, not even the company can touch you. Besides, Lablanc is a practical man. He won't waste the time or effort to track you down."

Sasha had thanked him, smiling, but she had refused the offer. Then, because they would not leave the matter, she had told them what was really on her mind. She also told them because one of them would be essential to that project. She explained it fully.

Ah, the argument that had sparked! But her mind had been made up long ago.

"You see," she said, "I know about that tunnel. I was raised on this island, sirs. We children found the other end of that tunnel long ago. Some of us played in it, daring each other to go farther and farther toward what we knew had to be the fort. I expected it would lead to a cell, or from it. So you see, I would have been out of here eventually, anyhow. But now that you know, you can help me with my plan."

Further argument came, but further argument was useless. Sasha had made up her mind, and that was that.

She waited that second night until long after sunset, when the guard changed, and when the new guard had had time to fall asleep. Then she dug in one corner of the room, until she came on the ring that was attached to the tunnel door.

Major Drouin watched carefully as Leon Lablanc confronted Captain Tousaint at the gangplank of the latter's ship. Lablanc had several men with him; tough-looking characters, part of the crew he had brought with him from Saint-Louis, and no doubt, originally, from France. But Tousaint had some men too, and quite pointedly at his side was the fellow known as the Claw, with a huge hook at the end of one arm.

Drouin was ready, too. He had brought enough soldiers, he felt fairly sure, to handle any confrontation.

"You say the bitch isn't aboard," Lablanc said to Tousaint with some force. "I say that I must search, nevertheless."

"I didn't say that," Tousaint growled. "I gave you my word of honor that Sasha Fara is not aboard my ship. If you search my ship now, Governor, you are casting doubt on that word. No one will hinder you from a search, should you choose to undertake it. But, when that is done, you will give me satisfaction."

Instantly, all of the men at dockside tensed up. Lablanc's eyes widened. His tension was perhaps greater than the rest, for everyone knew this language presaged a challenge to a duel. And it was a challenge which, under the circumstances, Tousaint would have every right to make.

Drouin watched Lablanc's face closely. The dark color was draining, all right, but if there was fear, there was also a measuring glance. He was probably thinking of Tousaint's age, and his seagoing habit. No doubt he would choose swords, if challenged. Lablanc was no fool, and he was not likely to risk pistols against a man who had learned to shoot one accurately on the careening deck of a ship.

But it never came to that, for on shore a man raised a cry and the Frenchmen's attention was directed to a rising pillar of black smoke. At first the Governor expected it to be from a small ship, but it wasn't. Instead it came from a small raft. The raft, caught in the pull of the current, was on fire.

Spyglasses snapped up to faces, several of them, including Drouin's. Some of the sharper-eyed islanders could see clearly without these aids, and they set up a wail. Drouin studied the raft in detail; it was blackened now, and parts of it were beginning to break off. The outline could still be seen, however. It was an oddly wrapped shape which had been strewn with clothing and ornaments, all the finery of a *signaré* of Gorée.

"What are the damned macaques muttering?" Lablanc demanded of Drouin.

"A new legend, *m'sieu le governeur*. They say Sasha Fara has gone free the way her mother did, only this time she has deprived the sharks of a meal by giving herself to the flames instead."

"Those giants," the Governor snapped. "They must have helped her. Well, we shall find them and hang them instead of her. As for the bitch herself, why, good riddance. In a way, it's appropriate punishment." Lablanc's grin was repulsive.

Drouin, however, shrugged it off. He could not be perturbed by the likes of this man. At least, he wasn't about to show that he was.

Lablanc shouted an order, and his men turned and left to search for the tall Africans. The Governor turned back to Tousaint.

"Sail, go ahead and sail. Get out of here before I change my mind. I shall report your defiance, Captain Tousaint. You can be sure of that."

"I have reports to make as well," Tousaint answered.

"Yes, of course. Do be prudent. I have friends at home, Captain. They are quite strong, if you get my meaning."

"They must be strong, indeed," Tousaint growled as his men cast off, "if they are able to eat the same shit as a dog like you."

Lablanc roared an angry reply, but Tousaint had already turned on his heel. The ship pulled away almost immediately, leaving the Governor of Senegal blustering. With no other target, he turned on Drouin instead.

"And you! You are as incompetent as you are arrogant; letting a tunnel like that be built beneath your very eyes! Have it filled in at once! With stone!"

Drouin shrugged. "I did not let it be built, sir. It was designed in... when this fort was erected on the foundations of the old Portuguese works."

"What!"

"A prudent precaution, sir, known only to fort commanders ever since. This island is vulnerable, Governor. It has been taken many times. One day you or I might find ourselves confined to that back cell, no? But I shall do as you wish, and fill it in."

Lablanc stared at him, and swallowed. "Forget that order. But put it about that you have carried it out. And some night, get your men to work and have them redirect that exit, and fill in the original. Do you understand?"

"*Oui, Monsieur.*"

Drouin called out an order, and his soldiers began marching back to the fort. With the ship safely in the distance and Lablanc's men gone, the only people left on the shore were the islanders. Softly they lamented as they watched the raft burn away in the distance.

Drouin's eyes followed their gaze. He was puzzled, and sad, but perhaps not as sad as he might have been.

No one had told him what Sasha's plan was. Neither Tousaint nor Hadithe Zakale, nor the two black giants who were bound to turn up missing now, one way or another. He knew Tousaint well enough to know, however, that the man's word of honor was decisive. Whatever the situation, ruse or not, Sasha had not been aboard his ship.

Still, he found it hard to believe that Sasha was really on that raft, either. But, as a soldier and a man of honor, he was glad he didn't know what really became of Sasha. After all he would have been bound to report it...to someone, sometime.

Drouin gazed after the raft thoughtfully, remembering the vibrant young woman as she had been just a few days before. And he realized the source of the sadness. Whatever might really have happened, one thing was fairly certain. Marcel Drouin would not see her, or the like of her, again.

East of the island, the coastal lowlands of the African mainland ran almost unbroken as far as the eye could see. Just at the edge of vision, a small headland jutted forth into the Atlantic. The rise marked a dividing line on European maps, if not in the minds of the African peoples. Beyond this point, Gorée dropped out of sight, and the Little Coast, as the French called it, formally began.

Two mornings after Captain Tousaint's ship sailed for France, Hadithe Zakale climbed this rise with three companions. Two of them were the lame black giants, Samson and Hercule; the third, a woman of much lighter complexion, wrapped in white and wearing a simple headdress with a veil.

The veil came up, and the four people stood looking at the island, saying nothing for a long time.

"They won't have been fooled," Hadithe Zakale said at last. "At least, not all of them. Some will suspect you escaped, Sasha."

"Of course," Sasha replied with a show of unconcern. "But they will have an explanation, and an excuse to forget about me. I know how those Frenchmen think." She frowned slightly. "At least, most of them."

"You are talking about *M'sieu* Lablanc?" The storyteller said solemnly. "You are feeling unsettled because he was able to fool you...you who is not easily fooled."

Sasha's eyes flashed with wounded pride.

"He did not *fool* me, teller of tales. I simply misjudged his intelligence. He is no *Monsieur* Bruie, I can tell you that. Imagine, thinking a woman like Desiree is capable of running this island. Surely, *M'sieu* Lablanc will come to realize that I was an effective leader."

Hadithe Zakale was amazed by Sasha's naivete.

"That is where you are fooled, Sasha. *Monsieur* Lablanc is not interested in a leader..."

"Then *Monsieur* Lablanc is a fool!" Sasha's words were cold and harsh. Her eyes held an icy, vacant stare.

Turning to the storyteller, Sasha lowered her voice. Her eyes softened a bit. "Well, that's all in the past now. I must look to the future. Please, tell me, what's in the future? Where will we go, Hadithe Zakale? I would like to be prepared."

Hadithe Zakale chuckled. How neatly she turned the conversation, when she wished to! But, after all, he was able to spot such things, and was equipped to deal with them better than most. It would, no doubt, be an interesting journey.

"Dahomey," he said after a moment. "Ashanti, perhaps not again for a while. There are tribes on the fringes of the desert that I haven't been among for a long time. And... " he hesitated "... perhaps even my homeland. It seems I have not been entirely forgotten, as I supposed."

Sasha looked up at him. "How would you know this?"

"From Samson, and Hercule. You said, Sasha, that I knew their tongue. Say rather that they know mine. They are Masai, men of my tribe. You remember that Samson spoke to me when he first saw me, at the Stone House?"

"Yes."

"He asked me if I was the son of Singlehand, who had become a teller of tales." Hadithe Zakale smiled. "Most of our talk since then had been catching up on a generation of events among the Masai. It seems they've followed my career, when they've heard of it; and I'm assured of a legend's welcome in my own right, if I should visit there again."

Sasha smiled, her eyes very bright. Her expression resembled that of a child.

"Then I shall be your companion." Her words were more of a question than a statement.

The story teller nodded with admiration *and* doubt.

"You are not a simple person, Sasha Fara. I fear you may find the life of a storyteller's companion less exciting than you expect." His voice was steady, yet kind.

Sasha's face filled with eagerness. " I will not! I will learn, Hadithe Zakale. Then turning back to the island, she lowered her head. "I can see now that I have much to learn."

Sensing her sincerity, the teller of tales nodded assertively. "Well, then, I will be glad to have you." Instantly his thoughts shifted to Helene-Marie. He smiled as he remembered her last wish, and his promise to fulfil it.

"But if you ever tire of my company, please, say so, Sasha. You and your men are free to go at any time."

"My men?" This time it was Sahsa's turn to chuckle. " You overestimate me, Hadithe Zakale. I have made it very clear to Samson and Hercule that they are free men now. Besides, I suspect that they would be more inclined to follow you if we ever parted company."

Hadithe Zakale laughed. It was a large laugh, a kind he had not experienced in a long time.

"No! My dear, Sasha. I do not overestimate you. You underestimate yourself. Your humbling experience has made you too much so. These men will never abandon you!"

Sasha cocked her head to one side, intently thinking the matter over. Then she faced him. "But I will not hold them, storyteller. They must seek their own destiny. Just as I must seek mine. I shall find what I seek."

The teller of tales nodded.

"That, Sasha, I can well believe. But what is it that you seek. Do you even know?"

Sasha was silent for a while. She stared at the island, then broke away and turned her back to it.

"It is difficult to explain, Hadithe Zakale. I am sure that you have always wanted to be a teller of tales. And I...I have always wanted to rule the island where I was born." Suddenly Sasha lowered her eyes to the ground. Her voice wavered a bit.

"I am not proud of some of the things I have done. But, it had nothing to do with power. I did what I did because I knew I could make the island and the people prosper."

Then, Sasha looked up at him. Her eyes were intently focused. "I have no regrets."

The teller of tales nodded. Her statement needed no reply.

"I will be your companion, then," she continued. This time Sasha's tone was emphatic.

Hadithe Zakale remained silent. His eyes searched hers. It was difficult for him to read her expression. Difficult, but not impossible.

"I shall be your companion in all senses, sir, but I must make one thing very clear."

The storyteller simply grinned, admiring the determination in her tone. He had already suspected her terms.

"I do not ask that of you, Sasha," he remarked patiently.

"But I must make it clear. I won't deny you my body. But I cannot bear your children. Destiny has something other than motherhood in store for me. Men must be...part of my life, rather than the whole of it. Do you understand?"

Though her words were harsh, Hadithe Zakale detected a bit of uncertainty in her tone. It was as if she was trying to convince herself as much as he. Still, he shrugged.

"I leave it in your hand, Sasha."

Abruptly, she cast a long glance over her shoulder to the island, now gripped in the mist of the Atlantic.

"Well, it's finished, then. I have seen the last of it!" With that she laughed, and began walking down the hillside.

The storyteller remained for a moment longer, his eyes devouring the landscape of the island.

"Long ago, Mama-Lise told me that if I didn't quit being a bad girl, she would pack me off with Hadithe Zakale the next time he came by the island. She was trying to frighten me, by making you a boogey-man. But bad girls aren't afraid of boogey-men, any more than they are of exile. Truly, I must be one still."

Hadithe Zakale, beside her, made no comment. He satisfied himself, taking a long look at the misty spread of land in the distance. This would be his last visit to the island. But as for Sasha Fara, that was another question. It was a riddle not unlike the woman herself. It would resolve itself in time, and if Hadithe Zakale had learned anything in his travels, he knew it would resolve itself in a way no one that day could hope to predict.

And she was young, with plenty of time left to spend.

Mid-17th-century African woman taken to
Gorée Island. Sasha's mother's character
is based upon this illustration.

Illustrations: Darondeau; Source: *Côte Occidentale d'Afrique;*
Henri Nicholas Frey; Paris; 1890

First-generation Signaré
of Gorée Island.

Signaré of early 18th century
Gorée Island.